THE GOLD FACTORY

Critical praise for
Djelloul Marbrook's fiction

Guest Boy (2018, Leaky Boot)

What Marbrook does so well in *Guest Boy* is the contradictory elegance he showed in *Saraceno*. He finds the tender and poetic heart of very tough men. In *Saraceno*, it was low-level mobsters; in *Guest Boy*, it's men of the sea. They're a horny-handed bunch, and Marbrook's familiarity with ships and the characters of mean-street ports is deep and exciting. But Marbrook knows that these guys have a lot more going on within, and are simultaneously deeply tender philosophers. It's a mesmerizing book... You'll find yourself thinking about it long after you've finished reading.

—Dan Baum, author of *Gun Guys* (2013), *Nine Lives* (2009), and others

Guest Boy is a complex work: deep, passionate, exciting and beautifully written with flashbacks and imagery merging real and surreal. By opening up routes to the culture and history of the Arab world, *Guest Boy* helps us understand that world and our own.

—Sanford Fraser, author of *Tourist* and *Among Strangers I've Known All My Life*

... it is in books like this that I seek answers and guidance as I travel my own path to enlightenment and contentment. This book opened a struggle in me...

—Isla McKetta, editor, *A Geography of Reading*

Artemisia's Wolf (title story, *A Warding Circle*, 2017, Leaky Boot)

... Djelloul Marbrook's impressive novella ... successfully blends humor and satire (and perhaps even a touch of magic realism) into its short length ... an engrossing story, but what might strike the reader most throughout the book is its infusion of breathtaking poetry ... a stunning rebuke to notoriously misogynist subcultures like the New York art scene, showing us just how hard it is for a young woman to be judged on her creative talent alone.

—Tommy Zurhellen, *Hudson River Valley Review*

... lets his powerful imagination run wild, leading the fiction into unexpected corners where weird performers hold court and produce endings that both astonish and are frequently magical.

—James Polk, *The Country and Abroad*, former contributing editor of *Art/World*.

Saraceno

Djelloul Marbrook writes dialogue that not only entertains with an intoxicating clickety-clack, but also packs a truth about low-life mob culture "The Sopranos" only hints at. You can practically smell the anisette and filling-station coffee.

—Dan Baum, author of *Gun Guys* (2013), *Nine Lives: Mystery, Magic, Death and Life in New Orleans* (2009), and others

...a good ear for crackling dialogue ... I love Marbrook's crude, raw music of the streets. The notes are authentic and on target ...

—Sam Coale, *The Providence* (RI) *Journal*

... an entirely new variety of gangster tale ... a Mafia story sculpted with the most refined of sensibilities from the clay of high art and philosophy . .. the kind of writer I take real pleasure in discovering ... a mature artist whose rich body of work is finally coming to light.

—Brent Robison, editor, *Prima Materia*

Alice Miller's Room
(title story, *Making Room,* 2017, Leaky Boot)

This enchanting novella is a delicately wrought homage to Jung's famous principle of meaningful coincidence...

—*Breakfast All Day,* UK

... the story draws us into that mysterious and terrifying realm where the heart will have its say and all who enter leave transformed...

—Dr. Patricia L. Divine, Head Start program lifetime service award winner

Mean Bastards Making Nice (2014, Leaky Boot)

I love it. I admire it. It is you at your best.

—Novelist Gail Godwin on "The Pain of Wearing Our Faces"

❧

Critical praise for
Djelloul Marbrook's poetry

Far from Algiers (2008, Kent State University Press)

... as succinct as most stanzas by Dickinson... an unusually mature, confidently composed first poetry collection.

—Susanna Roxman, *Prairie Schooner*
(author of *Crossing the North Sea*)

... brings together the energy of a young poet with the wisdom of long experience.

—Edward Hirsch, Guggenheim Foundation

... honors a lifetime of hidden achievement.

—Toi Derricotte, Wick Award judge

... wise and flinty poems outfox the Furies of exile, prejudice, and longing... a remarkable and distinctive debut.

—Cyrus Cassells, National Poetry Series winner

Brash Ice (2014, Leaky Boot Press, UK)

...resonates with wisdom and a keen eye for the beautiful things of this world ...a poetry that would make brash ice melt again.

—George Drew, author of *The View From Jackass Hill*

... a precision that occasionally recalls Yeats ...

—James Polk, *The Country and Abroad*

... aesthetically pleasing, thematically intriguing ...

—Michael Young, *The Poetry*

Brushstrokes and glances (2010, Deerbrook Editions)

Whether it is commentary on state power, corporate greed, or the intensely personal death of a loved one, Djelloul Marbrook is clear sighted, eloquent, and precise. As the title of the collection suggests, he uses the lightest touch, a collection of fragments, brushstrokes and glances, to fashion poems that resonate with truth and honesty.

—Phil Constable, *New York Journal of Books*

... looks at art the way a drinker drinks—deeply, passionately, and desperately, as if his life depended on it ... makes you want to run out to your favorite museum and look again, as you have never looked before, until the lights go out.

—Barbara Louise Ungar, author of *Thrift*; *Charlotte Bronte, You Ruined My Life*; *The Origin of the Milky Way*

... one of those colossal poets able to bridge worlds—poetry and art, heart and mind—with rare wit, grace, and sincerity; a soft-spoken artist with the courage to face the "fatal beckoning" of his muse ... crisp intellect, seamlessly interwoven with loss and longing. ... poetry at its best: at once both gritty and refined, private and political, tender and tough as iron ... well worth reading."

—Michael Meyerhofer, author of *What to do if you're buried alive*, *Damnatio Memoriae*, *Blue Collar Eulogies*

...delicately wrought... highly recommended reading...because, ultimately, this witness so clearly loves his subject.

—Eileen Tabios, Editor, *Galatea Resurrects*

Riding Thermals to Winter Grounds (2017, Leaky Boot)

... some very powerful lines, such as: "And then, near the end of my life, I become the man I wanted to be without the fuss and bother of giving a damn."

—Sidney Grayling, Editor, Onager Editions

THE GOLD FACTORY

Book 3 of the
Light Piercing Water Trilogy

Djelloul Marbrook

LEAKY BOOT PRESS

The Gold Factory: Book 3 of the Light Piercing Water Trilogy
by Djelloul Marbrook

Hardcover: ISBN: 978-1-909849-64-8
Softcover: ISBN: 978-1-909849-58-7

A full CIP record for this book is available from the
British Library in the UK and from the Library of
Congress in the USA.

Every visible object that is not a direct light source
is a kind of mirror.

Ibn al-Haytham
966-1040 A.D.

I have seen a wicked and ruthless man
flourishing like a green tree in its native soil ...

Psalm 37, Verse 35
King David

Author's Acknowledgments

Endless thanks are owed to my wife, Marilyn, who has in so many ways made all my work possible; to James Goddard, my publisher, whose steadfast faith in my work brought it to light and buoyed me in rough waters; to Sebastien Doubinsky, who published my work and introduced me to James Goddard; to Brent Robison, whose wizardly videos and deft hand with e-books still astonish me; to Kevin Swanwick, whose radiance as a reader and advisor unfailingly enlightens me, and to Emily Brooks, whose artistic taste, good cheer and resourcefulness seem fathomless.

for my beloved wife Marilyn

Characters

Amir (Bo) Cavalieri—American merchant seaman, owner of two priceless medieval manuscripts, *The Book of Secrets*, on Arab alchemy, and the rutter of the fabled navigator, Achmed ibn Madjid.

Said bin Taimur—Sultan of Oman, who gave Bo the two manuscripts.

Ulrike Theiss—painter; Bo Cavalieri's mother.

Alessandro (Sandro) Cavalieri—Bo's stepfather.

Adeline (Addie) Compton—English conservator of ancient musical instruments, aikido adept.

Margaret Wadeleigh—Oxford mathematician, Addie's lover and friend since childhood.

Weybrandt (Gundy) Gundersen—Merchant seaman, Bo's closest friend.

Jolene Gundersen—Gundy's Icelandic wife.

Dacia Wynne Wadeleigh—Margaret's mother; Bo's childhood friend at Cairnhall, his boarding school, whom he's always loved though he hasn't seen her since she left Cairnhall at the end of the war.

Woofy Poofy—the rag doll Dacia left behind at Cairnhall in Bo's care.

Rose MacQuarrie—Wealthy Scot who nursed Ulrike back to health in Algeria before Ulrike's liaison with Rose's lover, Ben Aissa.

Sheik Mutawakkil ibn al Quereishi—Medieval Arab alchemist and mathematician.

Si Sliman Hamidaoui—friend of Margaret and Adeline; old Algerian rebel who slipped out of the hands of General Jacques Massu's torturers to retire to England.

Klement Gruber (the Bison)—employee of Commodus da Cunha, who wants Bo's *Book of Secrets*.

Khaled ibn al Qwarzimi (the Crane)—assistant director of Omani intelligence tasked to acquire Bo's *The Book of Secrets*; his true boss is Bayazid Qadir ben Saadi, a pan-Arabist Algerian marabout who dreams of restoring the caliphate.

Hettie Warshaw—Former assistant to Dr. Josef Mengele; Ulrike's and Sandro's lover.

Ute-Britt Broghammer—Barmaid in Hamburg whom Bo draws compulsively.

Lakhdar Ali Wahab—Ute-Britt's co-worker and lover; Moroccan guest worker.

Joseph Minihan—Manhattan barkeep, retired Irish Republican Army bomber.

Si Larbi ben Hamrouch—giant Algerian al Fatah assassin.

Peter Tomlinson—Wealthy British writer of "famous route" books; owner of the North Sea trawler *Morgaine*.

Moira Sayre—Peter's companion; marine photographer.

Uthman al-Biruni—Pearl diver, Marxist rebel, Bo's friend.

Commodus da Cunha—Portuguese arms merchant, collector of incunabula and art.

David Llewellyn—Bo's therapist.

Glossary

Some terms in this novel may be unfamiliar; see pages 251–254.

PART I

1

He smells ice at sea when radar's blind. He knows the hyacinth of a woman's craziness. He knows the scent of rogue seas, fanatics, berserkers, cockatrices and banshees, the feeling of privilege and sorrow when you're in someone's crosshairs. A ship changing its course unaccountably bears watching. This is different. Something he hasn't smelled before has him in mind.

Who stalks a rootless seaman? What odor survives mustard and sauerkraut, paint, disinfectant, gum arabic, carbon monoxide, rain in filthy gutters, scorched coffee, roasting chestnuts, cheap perfume, stale beer and piss, the excreta and degassing of people in their mazes?

His first profession was to kill by stealth. Now it is to shiver and sweat under many flags in all weathers, but he can't weather his mother's contempt. That's his sickness.

His sketchbooks define him, keep him in deep waters. But a lockbox at the Irving Trust on Union Square draws him into waters where be dragons. These priceless manuscripts bequeathed him by the late sultan of Oman, who called him Sindbad, consume him with the question: why would a sultan give them to a sea bum?

His Navy medals and ribbons are safe passage through jackbooted caricatures whose eternal demand—*Your papers, please*—provide us the ghouls we'd have to invent had not the Nazis been so obliging. Born with his papers out of order, half German, half Bedouin, he slips past every demand for them in a country where some of us are less welcome than others.

★

For all its glitzy jut, Manhattan never seems masculine to him. Dumping the black box of Margaret Wadeleigh's beeping hang-ups into the Hudson felt like a coup d'état. He feels younger. His jadedness peels away. This isn't his old town, the one he calls home for lack of a better place. This is a new city given to him by Said bin Taimur, late autocrat of Oman. Sindbad had his Basra, his hags and pestilent geezers, giant rocs and sea serpents. Bo Cavalieri has Manhattan. Its creatures, black, brown, yellow, white, purple and green, are all *ifrangis* to him, infidels. He feels it like an Arab garbageman in Paris: it isn't his city, but it would stink without him. This is what it's like to be a djinni, but not in Aladdin's lamp.

He likes to walk up Fifth Avenue to Bryant Park, the former reservoir where the lions Patience and Fortitude of the city's main library lord it over readers and shoppers. There he sketches, as his mother Ulrike once sketched in Bou Saada, gateway to the Sahara. He draws a three-hundred-pound infidel in a motorized chair with a white poodle cowering on a shelf in the back. Her companion (husband?), who wears the face of all the world's diasporas, whines, *Why don't you explain to me what's going on?* She looks at him as if she doesn't think he deserves to know. Bo's hand shakes, wondering if it can capture the zaniness of the contraption and the woman's expression at the same time. A tall black woman in a flowery brown and yellow dress heaves into view, her rear enjoying its own tidal life. How can he catch this wondrous samba?

Daumier's wry eye and Goya's accusative eye inform Bo's work, but his own eye is cooler. His two great forebears had too much to say. That's what worries him about the motorized lady and her entourage: he can do the poodle, he can do the contraption, he can do the faces, but doing them together would be punditry. Had he not lived so long in Ulrike Theiss's shadow he would have said more and seen less. A life under her sore unwitting tutelage—he never let her know he drew anything until she was dying—made him a spare and shrewd draftsman. His tentative use of color once she is dead is paranoid. He doesn't trust a single hue. He engages color as if trying to operate an alien spaceship.

As a seaman he regards paint as a necessary evil. The Navy chips and paints with zeal. The merchant marine covers neglect with paint. He prefers the Navy way. The difference incensed him so much it drove him off the deck and into the chart house.

Now he experiments with pencils, Conté crayons, chalks, charcoals, stick and ink as lasciviously as he saw Turks in Korea sharpening their bayonets. But he and color hold each other at bay. Only when a drawing makes a diplomatic request for a daub of color does he relent. Often he works in his Soho loft only in khaki shorts and a wool watch cap, trailing blue Cohiba smoke as he strides barefoot from one sketch to another. He once carried his sketches in a pad like a back brace under his wide black seaman's belt. Now he sometimes works on one of several easels stationed like blue herons around his loft. He built a chest-high rectangular table twenty-two feet long in the middle of the loft and partitioned its sides into masonite compartments for his portfolios. He constellates his life around this table, walking, sketching, eating, drinking coffee, croaking scat and boogieing backwards. It's his drydock chart room. Here things make sense or founder. Here he imposes his seaman's sense of priority: navigation first, then maintenance. Keep the ship afloat. Failing that, abandon her smartly. But still there's not a yard of canvas in his loft. Paper doesn't presume like canvas. Ulrike lived a life of presumptions, and he continues to distrust her medium. Wide seas and star charts never daunt him, but a thirty-by-forty-inch canvas fills him with dread. Ulrike and her fellow dybbuks rule the woven surface; her son does his best not to draw their attention. That's the sum of his wisdom. It never occurs to him that Ulrike painted fantastical things because people interested her not a whit. After he was born in horrific gushes of blood and tissue, worthy of her brush, she saw nothing in people. If he can someday draw and paint his way to this knowledge, he might perhaps believe she really died, but for now her death is merely an intellectual challenge. He gave her a Viking funeral somewhere south of Cape Cod and watched her grin in the flames. He hopes the sea is wide and deep enough to hold her imagined entitlements. As it is, the shame of not having been loved convinces him that color is a privilege he has not earned and an invitation to become a target. And yet he is a naval commando, and in this guise he comes up on color in the dark and garrotes it. It's miserable work, and he likes to give himself leave to regress to the grays of a dog's life. Dogs are not confused by nuance.

2

On her last night at Hatteras Addie Comptom wakes gasping, then falls back to sleep and dreams she's wearing a white burnoose and a cheche, one of those whorled Maghrebi turbans. She's suspended in air and the cauldron is like a sea. She's one of Giordano Bruno's star beasts, the ones that got him burned at the stake by the grand inquisitors. She's thinking of Bruno when a ship's horn awakens her.

The church's wicked act calls to her mind the cruelest thing she ever witnessed—the habitual taunt of a little friend's mother. Sabine Truscott would ask her daughter Emily: *What're you looking at?* Sometimes she didn't even bother to disguise her taunt in humor. The word *you* was meant to exile the child, crippling her spirit, darkening an eye shining too brightly. Addie could never cross the taiga of Sabine Truscott's question, and even if she did, what would be there? Not her mother, not Annabeth Compton, who was unfailingly interested in everything Adeline had to say. What finally spared Addie Compton the injury of Sabine's question was that she came improbably to like it. What was she looking at?

Emily had been looking at indifference and resentment. Her mother knew it and salted her tone with mockery to disguise her shame.

Had their two cottages not been so close, Annabeth and Brian Compton would have tried to wean Addie from Emily. They didn't want her to share the desolation of the Truscott home. Mrs. Truscott yanked Emily around her house by the hair—her house, not Emily's—sucker-punched and backhanded her at the slightest provocation, sabotaged her confidence with

23

derision. "There's something wrong with you, girl. You're not like other children. Other children love their mothers." It was easy for Emily to believe. Something was wrong with her, because she wasn't like other children, and she didn't even like this tormentor she was supposed to love.

One evening Addie blurted at supper, "I hate Mrs. Truscott, I despise her." It was the signal event of her childhood. She was testing Annabeth and Brian to see if underneath their tenderness they were not unlike Emily's mother. Annabeth ladled her some stew and said, "Have some more, dear, it's delicious." Brian sat back and studied her. "Yes," he said at last, "I can't say I care for her myself, Adeline. Still, I think we can do more for Emily by not bringing our dislike of her mother to a boil, don't you think?"

"But what about Mr. Truscott?" Addie said.

"Well, these things—this awful behavior—always take two," Annabeth said. "I mean, Gordon Truscott has clearly not put his foot down, has he? So I don't think we can absolve him."

"But we're called upon not to judge, Mr. Creighton says," Addie said, paraphrasing their vicar. "Of course he doesn't live next door to the Truscotts."

"Yes, it's one of the few good things we can do for the poor man," Brian said. "Even our Lord's patience was tried from time to time, and, well, Father Creighton, after all, is called upon to say such things." Brian winked at his daughter. Nothing could have entrenched her faith in her parents or in her own judgment more than this slender conversation.

★

She doesn't know why in Salvo, on Cape Hatteras, among sinister contraptions stilted on pilings, their windows slathered in red each evening at sunset, she understands everything. She grows afraid of the place. Clarities, like the wind and the sea, are relentless. After two weeks she leaves.

Entering the Lincoln Tunnel reminds her of muskrats and sand crabs burrowing. Somewhere in the hedgerows at Saint Agnes in Rolle on the shore of Lake Geneva, long before menses heralded a difficult life, she realized that Adeline Compton was an impostor. The hidden Addie was a magus so austere that speaking to her was life-threatening.

Once unpacked in Chelsea, Addie addresses her companion as a godlet at an obscure altar. She's convinced that the hidden Addie, pointedly silent in Salvo, would reveal nothing if not treated decorously. She always asks if they might speak, always waits patiently for an answer, and always hears a voice more hieratic than her own. But now she hears nothing. Her companion is as silent as she had been at Salvo. She sits by a window, smelling the sun in her hair, hair so fine only an elastic band will hold it. She goes to her little gray Olivetti and composes a flowery apostrophe to the longed-for Margaret.

★

"Flying over McKee's Pond as the earth with its presentiment of spring melted the littorals and made them dark and menacing, I learned that I would never have to grow up. I was a changeling. Why should I have to learn to love wood grain, blue-snow smell and pond freeze only to end up barely knowing how to make toast? Not me, not Addie Compton. My pigtails would stream forever over McKee's Pond. I would dare the dark woods forever with long green eyes. That is why I make musical instruments and resurrect ancient ones, so that I will never lose my knowledge of the secret wont of things.

"We bring suspicious baggage to our seeing; the result is distortion. Something else I learned on McKee's Pond: the edges of anything are unreliable. Stay in the center: hard advice to follow. People are drawn to rotten ice and the mutterings of the forest. I preferred skating to sledding on the pond. A long-legged girl with cavernous lungs would, but sledding had one advantage: I could study the ice, the bumps, the trapped twigs and leaves and labels of things, the way it wanted to freeze, and I could feel the intimate menace of the black melt. I suppose in time that is why, however many friendships I've made with men, women please me more. Women are not so willing to sell what's closely studiable for a song. Nor are they half so apt to flinch. Did you ever know a man who knew that?"

It takes her two days to write and revise, and when she

finishes its polish hurts her eyes. It's like the essays she used to write to dazzle professors and throw them off the scent of her derelictions. But a week later, she reads her words again and sees an Addie who can't afford such wistfulness for Margaret, an Addie who has parted company with Margaret in a way she can't quite see yet.

3

Bo's long friendship with Weybrandt Gundersen has survived
the perils of sobriety. Few dry drunks stay friends. But he and
Gundy, only two years sober, still ship out to sea as when they
were fools. Only now Gundy is the skipper and Bo his chief
mate. That's their compact, the one Bo proposed one night in
Weehawken when Gundy was struggling to sober up. He'd stop
hiding in chart rooms as navigator and take on the responsibility
of chief mate if Gundy would stop hiding as chief mate and
sail as a captain. They had long been suited to their new jobs,
but the fuck-you machismo of booze left open circuits in their
brains. Now, as sober drunks, they not only make more money
but are negotiating the middle strait between boyhood and
manhood: Gundy, the Viking chief, fearsome and remote; Bo,
lanky, taciturn, at one with the crew. They are what they'd been,
good men to sail with, but now quieter and more deliberate.
They're getting acquainted with themselves. They're not quite
the men their shipmates knew. Drunks fondle an adolescent
belief in immortality, so now age splotches, lazy dicks, sore hips,
sour guts and respect for sleep hint to them that old men and
women are brave in ways no one else can imagine. Most of
their shipmates think the two hide their drinking in tanks too
pricey for the rest of them and would freak out to find them in
museums or motorcycling around foreign countrysides. They'd
done their drinking and their whoring, enough for twenty men.
Now they're plumping up their pensions and provisioning for
final passages.

Gundy proves a pensive captain. He'd once been a
rambunctious mate. He takes at least one meal a day in the crew's

27

mess and tries, it seems to Bo, to take a leaf from Bo's own book. But the crew's lives wash over him and he falls far short of Bo's habit of becoming the repository of everyone's story. Still, the crew knows Gundy is one of them, having worked his way up the hawsepipe, starting when he was fourteen, and they spare him their contempt for academy officers.

Bo as chief mate seems to touch every rivet and visit every space, except of course the engineers' fief, but the need to give orders fails to make him more voluble. If anything he seems to speak even more than before in a kind of sign language that unfailingly amuses Gundy. It strikes Gundy as pantomime, and in booming high seas it's a big asset. That it has more serious virtue never dawns on Gundy: Bo's signing never poisons an order with tonality or edge. It puts him at one with the crew's physicality. If Bo ever says, Well, I guess that's one way to do it, it stings worse than a reprimand. Gundy's response in a similar circumstance is to do the thing his way in silence.

Men whose delusions can't withstand eye contact find other ships, for neither Gundy nor Bo are men to look away, which pretty much defines the crews they sign up. The companies for which these descendants of Eric the Red and Sindbad sail value their ability to size up men. They're not to every seaman's liking, their eyes being too steady. But there are men who have broken down and wired themselves together, men more fragile than their looks let on, who swear by Gundy and Bo, who seek out their ships, a fact not lost on employers. Few men, usually strangers, call Bo chief; fewer still call the captain Gundy. Bo is a fellow seaman, only accidentally an officer, while Gundy, whatever his origins, can hardly be imagined not to command. Bo often eats with the unlicensed crew as if he's lost his way to the officers' mess. He commands as if the company can't find anybody else, but he doesn't fool anybody.

As drunks they chose ships by whim, depending on where they felt like spending the winter. Now the shippers seek them out. Gundy still dreams of certain streets, waitresses, harbors, but Bo dreams of earlier lives and places, and he hankers for his cast-iron Soho loft and the ascetic regimens he observes there.

Sindbad probably finished his astonishing life cushy in Basra. Bo intends to finish his by deciphering the sultan's *Book of Secrets* and navigating through Manhattan's tides and storms of people.

Gundy sees Bo as the Flying Dutchman, sails full-set in any weather, destination under lock and key. What Gundy knows best about him is that you never know what he'll do, and neither does he. What Gundy doesn't know is that the world is seeded with busboys, waitresses, hookers, widows on park benches, elemental girls in museums, Sufi sheiks and Hindu holy men—who remember Bo as an epiphany.

Bo and Gundy talk of fitting out a sloop in Edgewater or City Island and engaging the sea as Eric and Sindbad knew her. They know they will die as seamen. They think of landlocked countries like Switzerland as jails.

★

Suddenly Bo puts a name to what he smells in the dank nightfall—hate. Stronger than cat piss. It's risky to work on ships with a bad nose. His mind fumes with paint lockers, grinding gears, molding rope, rotting teeth, and the solvents of loneliness. Hate doesn't smell like these. Hate smells like burning flesh.

Only one smell is more memorable, the smell of Ulrike's mind when he entered it. Battery acid and corrosion.

Manhattan's aromas dizzy the mind and send it staggering down half-remembered alleys. He knows he's smelled only two women. In all other encounters he smelled his own fantasies. Dacia: lemon, piss and new-mown hay. Margaret: apples and falling snow.

And now there's apple and juniper in his nostrils.

Scat asks, How ya wanna smell, Bo? He's almost forgotten the name. They called him Scat at a gym where he used to hang out in college because he could fake the sounds of musical instruments and make songs out of them. Hello, Scat, where you been? The name Bo, short for boatswain's mate, came later in the Navy. The conversations between Bo and Scat kept him sane. And if they needed a referee, there was always Amir, his given name, to jump in and say something smooth.

He pirouettes and boogies backwards a few steps, making like a sax and not attracting much more attention on West Houston than your ordinary syphilitic. How'd I like to smell, Scat? Like the North Sea, without remorse. He walks two more blocks before his own words catch up with him. Without remorse. He doesn't mean cruel. What does he mean? Could remorse be the corrosive? Ulrike invited him to feel remorse for the sacrifices she'd made for him. He's read about emotions he can't feel, proving himself a stranger, forcing him to turn to movies to learn to fake responses. The trouble with movies is you like to sound like Claude Raines but prefer to look like Trevor Howard. Too many decisions. You gotta respect your nose. Didn't James Joyce know that? People who say he's unreadable have ruined their noses smoking.

Sailors don't trust the sea the way soldiers trust earth. Like all seamen he knows the sea is peopled by demons. Earth beasts are lawful and predictable. Demons are lawless and unknowable. The sea doesn't mother fools.

He shrugs and scuds southward towards his loft. Manhattan is rewiring the connection between his eyes and his brain. He's used to distances, like seamen and Bedouins, and now the middle distance is as junked up as Rotterdam harbor. At sea his eyes don't have to pepper his brain with messages—a frigate here, a freighter there, a junk ahead, a dhow with her divers down. From Pernambuco to Alexandria to Kobe he's searched for lodging, and everywhere he's been a stranger more than here.

4

All Addie's written musings are addressed to Margaret and never sent.

"*Women are not so willing to sell what's closely studiable for a song. Nor are they half so apt to flinch. Did you ever know a man who knew that?*"

It was still sitting in her Olivetti, looking ridiculously grandiose. She felt like a drunk unable to decipher her notes the next day. What the hell did I mean? She snatches the paper out of the typewriter, crumples it up and throws it into the center of her loft. She shuts her eyes and imagines the floor as a pond, her words rippling out from the center.

"You knew a man who knew that and you threw him away. You did, you—" she cuts herself short, astonished at her anger at Margaret.

She studies her face in the darkening window and thinks it's a face she might like to have. This is how she stands back from an instrument to apprehend what it means to be.

Two days later, speaking with Margaret on the telephone, their conversation turns as it often does to Dacia. "But if she had loved you, what would it say about you?" Once she says it, the encrypted silence of their transatlantic line swamps her. Addie Compton and Margaret Wadeleigh speak more by caesura than word. But this silence is mean. Addie hears the bond between Margaret and her dead mother Dacia part strand by strand and finally snap. She has no talent for *le mot juste*, but now she has found the one way to put the matter that darts past Margaret's formidable intelligence and hooks her gut. It's like striking the first note on an ancient instrument she has restored. You can't know how it will sound. Hearing it corrupts all your efforts to tune the thing. After years of communion as girls and women she has finally said exactly what Margaret wants and dreads to hear, and she hears their own bond fray.

Margaret and Bo Cavalieri stared into the kilns of each other's histories and staggered back blinded. Not an image Addie is likely to forget, nor did Margaret intend her to forget it. She'd drawn the image as a kind of notation to herself, and handed it over to Addie. She can certify few things as real until Addie knows them. Addie is the repository of what eludes Margaret. It's the nature of their love, but how could Addie know that it can be spoiled so easily, by simply saying the one thing Margaret had unknowingly been waiting for Addie to say?

If you ask her Addie will be unable to say when she has last been angry. She probably can't remember being angry. She has not had that kind of life. But at this moment she's furious. She feels betrayed by Margaret and by herself and she hardly knows which of them deserves her fury more. In a salad of signs, a babel of emergencies, Addie listens vainly for the only voice that ever struck her as true.

Nothing in her exhilarating friendship with Margaret has prepared her for this. They became lovers by experiment, then by preference, slowly by love. At first it felt like incest. In time it was comfortable and intimate. Their lives came to rest on this unbreakable bond, even across a sea.

When Margaret returned from her lectures in North America she told Addie in detail of her encounter with Amir Cavalieri. She'd met Amir in the attic of the deserted boarding school where he and Dacia had lived during World War II. Dacia and many English children, particularly those from East Anglia, where American bombers massed, were sent to safety in Canada or the States. When her mother called Dacia home after the war, tearing her from Amir, it blighted her life. She never regained her footing. She remained difficult, enigmatic and unloving for the rest of her short life, mourning Amir but afraid to look for him.

The choreography when Margaret found Bo was so surreal that she lost her way. The more the taciturn seaman attracted her the more he frightened her. At first Addie thought her friend had been unable to resolve some sexual conflict, some issue of identity. She wondered if perhaps Margaret's connection to Bo had become more sacrosanct than even Addie imagined. But the more she heard the more she understood that Margaret's body had opened like an autumn rose to a pale sun but had been checked by a perversity Addie had never seen before. Margaret had longed to take what her mother was denied. She longed to exult doing it. Margaret's account conveyed the fragrance of her desire, but not the one thing that was most apparent to Addie: Margaret had simply fallen in love. Whatever that means. Until then it had always meant what they felt for each other.

Because it was her agreed-upon job, Addie listened silently. She rubbed Margaret's feet, huffed a breathy zephyr up her pubic knoll and laughed, traced her finger around Margaret's nipples, and finally made resourceful love. But she was furious, all the more so because she hid it.

As she sits in her window watching the setting sun pink the buildings across the street, she understands that her profession prepared her to be furious with Margaret's behavior. You have only one chance to restore anything like the original sound of an instrument, and you have to seize it as boldly as you can. Instead Margaret pitched an eight-year-old's tantrum. She isn't even worthy of Addie's love any more, is she? She probably thinks, brilliant mathematician that she is, that she can go back and work that equation again and again any time she wants to: erase it, write it down again, leave it on blackboards, neglect it. Is that what she thinks? Foolish girl. Or did she think at all? She's thrown away not only Amir Cavalieri but Addie's respect. The perversity of the act infuriates Addie. All her life Margaret complained of Dacia's perversity; now she's trumped it.

The more Addie plays peekaboo with such thoughts, the more she sees her own anger as facile. Packing off to Salvo because your lover dumps the inevitable man doesn't parse. She didn't pronounce herself dead and go off to Salvo to enjoy her death because Margaret had turned their world topsy-turvy and was acting as if everything is business as usual. No, something in

Margaret's story belongs to her, something Margaret is treating cavalierly. Bo cavalierly? She smiles. Put on your running shoes, Addie, run this puling thought to death. You're angry because Margaret is a prat, because she hurt this man who doesn't deserve to be hurt, who's had enough hurt, who . . . put on your running shoes and sweat out this nonsense.

5

"Now I lay me down, not in this gated vault—too public—nor under these fatted cherubim, nor this veiled obelisk—gauche— but in that pale-lit glade between the stones from which I can rise and visit my peers like a deer at twilight. I can speak with these wise people but not with the busybodies who beset the body of God like gnats."

Oh my God, what tripe! Margaret says whenever she revisits this passage in her journal. She wrote it the second night of her return from America, after her stay in Addie's place in Murray Hill and her encounter with Bo Cavalieri. She stood at Heathrow the night before, looking around for Addie to embrace her, reward her for leaving the past where it belongs. But Addie hadn't been asked to be there, and Margaret felt like an immigrant disembarking from Lahore. New York at her back felt more familiar.

She has no idea which gated vault she means, which cherubim or veiled obelisk. It sounds like a horror flick. She buried Dacia in Paris and not in a gated vault or under cherubim, but in a sunny clearing, because all she'd ever loved of Dacia was seeing her eyes dance in the sun.

She decides her over-ripe journal entry is a memento mori. It fits because she often apostrophizes Descartes, Pythagoras, Al Jayanni, Napier, the divine lot of them, her true forebears.

Margaret is at times—in her garden in Lechlade, before a fireplace, when flustered—embarrassingly ripe, but it's unlikely her colleagues see anyone but her usual statuarial self behind which she defends her altar from Dacia's fickle enthusiasms. And yet from Dacia she learned the importance of disguise. Dacia's enthusiasms were nothing but the masques she wore over her mourning for her lost friend Amir, the severe Cavalieri whom Margaret found in the attic of a ruined boarding school, sitting in a shaft of golden dust, sewing up Woofy Poofy, Dacia's ancient rag doll. Now Margaret joins this mourning, marginalizing herself as Dacia had done, because later in life neither Dacia nor Amir sought each other out, preferring to cut their losses, fearing the changelings they might find.

★

Margaret owes her success as a mathematics professor to ice and sleet. Sleet was tearing at her pneumonia hole—bearing in mind Isadora Duncan's bizarre death, she regarded scarves as nooses—so she ducked into a lecture hall at Cambridge one evening and studied the announcements. Doctor John Croyden, guidance systems coordinator of Roitmann Rocketry, Ltd., was the speaker. She smiled at the idea of limited rocketry. She peered into the empty hall and saw a flustered scarecrow fidgeting with his papers at the podium. With the sleet puddling her neck she felt some empathy with the linear man's discomfort. She took a seat in the front row, like an ambitious student, and smiled reassuringly at him. He blushed, which amused her. Her beauty was usually so forbidding that it rarely invoked so boyish a response. She trusted men—women too—who responded to her as if they couldn't help it. Margaret groaned within when Croyden began to speak. She expected Americans to be less verbal than their British peers even when they were smarter, but this man's thoughts couldn't survive his lips. She freed him of her gaze, which was in any case unsparing, and began to read his brief biography: M.I.T. doctorate in speculative mathematics, Stanford doctorate in quantum physics. Dear God! She looked up at him in awe and consternation, and in that instant, as if emboldened, he turned his back to his audience and then wheeled back around, a different Croyden.

"Look," he said, seeming frustrated, "rockets, guidance systems, smart bombs, they're toys really." Seats creaked as his modest audience leaned forward. "If you want to savor a really sophisticated engine, an engine more powerful than any we've imagined—consider a poem. Riding a poem to Pluto is like a spin around the block. A poem can take you to places you haven't even imagined. And if you think that's something, let me offer you an even more elegant engine—a mathematical formula. No, I'll make it more beautiful than that: the simple zero. Consider it. Oval or round, it's close to God's mind, uh, with apologies to the atheists among you. The Hindus imagined it. With their embarrassment of gods and goddesses, they were the predictable people to imagine it. I'm not a Hindu, but I can see the zero being dedicated to Kali, the goddess of death. Then came the Arabs, night travelers with their heads stung by the stars, and they took the zero and developed a mathematical science so that the idea of number could be liberated from Roman stick figures. They pulled the heavens down into our minds."

This different Doctor Croyden went on for another five minutes. Then he looked straight down at Margaret Wadeleigh and stopped. His audience took it as a caesura, but Margaret understood it better. She rose and walked straightaway to a side exit near the podium. She did not acknowledge John Croyden. But at the door she turned and found his gaze. Slowly emotion warmed her long, unfathomable face until she beamed. John Croyden had earned a smile no one had seen since Margaret was eight. It beatified him.

Margaret had no business being at Oxford, as the sherry sots and pooh-bahs at Cambridge were always telling her. Cambridge was famous for its mathematicians and scientists, Oxford its arts and letters. Indeed some of her peers at both universities suspected that she chose Oxford so that her star might hang a bit higher than it would at Cambridge. It wasn't true. Her choice had nothing to do with university.

The day she graduated from Oxford she celebrated not with beery chums but biked alone in the Cotswolds and fell in love late in the afternoon in the headlands of the Thames in the pleasant village of Lechlade under the shadow of the Saint Lawrence Church spire, the one Shelley called "an aerial pile."

She'd passed it briskly. She was tired and looking for a place to eat. A stone cottage winced from the road, facing east. Actually it faced Clare's Way, which intersected with the east-west road she was following, so that she first saw the south and east sides of the cottage. She wheeled around, just barely getting out of the way of an oncoming lorry. Once on Clare's Way she could see the sun setting behind the cottage through its front windows and she sensed it was vacant. The architecture struck her as melancholy. She imagined that even when this classic Cotswolds cottage had been built during the heyday of the wool industry it had conveyed a certain grief. This isn't what the famed honey-colored Cotswold cottages are known for. They're known for tidiness, sturdiness, palpable pleasantness.

Her pulse quickened as she peered into a window. The place was in the final stages of disrepair. From a distance it had looked intact, but up close she saw it couldn't bear many more winters of neglect. The ground that sighs and settles towards the Thames had conspired with the builder to pervade the place with melancholy. The gardens had never been well designed, but they had been loved, and now they were a morbid palette.

"Yoo hoo, what is it, dear? Yoo hoo."

Margaret came around from the back to confront a wiry, snowy woman.

"What is it, dear? May I help you?"

Margaret, never chatty, found it difficult to say how she might be helped. She gestured dumbly at the cottage.

"The Strayhorns lived here, dear. Yes, but they've been gone, oh so long I forget. Thirty years, I should say. There have been some renters. You're not a Strayhorn, are you, dear?"

"My name is Margaret Wadeleigh. I'm from Lowestoft, Suffolk."

"Mary Lambert. It should be Marie, don't you think? The Norman strain, I mean."

"Would you like it to be Marie?"

"Oh yes, dear. That would be nice."

Margaret thought dottiness divine and was adept at inspiring it.

"Well, Marie, actually I'm a student. Oxford. Well, that's not quite so any more. I graduated today."

"Of course you did. And that's exactly why you're here."

"It is?" said Margaret, smiling.

But Marie Lambert was not pursuing this line of nonsense. "Would you like to go in? I have the key."

"Is it haunted, Marie?"

"Of course, dear. Everything is haunted, don't you think?"

Two weeks later, after a flurry of telephone calls, Margaret bought the Strayhorn cottage from a bank with her father Colin's legacy. With its falling plaster, rotting roof shakes, musty closets, soggy moldings, lopsided windows, skewed doorframes and support posts, creaks and sighs and nameless ghosts, she inherited Marie Lambert as aide-de-camp as if the old woman had been waiting there all along.

The place was a wind harp and she could hardly wait for Addie to tune it.

6

At home he cooks simple fare. It's hard to find a modestly priced eatery that doesn't sprout exhibitionists at the bar. But The Red Tam on Spring Street serves up decent food and bottles the drinkers behind etched glass. He enters wearing an open peacoat and Navy watch cap low on his brow. The Red Tam reminds him of Rose MacQuarrie in her sixties when he found her in Edinburgh. She'd been betrayed by Ulrike in Algeria, and he was the result of that betrayal. He and Rose made love that snowy night and in the morning she made him breakfast wearing her nightgown, an ancient blue sweater and a red tam. He presses his eyes with both hands to repress tears.

Finishing his veal piccata, Bo glances through the clear border of the glass corral to catch the gaze of a bozo whose graying blond hair is a ruckus of horns. We know when we're watched. We've all turned in a crowded room to stare into the eyes operating on us. This watcher is not an admirer. He's not, like Bo, a man who fancies faces. Bo allows himself a sigh and scribbles in the air to the waiter to bring his bill. Occasionally he signs a drawing Soren Tired, and Soren Tired now pays the bill, gets up and leaves without another glance toward the bar.

There are nights when it takes too much to meet eyes in the street. There are other nights when he meets all eyes and seeks some out. He's a man of whom eyes demand much, and he has no escape route from this to the sea.

Worse, he's being stalked. Men who've lived on ships know sooner than others when they're being watched. It's not someone who hates him. If you have to be stalked it's better to be hated than for it to be a cold piece of business. Hate's hot and dimwitted—you can smell it. You don't have to do much to earn it. It pops out of someone's craziness and you just happen to be standing in the way. It hangs around like cat piss.

Soho in its artsy reincarnation remains infernal, haunted by the swindled clerks and laborers denied sweat equity in factories and shops. He sees their drawn and foreign faces. He's comfortable among the exhausted immigrants, not today's purveyors of pretentious kitsch and their avid dupes.

He's comfortable among the sweatshops' ghosts because his mother spawned him somewhere between Bou Saada and Algiers, then cubbyholed him under the shadow of Ebbetts Field with her German family, ever vigilant for predictable signs of his negritude, therefore his cinematic inferiority. Children born on the sly, especially those whose birth importunes others, are haunted. But hunted is the operative word—they're hunted by the injured, the betrayed, by the moment lost to cowardliness, by the trashed opportunity to soar. Ulrike conceived Bo behind her friend Rose MacQuarrie's back, probably in her bed, and Rose uncovered the betrayal soon enough.

All his life Bo Cavalieri navigated for others so as not to navigate for himself. Even before he became a navigator he was navigating the shoals of his precarious life in this, Ulrike's country. That's why he gave her a Viking funeral out beyond the twelve-mile limit, so he could finally have a chance to hoist his flag in the country she had made so foreign to him, even if it's a country for which he's killed men. Now that he's being hunted he has to do his own navigating. Whoever's stalking him—it doesn't occur to him he might be imagining it—stalks a man who has already used fourteen of the eighteen ways he knows to kill without a weapon ... but not recently.

He isn't old, but at fifty-two he's working on it. His last victim was a zarook captain in the Arabian Sea. He killed Khaled bin Aissa Al-Maeini with one clean cricoid chop to the larynx. Then he fed him to the sharks, brought the zarook about and headed her with her cargo of wretched Somali slaves bound for Nishtun—young women and children—back to the East African coast. There he distributed Al-Maeini's booty to the

Arab crew and the Somalis, keeping nothing. He'd hired on with a letter from the sultan of Oman to teach Al-Maeini modern navigation. It was rather like Vasco da Gama teaching the Arabs how to navigate, but as usual he was running from something or someone, in this case an engaging British millionaire who wrote about famous trading routes and his sister Moira, posing as his girlfriend. Bo owes his fifty-two years to the fact that such spicy imbroglios waste their charms on him. Much as he liked Peter Tomlinson and more than liked Moira Sayre, he knew the sea was safer and in the worst case offered a better death.

Integrity attracts enemies, but his own view is more metaphysical: at every checkpoint in life somebody wants to see your papers. A Jew might understandably indulge this morose notion even in self-congratulatory America—and an Arab-German-American improbably called Bo might at least empathize. Maybe he acquired more papers than most men—citations, certificates, Coast Guard licenses, discharges, the sultan's *Book of Secrets* and the fourteenth rutter of the fabled navigator Achmed ibn Madjid—because he'd never believed his papers to be in order.

Never trust a man without enemies. But that makes it no easier to decide which of your enemies might be stalking you—some wacko from a forgotten scow, nursing an improbable grudge? What wrong has survived the rub of time, the corrosion of the sea, the leathering of the liver? What does he have worth robbing? And if he has such a thing, why not just take it?

Perhaps because the two treasures are in a strongbox in a downtown bank. There would be people who knew he had *Al Kitab as Sirr, The Book of Secrets*, and Achmed's rutter.

Said bin Taimur of Oman, that charming troglodyte, left the illuminated manuscripts to Bo in his will. They'd met only twice in the sultan's palace. Tomlinson, a veteran of the Artists Rifles, had fought in a civil war to keep the despot on his throne. Peter wanted to dive off the Omani coast for alchemical artifacts. At first he wanted to write about the Pearl Route from Oman to the Mughal court in Delhi, but then he read a UNESCO book about Arab alchemy. He knew the Omani coast was a fabled cache of wrecks and he reasoned that some of them would have contained the paraphernalia of alchemy. It was an inspiredly dotty pursuit, and the wily sultan—thinking of deadly sea snakes—entertained it. In fact, he was more interested in Tomlinson's captain, Bo Cavalieri. He took to calling Bo Sindbad. He liked the hawkish, taciturn seaman and told him stories of the naval wars between Portugal and Oman for control of the seaways to Asia.

Later, when his modernist son deposed him, he took up residence in London and lived the rest of his life strolling in parks and reading. His priceless gift to Bo, delivered to Bo's loft one morning by a decorous emissary, had been a shock. Did the book contain a secret that the old man wanted to share or was the secret in the giving of the gift?

Bo by now has read the English translation provided by the emissary. He didn't have to know Arabic to know that Darby Featherstonehaugh had dolled up an alchemist's journal in fusty Victorian brocade. It annoys Bo and he resolves to translate the Arabic himself, perhaps even illustrating the book's many apparatuses and ideas, albeit the Arab miniatures could not be improved on, and certainly not the Kufic calligraphy.

Bo, unlike Margaret, doesn't have it in him to be a hidden observer. Nor has he Addie's bemused benignity. He's the son of races of fabled severity. When he sits under trees, on park benches, in cafés, sketching people, they notice him, and to ensure that they take no offense, he holds up his sketches and salutes their subjects. Otherwise his gaze—a Malay cook told him he could rivet steel plates with it—disorganizes people.

Bo, alert as an osprey, counts two of them, distracted, at odds with each other, slow. Then he sees another, fleet, separate, fond—watchers in conflict with each other. This is too far a stretch even for a man who trusts animal instincts. But he never forgets Chief Boatswain Sol Ederheimer's dictum: "Cavalieri, if it looks like a duck, quacks like a duck, and shits like a duck, it's not a goose." Later, trying to get off the roller coaster of depression and booze, he learned that children of abuse lust for context and that's their undoing. They always look for the why of something when in fact it's just a duck.

In every environ, Singapore or Rostov, a man with certitude for marrow attracts the covert watcher—a woman, a boy, a peddler, a vagrant, old souls remembering and young souls hungering. Soho with its artists and writers has more than the usual number of such men and women. Surely this sense of being watched amounts to this only: three intent onlookers as drawn to him as he's drawn to others. His composure is the allure. He understands that. He shudders and thinks wistfully of a slug of Calvados.

Whoever you are, may you sketch as well as I do, and use more color.

7

Addie is a creature of the Irish Sea. Her eyes brim with its changeability. Her sharp features are cut, not formed. Her tall athleticism summons spectatorship. Manhattan gnaws at her privacy. Knowing that New Yorkers are inured to craziness, she disguises herself in her preoccupations. Eyes must not say what they see in cities. In the city her eyes turn the color of wet sand. Their grains sift others' thoughts and intuitions. "You have the most readable eyes in the world," Margaret once said. It would have meant little to Addie—she knew it wasn't true—except that Margaret's own sapphire eyes are unreadable. And having returned to Manhattan, it seems to her she is lost at sea in Margaret's eyes, tossed like a Dixie cup in a summer squall.

She flies around Chelsea in her Nikes, winning the salutes of bent old gentlemen and vendors from Bangladesh and Bolivia. She cartwheels in her cavernous duplex, the one she herself gutted to its lushly parged brick. She practices her aikido rolls, glues a bridge to a lira da braccio, strokes a neglected lute, and listens to Telemann and Tallis.

Addie lives on Cushman Row, an iron-grilled north-facing march of seven Greek Revival houses on West 20th Street. A small inheritance from Brian's Norse mother Solveig and erratic fees for her work enable her to lease the fourth and sky-lit fifth floor overlooking bowered General Theological Seminary. Soho has not yet disgorged its artists and galleries, fleeing their faux arts haven where preposterously priced beds will replace paintings to bait Long Island dentists.

She has migrated with the sun from morose Murray Hill to Cushman Row, partly because stingy light depresses her, partly because she needs room. Dangling from the handle of a skylight is a glazed 19th century hunting horn. It turns in a draft and emits an amber glow when the sun strikes it. A barrel piano with its crank stands back against a bare brick wall. A self-important organ and a rather apologetic reed organ shaped like a Greek kithara seem to converse in the rear of the fourth floor. In the front between two windows an upright harpsichord reigns like Gloriana. Seated in a stuffed chair is a contented lyre guitar. Dangling acrobatically in the air are a Belgian clarinet in B flat, a flageolet in C, two tatty shawms, a boxwood and ivory oboe and a muscular dulzian. A grumpy silver euphonium hangs underneath the suspended staircase rebuking Addie for its embarrassment. The flared proboscis of a French horn tweaks its maker's pomp. On Addie's worktable a soprano ophicleide in B flat and dishabille, with nine arthritic keys, pleads to be left in peace. These are the notables, but the place is littered with mandolins, violins, lutes and hundreds of orphaned parts. Everything cries out for touch. Addie relishes being so much in demand.

Sprinting between umbrellas and puddles, lugging baroque cellos and bundles of arcane wood, Addie's a Chelsea familiar, a welcome bookmark to the glum studies of the seminarians. A Korean fruit seller waits for her each day so he can juggle Granny Smiths for her amusement. The Irish barkeep in Parnell's Hat stations himself at the head of his bar to snap her a cockeyed salute. The Peruvian busboy at Marsilio's awaits her with an Andean tune in his panpipes. Her minions are hard put to say it, but she cheers them with the possibility of goodness and they count on her like the moan of a romantic cello.

When she thinks of returning to England she worries about her people—the melancholic seminarians, the homesick busboy, the barkeep who'll be a little more sardonic without her, the round-faced jongleur for whom she is a kind of visa. Can she leave them to difficult America, America that needs so much understanding? But she misses the smiling verdure of the English countryside, the grave companionability of the Round Reading Room in the British Museum, the tempered zanies. Rowboating in Central Park is not as gracious as punting on the Isis. And sometimes the patois of Noo Yawk jangles her and is mitigated only by her ambition to cut up the passport of a certain kind of British arriviste who comes to the States to exploit Yank anglophilia. She boycotts the mouth-breathing British expatriate colony and despises its jaded plumminess.

There are people whose fevered antennae sense more than is good for them. Given love, parents' approval, circumspection and a poker face, they can survive in a world that punishes what used to be called seers. Others, writers for example, get into trouble for their exhibitionism. Addie's farsight and insight hide behind a carven face. Silence is her native tongue. That she hears people think and sees documentaries for which she has not paid admission never troubles her, nor does she choose that others should be troubled.

Only the Sunday before, she'd stood in the parish hall of Saint Peter's Episcopal Church, sipping coffee with the choirmaster, when she distinctly heard behind her, "God, what a lovely ass!" As she left the hall her eyes found the junior warden, who had parked that thought in the air. He was chatting up a claque of toadies. She looked over their shoulders and gave him a purse-lipped look that said dream on. Addie has neither the desire to offend nor the compulsion to be offended, but she has discovered in her lover a grand compulsion to be offended.

8

By the time Margaret earned her advanced Cambridge degrees, Cambridge had lost her. Wind Harp settled that. Marie Lambert's oddness advanced no further, leaving Margaret to speculate that Marie likely had been an odd child. While Addie was off learning what the craftsmen of Cremona and Venice had to teach, Margaret studied at Cambridge, and when she could she and Marie and a squadron of pub-based artisans refurbished the Wind Harp. Nothing pleased Margaret more on Friday evenings than to drive home to one of Marie's arcane meals. Marie was a vegetarian and proselytzed her found daughter, inveighing against the murderousness of milk.

Wind Harp was Margaret's secret, like being the bastard child of a mighty lord. She wouldn't name the cottage and its humble parcel, not openly, because she didn't wish to share her secret. No one at Cambridge ever saw it, so it took on mythic proportions, as if it were the Churchills' Blenheim, a process abetted by the fact that Margaret was already the subject of much speculation for having handled her own financial affairs since her first year at Oxford. That was the year Dacia had immolated herself in her celadon Maserati with its white leather interior when she hit a tree in the Bois de Boulogne. Her will said simply that she left her estate in its entirety to her daughter "who will, doubtless, handle it better than I have." That was the only personal reference to Margaret in the notably terse document. It was prescient.

Wind Harp had remained bland, if repaired, until Addie returned from her four years in Italy. She arrived unannounced on a June evening, toting her rucksack and little else. She walked down to the end of Clare's Way to find the fabled Marie Lambert.

"I'm Addie Compton."

Marie was up to her rump in herby ooze. "You must not only look like an Adeline Compton, you must feel like one. Do you?"

"Not at all, Marie. I think that feeling like one's name is rather like watering a garden at night, it shouldn't be done."

Marie looked at her latest daughter approvingly. Clearly this lithe girl was as wonderfully mad as she herself.

★

Addie wasted no time. Even before her tools and instruments and books arrived in the crates she had built for them she began stripping Wind Harp's beams, patching and refinishing its floors and making proper work counters. She stained the beams lightly and lightened the interior with white paint. She filled gouges in the floors with sawdust and polyurethane, plucked raised nails and tapped slightly bigger ones into holes carefully filled with splinters. All these transformations she accomplished in three weeks while Margaret was lecturing in Berne. By the time Margaret returned Addie was using the crates in which her instruments arrived to build closet shelves. She had already penciled bookcase and painting sites on the walls.

Margaret stood in the doorway cloaked in tatters of evening. Crouched in a cranny with a pencil in her mouth, Addie jumped up and shouted, "L'enfleurage!" In her joy at seeing Addie Margaret's usual eroticizing blush failed to appear. But as they embraced in the center of the spectral room all the ripened fields of her body stirred as she savored Addie's reference to putting neutral oils at risk of the fragrances of flowers. Margaret looked around, touching mantels and lintels, the walls, the refinished Christian doors. "You're incorrigible. It's magical. Did you have to do homework?"

"I grew up in the Cotswolds. It's a typical cottage. Nothing as grand and gloomy as East Anglia."

In a few days it was established that Addie was the resident architect, Margaret the master gardener. After years at their studies it didn't occur to them to discuss arrangements. Margaret knew Addie needed more space, much more, but for now Wind Harp was enough.

★

Wind Harp was Oxford's good fortune. Soon Margaret stood alone among her math and science colleagues in drawing students of the arts and humanities to her courses. She told each class it had come to build millennial engines that were desperately needed. In this way she cajoled each student back to an innocent time of dolls, doll houses, model airplanes and ships, and she convinced her students that this and this alone is what mathematics is about. Only a few of her peers approved, the ones who sail the seas of number hardly ever noticing the body politic. But the envy and ill will of the others didn't matter because a university is a business, and Margaret drew students, the fodder of such a business. She had the bean counters' admiration if not her department's—all that counts in a casino society.

The flustered, short-circuited John Croyden had made her a legend. But she never had the nerve to tell him. Sometimes she thought he knew. Other times she blanched in shame at her selfishness in not telling him.

9

There's a moment in the restoration of an instrument, indeed a moment in its making, when the sound it should have hangs in the air. A misstep dooms it to mediocrity. This is true in the making of a painting or a poem, but it's not as true. Addie Compton's profession is more dangerous than Bo Cavalieri's old profession of frogman. She has never lost her balance, never betrayed anyone else's work of art, anyone's true ear—until she says that one thing that breaks the string bridge of the instrument that was the love between her and Margaret, upon which no crudity had ever trespassed. Their love had always been a pure response to each other, not a revulsion from anyone or anything, and it had been broken the only way it could be broken, by one of them. Now, without this instrument, Addie doesn't know how to play any notes at all.

And then comes a conversation that moves her to long to be even less a thorn, even more anonymous. She's sitting behind the plate window in Rienzi's sipping a cocoa that would make an elephant diabetic. Rain strafes Rienzi's painted name. Soggy passersby look in at her. A Teuton god stares at her from within Rienzi's bowels. She leans her gaze across the wall against his mordant face and stops. Some men's faces tic when arrested in a woman's eye—they've been found in the odor of their thoughts. Others feign nonchalance and look away. Some smile genuinely or manipulatively. But this Teuton considers her as a god would. He's found a woman who can hold a gaze as impassively as himself. A handmaiden of Odin—he will let her near what he guards.

"May I?" he says, insinuating himself upon her table.

She nods slightly, wishing she'd given herself leave to read his mind.

"I thought we might be kindred souls."

Addie smiles, considering how a Noo Yawk chick might greet this lame ploy. She can't hear his tone. His beautiful bones have none.

"I like your face. I collect faces. Actually I paint them."

"For the walls of Valhalla?"

"Yes, yes, for the walls of Valhalla. You see, I knew we're kindred. I looked at you by the window and thought how beautiful this country used to be. But it's turning darker every day, dark and brutish and dumb. The greedy bastards with their Swiss accounts did it, opening the gates to cheap labor. Where are the blonds? I'll tell you, they're sex objects, sold like so many vibrators to the criminal horde."

"And you remember all this happening in your lifetime?"

"I've seen them coming, the caramel mutants, the ochre dwarfs."

She likes the cadence of his awful words.

He continues speaking. "The educated mind is capable of understanding history. We're short on educated minds. Do you know why? Because the swindlers who ruined this country needed first to make it dumb. That's why they've addicted it to violence and sexual abuse. They needed to coarsen it so that it wouldn't sense its own betrayal."

Addie's fate is to be told insupportable things. She shares this in common with the German nation. This Teuton god has struck a few true chords in the course of his racist riff. Good thing Goebbels hadn't looked like him.

She leans back and sets her surgical hands at the table's edge. Her anal sphincter shuts as kundalini rears. "The trouble, Horst, is that you have no affect. None." She rises and then looks down on him. "That's how it is." She walks out into the ballistic rain, her yellow slicker tearing open to welcome the purification.

Margaret Wadeleigh the never mistaken, Adeline Compton ever mistook, that's how it's always been, even in their lovemaking. Margaret a rose garden, Addie a spectral gardener, shapeshifting,

52

deft to a fault, answerable. To whom does Margaret answer? Only Dacia, the arbiter of their lives, Dacia who had the audacity to love only once, too soon and too much, Dacia who remained true to that one love until death, an act they could never top, the showstopper of their lives, damned Dacia dabbling even in their body fluids.

There are acts that are mere stage blood, albeit stage blood that would gag a vampire, and then there are acts that draw blood. Once at school, Addie, tipsy on smuggled absinthe, snatched a pair of Margaret's panties and inhaled. The moment stalled in the air between them. She thought only to make Margaret blush. But Margaret swarmed her with the blue of her eyes and said after a long spell, "Not lemon magnolia, I should think."

"Dacia actually."

Margaret ambled towards her, her pupils contracted. She lodged her long nose between Addie's eyes. Addie held her breath. She had gone too far. Much too far. With the middle finger of her left hand Margaret circled Addie's nipple, like an Egyptian priestess making a hieratic sign, and then she felt Margaret's other hand take the measure of her pubic mound. "This is a signal moment," she whispered in Addie's ear, "so say nothing more."

And Addie never did, nor did she ever really know what Margaret had understood by her tipsy remark. All she knew is that they decided that if Dacia were to haunt their sheets and lingerie, then perhaps her presence ought to be recognized if not formally invited. After that Dacia was no longer countenanced; she was accepted. Addie's only question was forensic: she might be expected to remember Dacia's special fragrance—new-mown, like Margaret's—but she would certainly not have known those other fragrances, and yet Margaret said only that she should say no more.

Maybe when they were girls they'd thought to be safe from Dacia in each other, but time taught them that she would be there tasting and seeing whenever nipple rose or pubis throbbed, whenever a thought turned to touch or a hair stood at its root. Dacia the sticky-fingered. How had Addie, child of dairy farmers, been caught in Dacia's web? Dacia hadn't wanted anything of Margaret and certainly not of Addie. Dacia hadn't wanted anything of anyone, and that's why polished stone can't keep her. Margaret must have known this or she wouldn't, couldn't have found Bo Cavalieri. His impossibly synchronous finding had to be Dacia's doing. That could explain Margaret's flight, her fright. But what of him? He isn't just someone's love object. What does he sense? Addie remembers his three calls on her answering machine in Murray Hill.

"Margaret, it's Bo." He'd paused. "I'll be here after ten and in the morning till eleven." She'd tried to place his accent. It wasn't Noo Yawk; it had been seasoned by the places he'd seen and the people he'd known. His voice was quiet, its cadence considered. He didn't hesitate to pause to form his thoughts. She heard melancholy, a strain of hope, and the long calm of truth. She played the message over and over and wondered if she should call him. Then his second message: "Bo Cavalieri, Margaret. Call." Did he think Margaret knew any other Bo? His third and final call conveyed a poignant introspection. He knew then that Margaret wouldn't call. Maybe he knew she was gone, although a seaman, Addie mused, would hardly think of being in England as gone. "*Bonne courage*, Margaret." He paused. "*Et adieu.*"

Addie fell in love with that third call. She hadn't imagined he would know French, but his accent bore the authority of a French speaker. So he was a man of parts. The dignity of his resignation gripped her. Margaret had wasted this man. He was worth knowing. Her mind sent for him but she decided her relationship with Margaret wouldn't allow it. He wasn't up for grabs. She felt resentful, thwarted. His voice haunted her, the wry, serious pauses as much as the few words. This man would never call again and it was Addie who felt bereft. What she didn't know was that Margaret before she left had exhausted the tape in Bo's answering machine with hang-ups until finally he'd picked up the box and dropped it in the Hudson. He was not a man who lived in the spaces between calls and letters. They were not the tools of his trade. Or of Addie's.

54

A man who understands gimcracks, gewgaws and doodads was bound to interest Addie. Walls on wheels, trompes l'oeil, faux windows and much more are Addie's stock in trade. She restlessly reshapes her workspaces and positions mirrors to reflect exterior spaces. She's fond of paneless windows on walls, or windows backed by mirrors. And locked inside one of these mirrors, sandwiched between two smaller facing mirrors, is Margaret's St. Agnes graduation portrait. The purpose of this cache is to force Margaret to face herself. Sometimes, before sleep, Addie wonders where she got the idea for this fetish. She must have read about it somewhere.

10

The silliest moment in his life, discounting getting himself born to narcissists, happened outside the Bay of Algiers. It haunts him with a question that strikes him both as nuts and as significant. It crosses his grain, reminding him of his innocence. "How much for the girl?" he asks whenever life stumps or trumps him. Then he waits for absurdity to tickle his brain. He was navigator on the *Onandaga Flyer* anchored off Algiers waiting for a Himmlerian harbor captain to permit her to proceed to a berth. Flo Hensen, one of the first King's Point women to sail, was walking purposefully on the deck, her red head occulting like a flashing buoy. She was handsome, more like a boy than a girl, her remarkable bosom notwithstanding.

"Yankees, Yankees, how much for the girl?" the *Terpsichore* radioed to the *Onandaga*. "Fuckin' Greeks," Pep Patterson, the chief mate, grunted. Pauli Mariano, the radio officer who had been slurping coffee while taking in Pep's orders, picked up the speaker and said, "*Terpsichore, Terpsichore*, you are cleared to proceed to pier six, over." Bo had been working a harbor chart and surveying the harbor. At first he thought the Algerian martinet had given *Terpsichore* her berthing orders. He was angry because it was *Onandaga's* turn. But then he saw Pauli's shit-eating grin and remembered that Pauli was a better mimic than sailor. The Greeks acknowledged, taking the fake port captain's order as a show of anti-Americanism, and weighed anchor. Twenty minutes later Pauli switched channels and they heard the port captain, sounding just like Pauli, swearing at the Greeks in French, English and Greek. Crazy Joe Hartshorn, their storm-loving skipper, said, "Don't ever do that again, Pauli." Then as he rolled up a chart, he muttered, "Goddam Greeks." Pep winked at Pauli. Bo stared at him. He couldn't bring himself to approve. Crazy Joe, who liked Bo, looked at him as if to say, *What can I do? They're all assholes.*

His fondness for the Greeks' question unfolds slowly over the years, its first inkling being that one day, months after Margaret vanished, he asked his mirror, "Yeah, how much?"

★

The first thing Addie does when she returns from her fantasia in Salvo is tape over the niggling red eye of her answering machine with a tiny square of black electrical tape. She's a gifted jackleg electrician, a good thing when you live in barns and lofts and greenhouses. She'll listen to the machine when she's unpacked and organized, when she's laid in food, reconnected with sensei's dojo, read a book. She considers with a shudder that Margaret left Bo's calls on her machine in Murray Hill like soiled panties on a doorknob. Everything else had been predictably spotless, a split of Taittinger Rheims in the fridge, the Borzoi edition of *The Voyages of Sindbad* that she apparently had found at The Gotham Book Mart, a fresh window scrub, sheets and towels laundered and folded in Margaret's distinctive four-ways-to-the-middle pattern. The more Addie considered Bo's unerased calls, the more contempt she felt towards Margaret's inconsiderateness.

They'd known as long-legged eleven-year-olds that they were winsome and longed-for, and if they were to give themselves permission to enjoy each other in trust, chivalry required them to do no harm elsewhere. Neither of them took offense, feigned or mock, at admiration, as dimwits do. They were at pains to take pity on anyone flummoxed by their looks. For instance, Margaret once looked up from her Graham Greene in the London underground into a boyish face jerked every which way in the embarrassment of being caught inhaling her. The poor boy's eyes darted away as if his life were in peril. But Margaret put down her book on her lap and waited patiently for his gaze to return, and when it did she smiled and winked to salve his masturbatory guilt. Beauty is accidental and not to be taken seriously, as far

57

as she and Addie were concerned. Whoever understands this about them has the key to their company. God, the great zero, as Margaret joked, unaccountably gave them each other so they'd never need another and would grow up untroubled by all the writhing that turns boys and girls into public nuisances. Perhaps that's why they sang their Anglican hymns with less than the usual academic desultoriness, to thank God for such untroubled lives—as long as room could be made for Dacia Wadeleigh.

11

Dacia touches the young women but has never summoned them. Now she summons Addie. Addie puts on her long navy duffel coat and patrols her loft beating her biceps like a flightless bird. She hopes the coat will banish the white burnoose and cheche her mind has been putting on her since her last night at Salvo. She feels encumbered yet ennobled by the Arab garb. And then she hears a question:

"Are you ready to proceed? My name is Mutawakkil ibn al Quereishi. You may call me master. Shall we proceed?"

"Proceed where?"

"At first to the point at which you perceive that you must call me master."

"That'll be the day."

"It will. First, sort yourself out. You're a mess."

"I weigh 110 pounds. I can easily run ten kilometers and sprint three. I speak English, French, Italian and German and am ambidextrous."

"You're a mess."

"You're referring to my feelings about Margaret Wadeleigh?"

"An alchemist is never sloppy. For example, grief is not despair. Sorrow is not depression."

"Have you anything good we can pour into little bottles?"

"Everything is good."

"Listen, Mooty-whatever, go hand out roses in airports."

"Call me master."

"How about shyster?"

As a detaching retina causes white flashes in the corner of the eye, so the sheik teases her gaze just out of sight.

Everywhere she looks in the room she sees a flash of white, then nothing.

"Yes, that would be nice. Call me shyster."

She recognizes the Sufi methodology: drive the adept toward holy madness. Plenty of self-ordained masters, all of them seductive and slick, pick your pockets for as long as they can. But this sheik doesn't exist, which makes him more dangerous.

"Mooty-whacky?"

"Yes, yes, I like that better than shyster, Adeline. Call me Mooty-Whacky. Shall we proceed?"

"We may proceed for as long as I say so."

"How else?"

She thinks perhaps she has tapped a part of herself that can offer wisdom as long as it's disguised as something, someone else. Margaret remembers little of anything Dacia said. Dacia said little, but now Addie remembers something Dacia told a bothersome acquaintance, "Your craziness shines in the dark." Addie wonders, Does mine?

"You're proposing to teach me alchemy then?"

"No one can do that. I can show you what is involved."

"Has this ever been done before? Surely it has."

"Why do you answer your own question? It's cowardly."

Her short hairs bristle. This is not how she'd talk even idly entertaining herself. This is more than verbal eroticism.

"Has it ever been done before? Really?"

"No. A thousand times no. Although a million charlatans say yes. Alchemy is consent. That's all it is. Consent to use your own powers. Therein is all courage and nobility and danger."

"I shall take you at your word, Sheik Mutawakkil ibn al Qureishi. For the time being."

"Fool's gold is the real gold. Value is always disguised. What you call true gold is a golden apple, forbidden and so doomed to be picked and eaten. The assignment of values is the root of blindness. These truths are worn on the foreheads of the occasional man. He is always reviled more than he is loved. It is necessary to torment and kill him. He is reviled most by those who would love him. It is necessary to betray him."

60

"How does he wear these truths on his forehead?"

"I have chosen you to learn. Whatever happens to you is part of your acceptance of my choice. Always ask yourself if you should ask more or keep your own counsel. The occasional man will always recognize you. Perhaps you have noticed?"

She nods, listens, but hears no more. If the sheik inhabits the brooks of her mind he's good at hiding in its trout pools. She can't conjure him, imitate him or even mock him once he leaves. He's as absent as a stillborn child and leaves the same kind of ache, the kind she and Margaret Wadeleigh learned to assuage in each other at Saint Agnes. The adolescent Addie kept catching herself daydreaming about the chain of loops and Palatino zeros that composed her roommate's body. Margaret was a riot of curves, freshets of blushes. She looked disturbingly fecund, and Addie, already more interested in musical instruments than in their sounds, longed to play her, to tune her, to repair her, before she knew how much Margaret needed repair.

Margaret was bolder, puzzling Addie's sinewy rhythms as she would equations on a chalkboard. She wanted to organize the bones under Addie's taut skin. She wanted to taste that mouth that could not hide its teeth, that seemed ecstatic even in sleep.

The two girls from their first encounter when they were eight would never need other friends, and yet it was their special politesse never to make others feel excluded. They kept their secret so discreetly that they were almost universally perceived as two typically reserved English achievers whose casual relationships with men merely bespoke discernment.

Margaret in her febrile bloom has more curiosity than Addie about men, but few men find a way to cope that isn't Florentine. They don't sense how approachable she is.

Addie attracts stammerers, the painfully shy and the rare jock whose synapses fire well. And less often she attracts the kind of man who loses his dignity to a spectacular pair of legs, which always amuses her. She pities his predicament.

Margaret is often perceived as a problem, a challenge. Addie is perceived as the possessor of a simple decency without which world order would collapse. The young women wear these roles lightheartedly, and yet they yearn for someone—a man?—to perceive them more simply, to like them for their pheromones, to act as if it would be pleasant to bask in their breath. They yearn to be sensed not by their auras but by their bodies, their odors, their essences, which they can't do anything about. Both of them understand—it's the weft of their gravitas—that they're the sort of people, once encountered, without whom the world can no longer be imagined. They accept this as a responsibility, not as power—and this serves them as well as Alexander the Great's *perpetua fortuna* served him. The given of this delicacy is that they themselves never should encounter anyone without whom the world can be imagined. Why should they? Have any so memorable, so indispensable, presented themselves? Not the beautiful and not the wise. Dacia, yes, but she's a wraith. It takes Addie, useful as a bank trust, to see that Dacia led Margaret straight to the unimaginable person. And Margaret, running true to form, ran away. But why has Dacia led stubborn Margaret to this threat to their equilibrium? Why not Addie, whom she favored? Why had she not said, *Here, practical Addie, you take care of this matter?*

She listens to her thoughts echo. Take care of this matter? Is that what Dacia would say? Bo Cavalieri, a matter to take care of? No, no, I've chosen my words as if I were explaining it to Margaret. Margaret, I've taken care of that matter, you know, the American thing.

At this point she comes up short as she realizes that when Dacia enters her mind she comes omniscient as God. Heedless, reckless Dacia, forever too affronted by fate. A thing broken can never be made whole, she'd told Addie, it can only be glued. She said glued through her nose as if evicting a gnat. And so of course Addie made a career of fixing broken things, arch lutes and bass guitars and Margaret's heart. But the heart broken by a parent or a child can never be glued; it wheezes and sobs and leaks and defeats conservators. A hint of that sometimes prompts Addie, a conservator of high repute, to tell clients, I'm sorry, but I can't do anything with that. As if the instrument tells her how it was broken and she respects its despair.

Margaret's brokenness hints at its willingness to flower in hybrid profusion. So Addie touches her until she understands the grain and wont, the songs that wait in their cells, and then she strikes the chord. Only she can do it, no matter how much Margaret wants somebody else. And now is there still something only she can do, something Dacia is arranging? Can Dacia be trusted? Yes, she can be trusted by everyone, except Margaret. Everyone else, it seems, takes pains to tell Margaret what a marvelous mother she had.

"You want her? You can have her," she once yelled at Addie from her shower. And when she stepped from her shower, a horn of fruit and spun gold, Addie said, "Easy for you to say, knowing damned well nobody can have her. Your father didn't have her, he mailed a letter in her slot is all."

"Yes, and here I am," Margaret said, "stamped and cancelled. Can you imagine anything plopping bloody and stupid from between those legs?" Only for a phantom had Dacia ever wanted to spread them.

"Let's do it thinking about Dacia," Addie had said one night in their room at Saint Agnes's.

"Shall we look at each other?"

"Oh no, that would spoil it. It would be just us that way. We must turn our backs."

Back to back, sitting on the bare wooden floor, they filled their room with fragrances and fantasies until Margaret shouted, "Ooh!" and jumped up. Addie waited a few seconds for her own release and then spun around to stare at nipples more distended and petals redder than she had ever seen. Margaret's index finger was rigored as if it were some ecstatic symbol. Her eyes had come loose from their moorings. Her lips shuddered. This vision burned itself into Addie's mind and became her erotic stock. She herself had simply imagined Dacia's golden silkiness—come, Dacia, she said in her mind—and then she welled up and flowed over like a new mother. But Margaret spent time with Sade and came back despoiled. Addie's whim ended in an introduction to their mistress of ceremonies and guide to nether places. They never mention the incident, but her glimpse of Margaret in that one instant vehemently eroticized what had been a companionable liaison. Margaret could have thought of someone else with her head turned away, but her bond with Addie demanded that she imagine Dacia. For this reason Addie knew she had incurred an unsatisfiable debt. Addie longed to see Margaret in that violate state again and knew she would long for it the rest of her life. And yet the incident had one reassuring result—it affirmed that men were far less than essential. Frills, fillips really, wholly unwarranted in their shows. Women know this, but it's a part of their self-denial to disavow it. Men know that women know it, which accounts for much violence and oppression in the world.

★

Now Addie has another wicked idea: marry Sheik Mutawakkil ibn al-Quereishi and Dacia Wadeleigh, dervish and wraith. They can play ring-around-the-rosy in the ether and leave the girls to follow their noses—Margaret to Addie's wildflower breath and Addie to Margaret's starry fruitiness. My ideas will get us killed some day, Addie thinks. But something far more true eludes her, that one of her ideas back at Saint Agnes will make them girls until they die unless they find a way to break its spell. They've woven a spell to ward off womanhood.

12

Addie had been quite content with her jury-rigged life in the Thames Valley. She lived over R.V.C. Creed's Rare Books in Harlequin Street and worked in a Victorian greenhouse on the Hamidaoui estate along the river. Si Sliman Hamidaoui was an old Algerian rebel who had slipped out of the hands of General Jacques Massu's torturers with the help of Sir Winthrop Phelps, a fellow historian of Al Andalus, Arab Spain. Si Sliman, spry and rich, could think of nothing better for the big greenhouse than that it should be filled with the tools, somersaults and baroque tastes of Adeline Compton. My zephyr, he called her. At first she expected the inevitable proposition, but she came to know Si Sliman as a man too refined to upset their equilibrium.

The high point of his waning life was tea with Addie. Their conversations in French ranged from the Arab lute to the adventures of Abd ar Rahman, the founder of the Andalusian Umayyad caliphate.

Addie could have imagined nothing to lure her away from this idyll—from Si Sliman's hospitality, Margaret's nearness, the riches of Oxford. But then her mentor, Nora Richards, died and left her a house in Tivoli in Dutchess County in New York's Hudson Valley, with all Nora's instruments and tools, some of them irreplaceable. It was her first glimpse of a world in which some people might be cheered in their dying, knowing she would live on. She wasn't sure this was a knowledge she could bear. She fretted for Si Sliman. She knew the health of the very old is often drawn from a dear one, sometimes even an enemy.

"You must go, Adeline, of course you must."

He paused. "Or you will upset your friend in heaven and she will become distracted and fail to enjoy her new estate."

"But perhaps in heaven such things are meaningless, and, besides, we can't allow people to move us about like pawns, can we?"

"No one will ever move you about, dear Adeline. You simply must explore her intent. I stay here to guard your work. Be sure. Remember, I am a terrorist. Did not the great Charles de Gaulle himself say so?"

"Pouf! He said a lot of tripe."

"Yes, that is true, but the man made good enemies. I should know."

"Si Sliman, you're as English a rustic as I know. Win Phelps has become a wazir and you've become a squire."

"Go, Adeline. We shall have our tea by telephone."

★

Nora's place was a Dutch stone house set in an apple orchard. Addie fell in love with it but could not work there. She needed urban hustle for energy. Si Sliman's had been near Oxford and its microclimate of ideas. So she took a place first in Murray Hill and then in Chelsea on Cushman Row and spent some weekends in Tivoli, two hours north.

She hadn't expected to be long from Margaret or Si Sliman, but almost four years pass, and Addie finds that she has less to contend with in America. That's her shorthand for the more problematical thought that she has ceded England to Margaret. If Margaret had not come over while Addie travelled, if Margaret had not encountered Bo Cavalieri while staying in Addie's Murray Hill flat and then abandoned him, Addie might have returned to Creed's and Si Sliman's greenhouse, but Margaret is taking up too much space and filling it with her ambivalence and bad behavior, so Addie takes comfort in a careening, contrary America that likes her.

The women regard their estrangement as temporary but are disquieted by its stubbornness. Si Sliman understands and counsels Addie to hold fast in Chelsea. But he misses his zephyr so much that in May he drags his scarred old carcass aboard a British Airways plane and comes for a visit. They spend the summer in Tivoli cooking for each other, taking long walks and minding the stars, one of his passions.

"I shall make the most magical marga for you," he says.

"And I shall . . . "

"You're not going to cook for me," he interrupts.

"I'm not?"

"Adeline, the English occupied most of the known world in search of a decent meal. You cannot imagine more toxic cooks, except perhaps the Scots."

"You must not betray your adopted country with such tosh. Besides, I cook in the Tuscan manner, as you well know."

Squire Si Sliman Hamidaoui looks away from the telescope set upon Nora's bluestone terrace as if his most admired star has condescended to stand beside him. He is the only person Addie enjoys teasing.

"You're a hopeless Anglophile, you know. Why is it La Belle France never seduced you? Because she was the enemy? Enemies can be seductive. I've known Pakky pooh-bahs to come through Sandhurst less anglicized than you."

"It's the untouchable arrogance of the Brit, Adeline. It's quite Bedouin. Oh yes, I would attend church and bathe in the posh liturgy if only I could deafen my poor old marrow to the muezzin's call."

"Why do I stay here, Si Sliman, do you know?"

His long face settled like trodden sand. She twitched her nose to deflate the moment, but he wagged his graven head to caution her to respect her own question.

"Because the Americans protect you."

"From?"

"Yes, yes, that's exactly the question. Shall I answer it?"

"No, Si Sliman, thank you."

He always gives more than she bargains for. It is their contract. She is neither the daughter nor the granddaughter he would have liked, nor yet the lover he would wish were he younger—she is his angel. He is not hers, but he is her marabout.

She doesn't tell him about Mooty-Whacky because she knows he'd take it seriously. You're speaking with a djinni, he would say. There are good and bad djinn.

No, Si Sliman would affirm something she wasn't ready to believe. Her relationship with the old man even in so permissive a time could pass in England for notorious, but together they project something reassuring and infinitely human, so that when they walk in town together or take tea in cafés they present a glimpse of a better world. He isn't a wog or a lecher, and she isn't a dupe. They are fast friends and voyagers, and of this friendship comes the truth about her American sojourn. She's come, like millions before her, for protection, and he's only told her what she knows and dislikes.

"Where has Dacia gone, do you think, Si Sliman?"

"To the only place where she ever wanted to be."

"And so I've inherited her, taken her off Margaret's shoulders, so to speak. Dutiful me."

"You do not fear and loathe and love her, as Margaret does. You and Dacia have no quarrel with each other. Perhaps she has a gift for you, one she cannot give her daughter, a gift her daughter does not have the mother wit to take. People do like you, Adeline."

"Even the dead."

"Especially them."

This is Margaret's province. Or Osiris's. But not Addie's. Why has Si Sliman brought her to this eerie recognition? Why introduce dead souls from whom not even the Americans can protect? She shudders. "I'm going in for a sweater. Can I get you something?"

He's in transit between stars. Her closest companions, Margaret and Si Sliman, inhabit great abstractions and leave earthly brokenness for her to fix. Tonight she resents it. She doesn't think she can bear this role without more warmth than a sweater offers, more warmth than her shivery love of Margaret, lost in its bottomless privacies. She ties the arms of her sweater across her breast, pours two fingers of Lafroigh and gazes out the bay window at Si Sliman, his frail old body wrapped in his pleasure at being here. How can she, being herself, which means never harming those whose lives lean precariously on her, keep her fire from going out? Who will blow on her faint coals and bank her fire against the night? She sets her mind in a dark space of the firmament to see what planets take up station around it. Only one gives up its name: Dacia. All right, all right, play with my hair, touch my face, show me, show me, and if I can give it to you without being Margaret's straw man, I shall, I shall, Dacia. I know you want something of me and have never wanted anything of her. I'm her guard against this knowledge, so let's deal: what do you want, and what's it worth to you? I'm gracious, Dacia, but not foolish. Surely you must know there is a price to pay.

She pours two more fingers to celebrate her audacity

Out on the terrace, back at the old man's side, she puts her arm around him. "Now we'll see what Dacia Wadeleigh's made of."

Si Sliman the Muslim abandons the heavens to confront her. Like a priest in Lent, he makes the sign of the cross on her forehead with his thumb. "We'll see what all of us are made of."

13

Margaret's visit to Cairnhall, no more than an hour east of Manhattan, had been like her graduation biking trip, whimsical. Addie had an important commission restoring a cache of instruments for The Metropolitan Museum and was in Italy doing research. Margaret had scheduled a series of lectures in New York and New England that summer and was using Addie's apartment in Murray Hill.

When Margaret wound up her lectures in Manhattan she knew Addie's work for the Metropolitan would soon end and her friend would return to Lechlade. Nothing in their intimacy hinted that the story of her encounter with Bo Cavalieri would infuriate Addie. She never dreamed Bo would leave messages on Addie's machine for her—or how those messages would affect Addie.

But in Lechlade Addie's bones felt sharp and unreliable, her own flesh felt dank and unfamiliar.

Soon, through the good offices of Si Sliman, Addie found reason to return to the States: a fat commission to make ready for donation to museums a fabled private collection of musical instruments. Margaret had begun to suspect she'd left something of her shame behind for Addie to find.

★

She held thoughts of Bo Cavalieri at bay until another Croyden-like encounter on Magdalene Bridge over the Cam. Clad in a camouflage poncho, she was listening to her Wellingtons smack puddles and running arcane equations behind her long blue eyes when she noticed an oncoming gentleman of a certain age admiring her. As she passed on his left she looked at him quizzically and then broke into her mischievous eight-year-old's smile, the one she had reserved for John Croyden. They passed and turned to look again. She saluted him and he steamed on to his professorship as if the sun were shining.

She was, she saw, no more able to go back to Bo than her mother had been. But she did manage to do Dacia one better. Several years after fleeing Bo she sent him a girlish telegram from Lechlade inviting him to come live with her "as it was always meant to be," foredooming herself to shudder every day imagining how he'd react. The way he did react would have crushed her. He'd been in Washington dressing for the opening of a posthumous retrospective exhibition of his mother's paintings when her message arrived. He crammed it in his pocket, not wanting to be distracted. At the end of the evening he walked out onto Constitution Avenue and read it. He stood for a few moments watching a gibbous moon haunt the National Archives, then folded it into a paper airplane and launched it into a menace of boxwoods and wisteria. Then he lit a cigar and strolled back to his hotel.

In the kiln of that Parthian overture Margaret had become nearly the sort of woman her mother had been, the sort of spirit Bo had loved as a boy and might have loved again. She'd gone to the States to see where Dacia lived during the war, the pretext of lectures notwithstanding. She and Bo had come to Cairnhall at the same moment for the same reason, mourning Dacia. The mathematical odds against their encounter awed her. You couldn't say he and Dacia had been lovers—too young—but you could say that they loved only once and hadn't survived losing each other. Margaret had seen that instantly and wanted it, wanted it and gotten it, and thrown it away in a fit of practical fact-finding. There were problems, of course. Bo Cavalieri was too old for her, and violent, and scarred. He'd used the phrase "comfort of the eunuch" to describe his condition. He wasn't a man to use words lightly. Why utter such a thing in the midst of a dizzying attraction except to forewarn? And had it forewarned her? What did she want in a man, this man? For the first time she entered her mother's soul and understood the one thing about Dacia that governed everything else. For the first time she wanted a man without ambivalence, without thought of Addie Compton, without arguing her nature. True that in her sexual fluster she wasn't able to imagine making love to Bo as men and women do in books and movies—her imaginings resembled her lovemaking with Addie—but it was just as true that she knew that any way she and Bo made love would be suitable to both of them. She knew there would be no rejections, no disappointments, and exactly that prompted her to flee.

Officially she attributed her flight to an interview with Hettie Warshaw, the magus-like crone who'd known Bo when he was a boy. That is, Hettie wished she'd known Bo, for she harbored a shamelessly inappropriate crush on him. Hettie had drawn a chilling picture of his childhood. It was like stumbling into a black cave lined with sharp outcrops. His mother had been theatrically unloving. Dacia had at least been considerate and intelligent. This was ample reason not to involve herself with him, but she'd hardly arrived at Heathrow before she understood that her real reason resided well below the navel. Why, she'd argued with herself, should she finish what Dacia had begun? Why should she allow the selfish dead to live again through her? It was ghoulish. She didn't owe it to Dacia. But by the time she sent Bo that telegram she'd come to see him as Dacia's legacy. Now she understood exactly what he'd concluded: Dacia had been taken from him by someone else; Margaret had taken herself. She was a hurtful person. There was no misunderstanding between them, never had been. Their attraction was in the histories of their bones, irrational and dangerous.

She didn't know that in the last three years she'd become a woman he might love. She didn't know she'd become a woman. She thought herself a genius girl, barely a sustainable notion at thirty-three.

When they met in Cairnhall's attic he'd said, "This is Woofy Poofy. Dacia gave her to me. I abandoned her. I feel bad about it."

Her heart had shouted. A violent chill had started from her crown chakra and lodged in her crotch. Icy, willful Dacia had a doll she called Woofy Poofy. She watched his long capable fingers and green eyes and would have preferred to go on watching wordlessly. "And will you again? Abandon her?"

He'd stared at her for a long time—it seemed like hours—and she knew he was looking at Dacia. "No, I won't."

"My name is Margaret Wadeleigh," she'd said. She hadn't offered her hand.

He's looked at her as if he didn't believe her. "Mine is Amir Cavalieri. Some people call me Bo. Dacia called me Amir."

"I've never heard of an Italian Beauregard." Instantly she'd fretted that this witticism would repel him, or hop over his head.

"Bo for boatswain, as in ship's boatswain," he'd said. "I'm not Italian, I'm Arab and German."

"How strange."

"The German?"

They laughed.

"Do you speak German? Or Arabic?"

"I speak Tourette's German."

Ah, she thought, Dacia's naval chum is literate.

14

The tall often have a dignity, a Lehmbruckian austerity, to which they may not be emotionally entitled. And so something about Bo's bone-crackling standing up proved foolishly reassuring to her. He was taller than Dacia's daughter, though not much. They stood less than two feet apart, far too close for any well-bred Englishwoman's comfort, locked in each other's gaze, stunned and unembarrassed. He was remembering Dacia's flashing legs, her startling sprints—he wanted to invite Margaret to race, having no way of knowing how pleased she would have been to accept. Everywhere he looked around Cairnhall he saw where he and Dacia had raced and tackled each other and wrestled, delighted in each other. Margaret noticed they were breathing in tandem, their bodies deciding something they'd neglected to tell their minds.

Most people are bereft and bland without their axes to grind. Margaret knew this and practiced what she knew until she swam Bo Cavalieri's green eyes in Cairnhall's golden attic—and then everything that gave her equilibrium sputtered and misfired. Later she could only describe her state to Addie as "twisted inside my head."

Her mother and Bo had been warehoused at Cairnhall to wait out not a war but their parents' terminal immaturity. Impregnable defenses had been raised against this truth. Dacia and Amir had loved each other so much—their pheromones haunted them—that nobody else ever fit, neither Margaret nor their grown selves. She'd rebuffed the idea of fitting Bo into her life in honor of her mother's lifelong inability to connect with anyone after Amir.

But now three years, two months, one week and four days from her flight from New York and Bo, the idea of making love to her beautiful, remote mother's only true love enslaves her. Her habitual battle order is to put people behind her cleanly, like Alexander the Great, who knew better than anyone how to move on. There are plenty of heroines for an educated young woman, a few goddesses even, but a woman communing with Alexander's shade is a rare thing. Like ancient Greek sailors, Margaret wears his crazed image around her neck. Only Addie Compton knows this and in Addie all secrets are safe. Addie once quipped, "If, like him, you take no prisoners, your sword had best be swift and you needn't think of growing old." On the contrary, she'd replied, Alexander beguiled his prisoners and made them allies if he could—but only those who fought him well.

What had happened to Dacia? Margaret knew what had happened to Bo—rape, near hanging, the indifference of a self-beguiled mother. She didn't want to finish Dacia's business. She wouldn't be a revenant. She had her own business, didn't she? Didn't she? Besides, Bo insisted on the proper order of burial, on the indecency of exhumation. He wanted no truck with her, or he'd have answered her telegram. But why? The shadowed turn of her calves aroused him, the sweat on her lips, the erotic creases beside her mouth, the bravura of her nipples, the flush of her skin. Had he not just once moaned her name and found his own release from the tension between them? Or had he moaned Dacia's name? She squirms to think he could guess that her own hand is often a poor substitute for him.

15

Addie walks like a prow cutting through chop. Margaret passes by as blue haze. People who notice her are likely to find elfin conclaves in the woods. Choosing among the cobblestones of Oxford, Margaret's sneakered feet are like a flutter of white doves.

She yearns for Addie to come home. Her body leans in New York's direction and she's always conscious of its western approach. She and Bo met, one might say, over Dacia's body. Woofy Poofy in Bo's hands told her what she needed to know, that her mother had been haunted all her short life by their pheromones, hers and Bo's. Nobody else ever fit, not Colin Wadeleigh, her gracious father, nor Margaret herself.

What had happened to Dacia? Her mother Zoe Wynne had been sharp-tongued, her certitude stupefying, like all manic-depressives. Hers was the only version of any story. Margaret thought it was this in Zoe, not her genes, that had thrust Dacia's lower jaw forward a little. Ultimately Zoe and her mumbling husband, Justin, packing his pipe and hiding in its haze, declared Dacia feral and lost themselves in the Irish Sea. Their sloop was found in a long green swell, its genoa muttering, its wheel lashed, the table in the salon set. No storm had struck it, but Zoe and Justin were over the side forever while Dacia pumped her yellow Becane from Seville to Cordoba.

Margaret had a childhood companion far more formidable than Woofy Poofy: the omniscient Mags. She clung to him until she began marveling at the length of the corn silk of her pubis.

She wished she'd known about Woofy Poofy. Perhaps it would have saved Mags from his fate. Dacia, after all, had been more tender. She'd entrusted Woofy to Bo.

We're cursed with our parents, they with us, strangers off the street. Encountering Bo Cavalieri in Cairnhall's attic pushed Margaret's face up against her mother's humanity. She'd written her mother off as an otherling. But Dacia had played games, had tea parties, comforted a rag doll, and loved someone beyond reason. This was not the mother she knew. Part of her hated Bo for knowing Dacia. She considered her differences with Dacia, looking for comfort. Dacia had been somewhat shorter, her beauty severe, her hair cut like a German helmet. Margaret pictured her vaulting from a dragon-prowed longboat in the Anglian fens, broadsword in hand, bloody-minded. Her Viking looks came from Zoe. Margaret, like Dacia, was startlingly fair, and yet her coloring was so high that she looked caught in the throes of some private ecstasy and seemed embarrassed for it. Her legs were meant for admiring, not for running. Dacia's rowdy look shivered the timber of a man, while Margaret's tested it. Margaret knew her beauty to be the kind that makes a man's lips twitch and his eyes tic. Dacia had the green pixie eyes of worlds within worlds. Margaret's were blue as a weatherless sky. She wondered how her mother had figured in the fantasies of men. Had they bent her over or had she slain them? She knew that only the most imaginative men indulged fantasies about her. Her only rest from her formidable beauty was her antic relationship with Addie Compton, musical instrument maker, conservator, jongleur and fool-savant.

She had been drawn to Addie's bed by Addie's anatomical witticisms. *Look at those jellubians,* Addie would whisper as a bra-less classmate jogged by. Or she would confide: *The sickness of that oyster is definitely its pearl.* Or, *Her tits' bark is loud.* Or, *Diver, beware that squid.* These sexualizing observations drew her to Addie's ecstatic mouth, the thrum of her groin, her honey pubic hair, the Vedic articulations of her fingers, her nipples alert as border collies.

Addie chose to live in New York—for a while, she said—because she loved to hear New Yorkers kvetch about each other. She called Manhattan a perfectly struck chord. "It's something in the schist below."

Margaret had never met a man she could remotely imagine rocking a rag doll on his knees or stitching up its wounds. That this man happened to be Dacia's gave him the cachet of the Lapis in her eyes, but also invited her contempt. That he drew people with all of Addie Compton's wryness, but also with a haunting fondness, put him exactly where he'd been in relation to her mother—the first member of the other sex to colonize her secrets. In her mathematical passion, Margaret thought to shut down a failed approach.

For more than three years the austerity of her psyche kept Manhattan from barging onto her private ice field. But suddenly in the onset of another rude spring a sheet's caress of a nipple, the ritual use of toilet paper, a feathering of lipstick conjures Bo's grave eyes, the attentive set of his mouth, the drama of his hands when drawing. In Wind Harp's crannies these erotic intrusions are as welcome as rosebuds. Her usual resistance falls around her ankles and she is unable to dress her nakedness. Predators don't wallow. Their skills are martial and urgent, their logic on point. Dacia and Bo accepted their wounds. They allowed others to strip off their childhood enchantment, to convince them that children do not love eternally—or even into puberty. They were raped in more ways than one. He returned to the scene. Dacia couldn't. He'd set down a strange and elegant paradigm, like all good mathematical formulae—and therefore he was clean prey, not some jackal or hyena, as were so many men with whom she'd coped. She doesn't know what she means thinking this way. She tries to exorcise the primordiality of it by musing that she's about to join a long line of English supremacists, like Richard Burton, Charles Doughty, Saint John Philby and T.E. Lawrence, stalkers of the Bedouin sensibility, if not the Bedouin. She shudders, preferring to be a beast rather than a triumphalist, but knowing there is no difference.

16

"And what is it you do?" the visiting don across the linened table asks Margaret at the Archimedean Society dinner for exchange fellows. Do? What do I do? Avoid boors like you. Even hidden behind her face she hears her hysteria. "I'm a numbers runner."

"And what does that entail, precisely?"

"Gambling." She gives him a snaky-haired stare that says, If you try to talk to me again I'll puke in your consommé.

Margaret isn't like that. Battleships simply do not fire on punts. Who then has spoken so meanly to this oaf from Sydney? Bo Cavalieri, she decides.

"This is ridiculous."

"I'm sorry?" says the spectacled professor Hakim Ali, sitting beside her.

"Oh, nothing, Hakim," she says to her colleague. "I'm grousing at an untoward thought."

"Perhaps even two of them," Hakim Ali says.

She smiles and engages him in a tête-à-tête about idiot savants and their bravura mathematical skills, but all the while another part of her brain speculates about Bo. No, Bo isn't uncouth. He would have indulged the Sydney boor. Why does she think of Bo in the bloom of her own rudeness? Because she never stopped thinking of Bo, because he scares her to death and that is finally a feeling she doesn't want to live without. Is it a sign that she wishes to be offended by Bo? She knows he suspected that of her—it is the hallmark of the man's perceptivity.

The beauty, the magic of number theory is that you don't obsess about anything. You just run the numbers. So in a sense her retort to the fellow from Sydney is on the money. The process is intolerant of anal retentiveness, utterly unproprietary. Aha, of course that's right. I've been doing an unmathematical thing. I've been counterintuitive, contrary.

★

That night she starts packing. She can't stay with Addie in her Druid's den in Murray Hill. Then she remembers Addie has moved to Chelsea. Would Addie ever come home, as she'd come home to Lechlade from Cremona, and, briefly, from Manhattan to Lechlade? Has she so handily become an American? She mentally feathers the artifacts of Addie's Murray Hill flat—the broken violoncellos, basses, mandolins, lutes hanging on the bare brick walls, the driftwood, arcane tools, vises, resins, the smells of the history of sound—and Addie in her coveralls, her Aikido hakama with its white top and blue pants, somersaulting from one end of the flat to the other, from darkness to light. Tears plop into her Vuitton. No, she can't stay with Addie. She gets on the phone and in an hour she jacklegs an exchange. Columbia has been after her for several years to lecture. I find I'll be in Manhattan on business for several weeks, she lies to Ari Salzman at Columbia, and I could, if you would care to have me, give a few lectures on an impromptu basis. I'm so delighted you thought of us, he says. I had rather feared that if you did ever come you would favor Stanford or MIT. Not at all, she tells him disingenuously, Oxford is an arts and humanities center and I naturally would feel just as comfortable at Columbia, I'm sure. She isn't sure at all. She detests the Columbia campus with its fascist architecture and its harrumphy indifference. You know, Doctor Wadeleigh, Salzman enthuses, it's serendipitous that you called. Conaboy Ayton—you're familiar with his work, I know—is lecturing at your Cambridge and I'm sure I could arrange with him for you to stay at his swish townhouse near Gramercy Park. That would be most kind, Doctor Salzman, she says.

Now her maiden voyage into impulsiveness is dressed in professionalism. Yes, Doctor Salzman, I can have my choice. And your pretentious pile certainly wouldn't be my choice

80

except that I want Woofy Poofy. I want something Dacia hugged every day. And he won't give her to me, will he? No, he thinks I'm unreliable. He won't entrust anything to me that was so precious to Dacia. He will not give me my mother's doll. I want that doll. I'm entitled to it. She spins around from her suitcase and stares into the long mirror screwed to her closet door. Her jaw is set. Its horrid rictus greets her. He-will-not-give-me-my-mother's-doll. The woman she sees in her mirror is mad. She's an intruder. She should call the police and have her put out. She has somehow gotten in and is menacing the landlord.

Absurdity takes a long time dawning as she stares down this furious stranger in her bedroom. I-want-that-doll, the stranger says. And to get her you will have to deal with Bo Cavalieri. Have you ever dealt with a skilled assassin? No, I'm not ready. I never will be ready. He'll always belong to Dacia. Colin never did. Remember my father? Dacia never belonged to Colin. She made me with him, I can't imagine why. He must have been careless. I can't imagine what she was doing with Colin. That's why I want the doll. The doll meant something to her. It's mine and I'll have it if I have to kill him. Or kill him so I don't have to have him, or—the stranger studies her unblinkingly. Go on, finish packing. I'm not leaving. I'm staying here. You go to America. I'll stay here. When you get back we'll sort things out, see what's left, who's who, so to speak.

The question is, Margaret tells the stranger, shall I be the child she should have had with this sailor or shall I have him for her? Now that's nicely enough put, isn't it? Or, you could ask, will he have me instead of her?

I-will-have-that-doll, the stranger says. If it harelips the world.

Well, it damned well will. She looks again and the alien is gone. Instead there is Margaret Wadeleigh, Professor Margaret Wadeleigh in her moist, inconvenient beauty.

You bitch. She laughs. An improbable happiness seizes her. She begins basket-shooting lingerie and toiletries into her suitcase from the edges of the room. This is me. This is me. Out of the box. She laughs again: out of the box was her and

Addie's private cryptograph for people who escape the box our everyday pretenses and denials build and seal. I'm out of the box, mad, totally mad. I'll lecture my damned fool head off, but what I want is Woofy Poofy. We all want something we'd lose our places at the table for naming, don't we? All the good people, the ones worth knowing, are out of the box. The others are all shipped express to Boorland, UK. Part of the cement in their relationship, her and Addie's, was that they'd always agreed on who was out of the box. Except in one instance: Dacia. To Addie, Dacia is gloriously out of the box. To Margaret, she is the box—and this lies throbbing at the heart of their lovemaking, a dissonance which, if struck exactly, achieves a barbarity that puts Carl Orff's *Carmina Burana* to shame. This discord is the tension that braids them. Is Bo Cavalieri out of the box? He won't give me Woofy Poofy. If he were in the box, he would. I'll have to kill him or—her crotch hurts and she doubles over. She goes into the bathroom and stares wildly at the mirror. She recognizes the face but not the eyes. The fingers of her right hand splay slowly over her left breast, leaving the nipple trilled. Her hand stops at the waistband of her panties. She pulls it up, then releases it and folds the blue silk into her mons. Still staring into those unrecognizable eyes, she tugs and relaxes—visions of Woofy Poofy's captor flood her brain—tugs and lets go, until she gasps, shuts her eyes and folds over the sink.

So this is a mission to rescue Woofy Poofy, she says to herself as she savages her teeth the next morning. Run the numbers, Margaret. Dacia left Woofy Poofy in Bo's safekeeping. He didn't keep her safe. He abandoned her, as he must have felt abandoned by Dacia. What parses? What locks in place? In the middle of his life he goes back to Cairnhall, finds her, sews her up. Sews her up? A grown man gets on the Long Island Railroad with needle and thread? No, he must have had a premonition that Woofy Poofy would be waiting for him.

Margaret loves ghost stories, especially the ones where the ghost hangs around trying to get someone to do some unfinished business. If I hadn't loved those stories so much I would have stayed in Manhattan in the first place, at least until I could figure out whether I hated Bo Cavalieri in my own right or because he was Dacia's. My story is I will get Woofy Poofy, and I'm sticking to it. But what if he gives her to me? Will I prop her up on my bed and let her remind me every day that there was a time when Dacia had a future? Not bloody likely. I'll just confront him and we'll read the entrails. Confront him with what? Me? My idiocy? He'll smile and not say a thing. Or he might not smile, he might just do something. He's surprising. You can count on that. He might just grab my crotch or throw me over his knees and spank me or boot my ass out the door. And which would you like, Margaret? Well, I wouldn't like the latter. He's like an untested idea in mathematics, this Signor Cavalieri. You do all the predictable calculations, and they don't work, but you know your question is sound, so where do you go? Well, if you're Margaret Wadeleigh, which is to say a polished iconoclast, you go to the cranks, because in mathematics cranks rule. Don't try to argue Professor Wadeleigh out of that, because she championed Abd al Wahid Sayyed, the self-taught Egyptian crank whom her sinecured colleagues worldwide ignored. But she answered the Alexandria cab driver's quasi-literate letters and when she'd struggled through his crude terminology she found him to be making formulations that had eluded them all, and she brought him to England at her own expense. Yes, cranks rule, and dons never learn, no matter how often they're embarrassed, because their status means more to them than their work. Cranks rule and God help every establishment that mocks them. Abd al Wahid enjoys a fellowship at Cambridge. What does the crank Amir Cavalieri enjoy?

★

A woman who sleeps in an igloo of pillows may feel ready for arctic drifts and bergs. Margaret feels she's checked her body hair with her luggage. She has clothing and toiletries but no cold-weather gear.

As the northerly latitudes bend upwards towards the depths of her mind she wonders how Dacia dealt with Amir after a spat. Did they spat? "Oh," she groans, remembering they were children. What use could their childish ways be to her? Would Dacia have stalked him? "Oh," she says again, "Stop it, won't you?" The matronly woman across the aisle leans forward and gives her a look that says, You are a bit young to be so odd, dear. The Indian gentleman beside her coughs to ward off something untoward. Dacia pounces from her grave. She sees them wrestle, Dacia and Amir, rolling away panting and laughing. It isn't like watching Dacia and Colin. They always seemed to fidget. Margaret is watching something she's lost. It infuriates her so much she turns on the overhead fan. It dements her with grief because she knows she's watching newsreels, no, the camera obscura of her mind. How can that mischievous child who loved only once and far too much have treated her so coldly? How did she fail to love herself in her child? Is it that she came to dislike Colin so much? He was everybody's idea of a likely chap, even if he had no idea himself who he was. Handsome but not too handsome, intelligent but not talented, considerate but not intuitive, and dumbly in love with Dacia. Perhaps he knew about Amir, but even if he didn't he would have known in time that he'd never engage Dacia in the amusements that entwine a man and woman. That's why he drowned his promising charmed life while sailing off the Devon coast one foggy November night, drowned like Zoe and Justin. He must have been baffled to have captured enough of Dacia's attention to marry him but not to love him. How could that be? his tidy mind must have asked. But why couldn't he have gone on being a respected MI-6 officer? Why couldn't he have found some measure of contentment in his little daughter? How could Dacia's indifference move this responsible man to abandon his daughter, his parents, his friends, his career? Dacia had hardly noticed him. She hardly noticed his child. She buried him with dignity, then deposited his child in school in Switzerland. Only Amir had ever won her attention. Margaret knows the answers to her questions: Dacia's remove demented people. No one knew it better than Margaret. It's the key to Margaret's personality, at least as usually perceived by others—the gratitude one feels when an icy demeanor hints at a tropical microclimate at its heart. By main force her good heart usually but not always breaks through her hauteur like a sundog. Most of her friends and acquaintances feel themselves secretly indebted to her for bestowing on them a warmth her physiognomy belies.

In the middle of this morose reverie Margaret smiles triumphally. She's doing what Dacia didn't dare, going back so that she can go forward, as Dacia was unable to do.

17

The Parthian sun pours through her skylights and slaps the white-painted brick as she practices her Aikido rolls and knows that all has changed. Addie draws a cardigan over her damp shoulders and turns up the heat even though it's not yet winter. A chill rattles her brain in its case. She lights fat candles and sits crosslegged on a mat for a long time, breathing deep and slow. She's as alert as a night heron. She's like a child who doesn't know she needs glasses. Her innate stillness inclines her towards the delta state where yoga adepts and remote viewers navigate time and place. Her mind fills again with frame shots and sometimes moving pictures: Margaret at her blackboard, a wintry trail in Korea clogged with frightened people, somebody's bedroom, a green-eyed face painted black.

These are Addie's unmentionables, and her bond with Margaret is woven with Margaret's tacit knowledge of her far sight. She breathes four times up from her crotch to her crown and empties her mind. All right, Dacia. Speak. But Dacia merely parts a curtain:

★

The sea oats lean away from the water. Addie strains to hear their whispers in the wind. She takes her time, conscious that she has left her shell sitting emptily in Chelsea. She accustoms herself to not knowing where she is. Evidence will tell her. Or maybe not.

A silver chop troubles waters the color of eels. Half sunk down by the bow is a coastal trawler, maybe forty feet long. Water smacks in her companionway. She is beyond salvage. Two great blue herons rise from the opposite side of the tidal gut. Hovering three or four feet above the narrow shore, she propels herself forward beyond the stern of the wreck and now she sees two children, their legs outstretched, leaning back on their hands. Their legs are outgrowing them. The girl's helmet of yellow hair shines in the reeds. Under her bangs her green eyes catch reflections from the water, eyes so bright they turn the fringes of her bangs green. The girl gleams in the happiness of being at one with place and time and person. She looks—Addie fights for the right word—perfect. The boy is taller. Where the girl's face is square, his is long, grave. His black hair flaps in the wind. His eyes, also green, are steady. The children wiggle their bare toes and laugh.

Their intimacy is so palpable that Addie tastes it, salty and urgent. It makes her bones ache. She has come upon angels unawares. Dangerous space, it should have been inviolate. Speak, Dacia, Addie had commanded her, and Dacia showed her, and probably not Margaret, her heart's pleasure and ease, her loss.

How old were they? Eleven? It would be their last year together, their last possible year, the end of their lives. And no parent will ever confess this desecration.

Addie feels the heat between them, the yearning, the currents dancing on their skin. I am the angel of death, she thinks. I have brought them their death. Here is the danger of far sight, to go back and forth and take responsibility for what one visits.

She hovers, longing to bring them safely to a later world. But hers is the tragedy of far sight, not theirs. We are sure such early love is inconsequential, sure of too damned much. They'll get over it, they're kids, kids are resilient, it's puppy love, life goes on—surely the adults said that.

But they don't get over it. Dacia becomes a cantankerous wraith. He becomes a killer and wanderer.

All this Addie sees in seconds, alight in another time.

★

Then she comes out of it, rubs her arms and puts on her cardigan. Her journey makes her colder. The candles flicker, bending to strange drafts.

87

Addie is an untrained natural. Others need discipline. They might, for example, imagine a magnificent skyscraper. They might hang a moon behind the building and paint some cloud nests for the city's reflections. Then they might descend. At each floor they might abandon their mental furnishings, their anxieties. They would want to be prepared never to see these encumbrances again. At the bottom they might seat themselves in a womb of light and begin to ship their minds to far places. That's one technique. But if, like Addie, you'd had this ability since your fifth or sixth year, you wouldn't need it.

She herself would have gone on thinking she was simply imagining things if Powe Haddon-Torrance, trying to bumble a little nookie from her in a sunny park, hadn't confided that he worked for MI-6 and was engaged in a top secret project that involved remote viewing. She listened to this silvery twit with her usual good humor. "Then Powe," she said, "if you would tell a tinker that you worked for MI-6 because she has a nice pair of legs, I think it's time to apply for statehood." He was crushed and she felt rueful.

Only later did she see that if intelligence people were doing what she thought everyone did, perhaps she wasn't imagining the scenes she saw. It put her in mind of Sari Voinivich, her Christian Scientist chum who thought everyone was as myopic as she was until the examining doctor at Cambridge told her she needed glasses. Her grades had been good enough to get her into Cambridge, but a pair of glasses made her a formidable scholar. Might this intelligence imparted by a toff with a plummy accent change Addie's life? Labeling things is not knowing them, although most academic testmeisters seem content with it. Addie is attuned to the nameless chord: what Powe really told her was either that MI-6 was hard at work reinventing the wheel, which might illuminate Britannia's declining fortunes, or she had a problematical gift.

She pours herself a bit of Merlot and empties her mind again.

★

Now she careens off the Williamsburg Bridge in a great arc. She skims the black water like a cormorant until she sees a disturbance. Just south of a pile of rocks now called U Thant Island hard by the United Nations she sees a swimmer making for Manhattan. His stroke is even and unflagging, his kick barely perceptible. A man is swimming the East River at night. Again and again she rides the catenary cables of the bridge like someone spotting a disaster and pacing back and forth helplessly. Then she flies upriver and watches the swimmer a few feet above the surface. She projects herself ahead of the swimmer. She hovers, watching him climb up to the street. He throws up, then sits hugging his knees and shivering as two cops get out of their cruiser and approach him. She thinks she recognizes this sea mammal. She watches him speak briefly with one of the cops, throw something into the river, then docilely climb into the cruiser. His name comes to her: Bo Cavalieri, two years before he encountered Margaret.

But how can she know it was two years ago? Why not right now? Or a year ago? Nothing would have changed except the make and year of the police cruiser, and she doesn't know about such things. She's accustomed to a certain kind of time travel. Listening for sounds that instruments originally made is an eerie preoccupation, so she isn't unnerved, just puzzled. She has no way of knowing if she has restored an instrument to its original sound, but she imagines the settings in which it would have been made, and that authenticates it. Or perhaps it's something other than imagination.

She rises from a cross-legged position in one smooth motion. She reaches down and picks up her glass, takes a sip, puts it down again and cartwheels twice over to her front windows. She releases the bamboo blinds and sits down again in a darker corner.

★

She watches Bo carted off to Bellevue. The cops josh with him. She can't hear them, she never can hear, but it doesn't bother her because she usually watches television, when she does watch it, with the sound off. She likes the images, but the time-serving blather and tone-deaf soundtracks annoy her. She cruises the river like a police helicopter. On the Manhattan side she flies from building to building. She lets the cops take Bo to Bellevue without surveillance. She sees a figure pass behind shaded windows. She follows a fire escape down to a steel door on a street. She sees a tall black man in a top hat holding a blossom of balloons. She studies a clever block and tackle used for lowering a door key to visitors once they're identified.

★

Then, curling up on the floor under her sweater, she tumbles into a fitful sleep. Sometime during the night she climbs upstairs to her bed. In the morning, as the sun hammers her apartment, she dresses and without eating jogs down Ninth Avenue, stopping twice for coffee after angling over to Broadway.

A. Cavalieri on Broadway had been easy enough to find in the phone directory. When she reaches Houston Street she reconnoiters. She right-angles around Bo's block just south of Houston. She's sure she will recognize him as her swimmer. She has circled his block six times when two men catch her eye as she approaches Broadway on Spring Street from the west. They're looking up at Bo's eleven-story building. One is tall, balding, wiry and jittery. He wears an expensive blue camelhair coat and is nervous in a Chaplinesque way. The other is a double-breasted blond bison, stuffed and top-heavy, a human carcass, his prissy patent shoes out of step with his heft and his eye-of-round face.

18

The rickety movie house on Irving Place that showed World War II oh-how-we-suffer Soviet propaganda films is gone, but Harvey's Tavern still draws more patronage than its cuisine can explain. Ulrike Theiss, Bo's mother, loved them both. Nobody suffers like the Russians, she'd say in Teutonic glee. It had been hard to tell what excited her more, the Wehrmacht's tanks chewing up shtetls or the Russian women ski troops whooshing down on the frozen remnants of Von Paulus's Sixth Army. At that time in her life Ulrike had a casual lover who wept when he watched these movies. His mawkishness disgusted her until he told her he was ravished by all those magnificent BMW motorcycles abandoned in the snow.

And what's better than the rancidities of 14th Street spiking your Manhattan while you sit outside Harvey's a few blocks from chaos: the whorish Academy of Music, S. Klein discount store, where suburban bashers poolshoot each other with their umbrellas, Union Square's old goats under the ticklish nose of Farrar, Straus and Giroux, inveighing in their East European angst against the conspiracies of the right, buses farting and taxis bleating in the tide and slop of dirty-water hot dogs, sauerkraut, mustard, stale beer and piss.

Margaret settles in on the north side of Block Beautiful, 19th Street between Third Avenue and Irving Place. She has Conaboy Ayton's brownstone to herself while he spritzes his student sycophants at Cambridge with baffling drivel. It's an exchange program, and the English are getting the worst of it, as usual. Ayton's house used to be an elegant brownstone, but an art deco nose bob disgraced it with Cubist facelessness. Ayton

91

pretentiously calls it a Cycladian look. Margaret is lecturing his erstwhile victims uptown at Columbia, as well as the professional societies that fall upon her in spasms of anglophilia.

The moon is void of course her first morning in the least beautiful house on Block Beautiful. That's one way of describing one of those days when the doorknob comes off in your hand, you chip your host's antique cup, and people act snarky. The heater in Ayton's bathroom can't be turned off, the tub takes hours to drain and smells like wet spaniels, the toilet runs, the door to the terrace won't shut and has to be wired, she drops an egg on the floor, the toaster burns her toast, the fridge sounds like a Boeing 747, the telephone bell can't be modulated, and the electric sockets bear acrid scorches. It all may happen that way because you've put on the wrong face or you're transmitting at the wrong frequency or because of solar storms or the intercepted intent of extraterrestrials. On such days the ante is up and everything we rely on breaks down—health, marriage, friendship, divorce, job. Some cosmic glue we can't identify lets go, or perhaps we're simply thinking about going home, though we know we've never seen home. For most of us, it's not the place where we grew up, thank God for small gifts.

Ayton's house promises much but doesn't hold up to scrutiny. Neither does his math. As a teacher he loses no opportunity to kitsch up a simple thing or shove a complex thing beyond an ordinary mortal's reach, implying that he himself is no ordinary mortal. His lectures and monographs infuriate her. She can't imagine how such a hornswoggler has gotten so far. His demeanor towards her has always been that of a schoolboy imploring a pal not to report him to the office for some misdeed, and she finds this foolishly endearing.

Margaret can't hear on the telephone without her glasses. This morning she can't find them. Without them she feels naked. Addie always urges her to try contacts, but she thinks them more deceit than conceit. She makes love wearing her glasses and imagines making love wearing them, except with Bo. With him she sees herself smaller, not naked but undressed, and if this distinction had been lost on her she would never have come looking for him. She sees him not as prodding but as offering. He's as ghostly as a theorem slipping behind a veil. For this very reason a purpose, something to catch sidelong, something over there in the dark waits for you, you alone. From the grave Dacia offers amends. Not having been able to love her, she offers Margaret the one she loved. In mathematics, in all high endeavors, there's a fleetingness and no shelf life at all. After more than three years, her quest is forlorn, in the teeth of the odds, and yet Margaret has a hunch that in the dark corner, between the light of the hall and her bed, between Cairnhall and Lechlade, her inevitable companion waits, as he has most of his life, and she won't need her glasses in his company.

19

Addie recognizes the windows and shades she saw the night before. They're on the eleventh floor. The men look foreign. Addie herself doesn't feel foreign: what does foreign look like in America? How do you do it? Well, you hold cigarettes strangely, perhaps. But these men aren't smoking. The bison's suit looks gangsterish but not necessarily un-American. These guys look much more unhomogenized than most Americans. The Gestapo or the KGB or MI-5 would pick them out immediately. The bison takes in the street. It would break his hump to look up. The Crane studies the building. They seem umbilically attached. They probably need to be cranked up every morning. Bison and Crane are definitely out of a Garfield movie. Bison has pretty good radar. He isn't missing much. Crane, on the other hand, is determined not to miss the pliant blonde runner who has just doffed her Yankees cap to shake out a spectacular cascade and stretch her calves. She's on Broadway's east side, about twenty yards north of Bo's tatty red door. And there's Addie's swimmer rounding the other side of Spring Street with a brown grocery bag in each arm. His head is framed by celery stalks and a loaf of French bread. Addie ducks into The Alec Crispin Gallery's entryway.

She recognizes the hawkish face. Soon Bo and the blonde, who has resumed her run, will be on a collision course, like everybody else in Manhattan. Addie likes this blonde, the ducky way she runs, a bit knock-kneed for all her elegance. Yes, she's drawn to this blonde. Always has been.

When Margaret finishes her hair shake, a device to keep distance between runner and quarry, she stiffens as if stabbed in the back. She's as observant as Addie, but Addie doesn't think she has been spotted by Margaret. I'm seeing something more unusual than that, Addie thinks. Margaret senses Bo, not Bison and Crane—I don't even think she's seen them—and she'll turn and slip away—exactly what Margaret does next. And Addie is glad of this because she needs time to process Margaret's presence. It never occurs to her that Margaret and Bo have reunited, that he's returning to his loft with their dinner, that Margaret is eager to join him. She knows her friend better than that. Margaret is stalking him, titillating herself, trying to straighten some jinxed equation that will enable her at last to consider Dacia's legacy with something like equanimity. This is a camera obscura of the damned. Only she, Addie Compton, is fully, sensibly here—Addie and Messrs. Bison and Crane. They fully inhabit the southeast corner of Spring and Broadway, while Bo and Margaret are holograms. A strong blow down from Lake Tear of the Clouds could sweep them away, but Addie and the two overly purposeful men will still be there. Sorrow like hiccups shakes her—those two specters, Margaret and Bo, have lost so much. They're Dacia's golems. She stands not more than ten yards from the corner, shuddering from a squall within, thinking that they lack an essential element—they have earth, air and water, but they lack fire, and she's the fire bringer, a priestess set apart to light the fires at their altars. I am to keep them warm. Do I want this? Is it enough? I've always been her priestess. Why should she not be mine? Why must I be creaturely and she deific? This last thought terrifies and delights her. Why should Margaret not be my priestess? How is it that the athlete, the sinewy one, becomes the fire bringer, and not the flowery, fecund one? Who cast these dies? I didn't. Margaret isn't some odalisque for whom I panted in school. She isn't some wan sleeper I aspired to waken. No, it's the lay of my bones and tendons in the shower that firms us in our orbit. How did I become the servant? Aristotle said slaves are born feeling like slaves. But perhaps, he allowed, an extraordinary master could educate them out of their slavishness. Has Margaret been an extraordinary master? No, she hasn't. She's been a loving master.

I deserve more. I-de-serve-more, her heart tattoos her rebellion. Alexander is dead, I will not serve Antipater. Dacia is dead, I will not serve Margaret.

She had known Dacia briefly. Dacia had a compulsion to toy with Addie's honey hair, to smooth her eyebrows with her forefinger and thumb, to trace her aquiline nose. It was heartbreaking to Margaret, whom Dacia never touched, and now that she thinks of it perhaps it explains Margaret's attraction to her. Even as a child she was glad of her clothing lest her body betray its response to Dacia's bemusing touch. Dacia was the white goddess. Trickily, she deprived Margaret of fire and assigned Addie to bear it to her.

Why can't she disapprove of Dacia as much as Margaret does? She owes it to Margaret. Is it because she still serves her? Like the four hundred pagan temples of Rome still stubbornly serving their perverse gods long after the era of the lamb begins? Dacia eludes Addie's disdain because she is of all things cool and certain. Had it not been for her long consideration of Dacia's nature she would not have been drawn to Sensei Haruki Norikazu's dojo in Paris. Dacia had an Aikido sensibility, an economy of behavior that left every ill-made move to someone else. As in Aikido, the heavenly road, Dacia had no enemies. She instilled in you a sense of otherness, and if you could bear it, it was much like having stood in the Sufi kiln: you would be fired to a perfection Dacia could touch; you would be perfectly mad.

She remembers Dacia's touch, cool, considered and divine. And Margaret's: hot, confused, instigative. How could her own mother, Annabeth, have fallen off her screen? She grew up in Annabeth's stone cottage in the Cotswolds, the house Annabeth inherited from her father, Hereward. She held onto Annabeth's apron while they watched her father Brian plow the fields behind Dolly, their black Shire who wouldn't work without a red scarf, a fedora in cool weather and a Panama in hot. She clutched Annabeth's skirt in church, unable to bear the pain of looking at the crucified Christ. Annabeth and Brian are gone, early and gracefully. Dacia is not.

20

As a drowned man could tell you, had he been luckier, the mind publishes treatises with speed that makes today's Internet seem pokey. Addie, watching Margaret's disappearing act and the statuarial poses of Bison and Crane, renovates her relationship with Margaret and computes the ballet in front of her eyes:

Margaret didn't take in Bison and Crane.

But it remains to be seen how long she's been spying on Bo.

The intentions of the two bozos won't unfold without further observation.

It's unlikely Bo knows he's being watched, his watchers are so sloppy.

Only Addie sees the complete chessboard, as she begins to think of it, and she has no idea how to play. All she knows is that if Margaret and Bo are the only players, she herself can withdraw. But if they aren't, if Bison and Crane are involved, then only she knows. It's a bad thriller. She hates thrillers. Thrillers are for dummies.

★

The next morning she waits in Café Diderot next to Crispin's for Margaret to take up station, but Margaret is probably lecturing bedazzled graduate students in a chalky amphitheater. At 10:44 she begins trailing Bo uptown. He seems never to walk, he lopes. Addie has to keep herself from overtaking him. He rocks along sole to heel to Irving Trust on the west side of Union Square. The usual Slavs and Jews are bloviating in the park, failing to ruffle the clockers playing the game of kings. Two smart-ass preppies, chucking the feckless avarice of Ayn Rand like rotten eggs, are heckling the over-earnest refugees. Bo stops outside the brass doors and draws a sizable pad from his belt behind him. He goes in and remains inside for about ten minutes. Addie spots Bison and Crane inhaling hot dogs in the tatty park across from the bank. She deduces that Bo regularly visits the bank and his stalkers mapped this out earlier. It's a stretch, but how else can their presence be explained? When Bo emerges he carries an haute couture brown briefcase. Bison and Crane begin talking to each other animatedly. If Bo runs, as he seems flexed to do, it's unlikely they can keep up with him. Certainly Bison can't. If she follows Bo she'll insert herself into the picture, putting herself under surveillance. They wait to see which way Bo will go. He heads northeast towards Fourth Avenue. Addie decides to stick with Bison and Crane. But what if they take a cab? Only in Hollywood's Manhattan can one cab follow another. They join the melée of bargain-hunters pressing into the lobby of S. Klein on the east side of the square. Crane shuts himself into a phone booth while Bison listens in. Addie saunters in, drops some coins two booths down and listens.

"*Salaam aleykum,*" Crane says. Uh oh, Addie thinks. But the next words out of Crane's mouth are French.

"*Bien entendu,*" says Crane, "*oui, oui, je le comprend.*" And that's it. He hangs up and turns to Bison.

"He says get it," Crane says in French.

"I don't care what he says," replies Bison, "I have to have my own orders. He's not my boss. We agreed to cooperate, that's all." Bison then makes his own call. She knows it's in Portuguese and that it's long distance, but she doesn't understand Portuguese. Bison speaks briefly, then listens. When he's through he hangs up without a word.

"Your world and mine," he tells Crane, "have irreconcilable differences." His French is smooth. "What we share is greed," Bison continues. "It goes to my boss first, that's the deal. We're messengers. The big shots will work everything else out. If they don't, fuck them. Your people are fanatics. Fanatics are untrustworthy. Money is always the best motive. Senhor Da Cunha is honorable because he is greedy. Fanatics have no honor."

The Crane smiles sardonically. "The Crusades were about greed. I am about the word of the prophet. You are for hire, I am for Allah. Why do you presume you know what you are talking about, eh? Tell me."

"Nobody knows what he's talking about," Bison says with a mouth that seems to crave a cigar.

"Well, then," the Crane says, squeezing Bison's arm, "Saracen and infidel agree about something after all."

Addie is delighted to have sneaked into this show. It's almost as good as peeking through a keyhole and seeing the autocratic nuns having at it at Saint Agnes. Bison is some sort of mercenary and Crane is some sort of holy spy. They work for different people, at cross-purposes apparently, and yet there's some sort of deal between them. What has Bison been ordered to get?

She stares at the dead phone pretending to listen and wrestling with a familiar dilemma. She is by nature a keeper of secrets, anyone's. The nuns, sensing what she knew, favored her because she loved the beauty of a secret. And she loves the secrets she just heard, the conflict between the two men, their motives and philosophies. Yes, they have philosophies, these thugs. She doesn't know what to do next, so she loses herself in the stomp, poke and swarm of Klein's. She can cobble no better plan than to take up station tomorrow and hope she isn't overtaken by events.

★

Addie avoids the Manhattan subway system because like her subconscious, it requires full attention, doors opening and shutting, exquisite faces flashing by, expresses hurtling through ventricles, stories streaming everywhere, a million unfathomable intents in a hurry. Dark and dangerous. Enter advisedly, expect nothing, never knowing where it will take you. You may be caught between doors, humped by ogres, thrown onto third rails, pushed before trains. Wherever she walks or runs it growls under her feet, an underworld with which sooner or later she must deal. Perhaps today. Yes, there will be no local stops today, she knows that. The trains will be moving too fast to read the station signs. If you manage to get on one, you'll never get off.

99

The entrance next door to Bo's Palladian loft building is a grimy bum haven. Every morning a janitor with a purple Mohawk sloshes it out with a pail of pink disinfectant. At eight in the morning Addie posts herself there, steeping her face in a piping cardboard coffee cup, dodging traffic to cross Broadway to Diderot's for refills.

Bo breaks out of his building at 9:51 and heads up Broadway towards Houston. She begins to grin as she follows him—he's boogieing, and he's good. She draws within a few yards in the comfort of knowing he doesn't know what she looks like. Unless of course Margaret showed him a photograph, which would be uncharacteristic. He boogies left and boogies right. He comes up behind the towering sinister balloon man.

"Make the kiddies hap-pee," Bo mimics him.

"Yo, mon, you be de craziest Ay-rab on de block," the balloon man says.

"I be de only Ay-rab on de block, mon, and I be half a very nah-sty Kraut." They laugh like brothers. A few paces on, with the same matronly briefcase she saw the day before in his hands in front of him, he stops, boogies backwards and chants, "Hoo-yi-yay, throw out the camera, hoo-yi-yay."

Addie lets out a squeak. This is not at all as she imagined him. His looks fit her picture, but not his demeanor. He repeats the refrain: "Hoo-yi-yay, throw out the camera, hoo-yi-yay." It seems Margaret's obsession is a man of amusements, a man who finds vendors and janitors and bums preferable to the likes of Margaret Wadeleigh. And Adeline Compton? She wants to shout Hoo-yi-yay to turn his head, to ask him comically what he's about, but he, whatever else, is a man in trouble and she has undertaken to pierce this trouble.

He goes straight for the Pierpoint Morgan Library at Madison Avenue and 36th Street, an ambitious walk. Well, he's like her in one way: he doesn't like subways. The Morgan palazzo has something of the mahogany moroseness of a Third Avenue Irish pub absent the smell of piss. But when she goes in Bo is nowhere in sight. Edwardian grandiosity has devoured him. She goes purposefully to each logical locus and only when she's about to abandon Bo to the woods of words does she spot him through a door upholstered in green leather. He is standing at one end of a long table pointing to a large open book. A wispy courtly gent in his mid-sixties is standing beside him. They speak gravely, nodding and pointing to something in the book. Bo's briefcase is at the far end of the table. She stands at the door of this alien dimension. She fears not that she'll be directed out of a private place but rather that she'll be caught within. The elderly gentleman will say, Come in, Miss, do come in, and stay forever. She will stand there naked, her past incinerating in a pile behind her, while tweedy gentlemen of a certain age examine her.

Had he taken this book in the briefcase from the Irving Trust to his loft and this morning to the Morgan? It seems possible, even likely. Is it the book that interests Bison and Crane? Some book. Codes, account numbers, security logs? Not likely, not in old Moroccan leather with gold engraving. Has Margaret pieced any of this together or is Addie the stupe in the piece? Margaret has more than a little of the idiot savant in her, and it fell to Addie at Saint Agnes to protect Margaret from her compulsive dupesmanship. Margaret becomes bemused by her predators and can't find her way around them.

This might be the nature of Margaret's current enterprise, except Bo's no grifter. What he doesn't need of Margaret would fill volumes. Addie wonders, what does he need of anyone? It's his melancholy at play. It stands out from him like dandelion seed. Some melancholies hurt their beholder, but his invites touch and a hunch that the touch won't hurt. I won't hurt, she thinks. A plan of action begins to take shape.

Margaret wants to touch his melancholy, so she lurks in corners and calls him and then hangs up. But Addie wants to hoot hoo-yi-yay after him, to josh and tweak and shove him playfully. She smiles. Hoo-yi-yay: What does it mean? It might be a Sufi zikhr, but would this nah-sty kraut, as he calls himself, boogie up a zikhr? Well, sure, why not? If dervishes can whirl, krauts can boogie.

21

The sap would have struck the back of his head if Bo didn't walk like a merry-go-round horse. It hits the inside of his left shoulder blade. He stumbles forward, breaking a fall to the pavement with his left hand. Bison is on him before he regains his balance, and Crane pours something out of a bottle into a handkerchief. Addie goes aerial four yards before both her feet hit Crane from behind, sending him crashing into the window of Cool's fern bar and wrapping a neon India Ale sign around his neck. The sign is still sizzling and greening Crane's head when Addie turns to see Bison straight-arm Bo's face. Bo staggers back, takes in Addie's help at that moment and then whirls around, catching the Bison's head with his foot and stunning him. She has rarely seen a more elegant spin kick. She sees Bo readying a lethal cricoid chop to the Bison's larynx.

"No!" she shouts. Unaccountably, Bison turns from Bo and comes at Addie with a switchblade that must have been strapped under his sleeve. She executes *tsuki atemi nage*, pushing Bison's solar face. Crane, noosed in neon, comes up behind her. Bo points to him over her shoulder and Addie suddenly lowers her body, throwing Crane over her back with a single motion like a passenger lurching forward when a bus driver hits the brake. Bison, his smashed nose blooming all over his face, isn't finished. He comes at Bo with the knife. Bo grabs his arm, pulls him alongside, then jams his elbow with his other hand, breaking Bison's arm with a muffled crunch, convincing the assailants that things could get a lot worse.

Bison flees without a thought for Crane, who is trying to extricate himself from the still-blinking neon sign. Addie watches Bo dropkick Crane's balls. His *sangfroid* is so palpable that she fears for Crane's life. So does Crane, who produces the snub-nosed S&W he'd feared to show in such a busy place. Bo looks unimpressed. She clutches the tail of his jacket and tugs to distract him. Crane sees his chance to break and run, signalling that they hadn't wanted to kill Bo.

A coughing fit seizes Bo as he watches them in a white limo with diplomatic plates jumping a curb on Spring Street to bypass two livery men rekindling the India-Pakistan border war. He leans over the gutter, gripping his knees, and watches black water streaked with red scuttle into a storm drain. It takes him a while to realize it's his own blood. He's checking himself for cuts or punctures when Addie presses her scarf, the one she wears to stop sweat from tickling her tits when she runs, under his nose.

"Your nose, see if it's broken."

He applies pressure here and there and shakes his head. She pinches his nostrils together.

"Tilt your head back." They hold this frieze as night rises out of the sewers and limns the teary windows of the bars and galleries. Other than to put his briefcase in the protective custody of his long legs, he does nothing to discourage this nose pinch. Addie too prolongs it. Their eyes play like children in a garden. She finally lets go and dabbles his nose with her ruined scarf. He reaches into an inside pocket of his gray herringbone jacket and with Victorian aplomb says, "Let me introduce myself." He hands her his card: "Soren Tired, Esq., 553 1/2 Broadway, No. 22, New York, NY 10000." No telephone number.

She reads his card inscrutably. "If you give me another card, I'll write my name on the back of it and we'll be even." He complies and she holds it in her palm and writes, "Destine Espionné, 744 East 36th Street, New York, NY 10021."

He reads her card and nods. There are no half numbers or 22-unit buildings in the 500 block of South Broadway, and 744 East 36th Street stands in the way of tugboats.

He studies her, starting with the carven shins and calves. Such a scan would have struck her as obscene if she hadn't been spying on him. He lingers awhile over her blunt and calloused fingertips and then circles her disquietingly ecstatic mouth on his way to the green quarry pools of her eyes. A Sufi calm settles in his long face. She thinks of Provence and imagines herself a village maiden encountering a Saracen lancer by a wooded stream. Too late to call for help, and besides, she likes the scrutiny. Something stutters in their eyes. Static moves along the rims of their lips. Then they burst into laughter, Soren Tired and Destine Espionné, phonies to the core.

"Well, Mr. Cavalieri, is it cavalier of you to laugh at your rescuer?"

"It was cavalier of you to rescue me."

She likes the way he says it.

"You must be mistaken, Sindbad. I am a magical roc, actually."

You're magical, all right—he doesn't say it, but she hears it anyway. The sidewalk tilts and he begins to spin. The buildings lean forward and sway sideways. The street lamps flutter and the traffic syncopates itself into Ravel's *Bolero*. He's still there, wrapped in his contemplation of her. Addie, Destine, the roc, the Cotswolds' boyish page to East Anglia's perfect rose wobbles on her feet. Better the street shuffle them off the board than this, she thinks. This what? But now he's smiling and it's too late to step back.

"About those moves . . ."

"Aikido."

Must she execute an Aikido move to break his gaze? Good question, Addie. What will break your own?

"Dinner." It isn't a question. "I'm thinking about veal scaloppine. I'd like to make us some."

He brushes the lock that always falls over her left eye. Men always long to touch Margaret's hair. Addie's attraction is her bones. Now Dacia's one true love has not been able to keep from touching her plain light honey-brown hair, to waken her to scaloppine.

She shucks her hair back in one of those what-the-hell gestures Margaret adores and puts her arm around his waist and steps out as if they were in a chorus line. She peers into his face and chants, *"Hoo-yi-yay, throw out the camera, hoo-yi-yay."*

"Yeah, it's a Bedouin song. They're venerating a saint, but when I first heard it in Oman it sounded like that, and I figure the saint won't mind. I hear things funny."

"I hope the saint won't mind," she says.

His tin ear and inability to carry any tune but the clunkiest Protestant hymns somehow vanished in Oman. Perhaps the insistent Bedouin rhythms called to his racial memory, just as the Germanic hymns had. He remembers a prayer for a safe return sung at the tomb of the saint Bin Ali at Mirbat. And while he's able to sing the entire prayer in Arabic, he likes to bastardize the chorus: *Hoo yi yay, throw out the camera, hoo-yi-yay.*

He wraps her shoulder in his arm and she thinks of Dacia, who also liked to touch her. Soren Tired, she decides, is a dervish, whether he knows it or not. And he knows the dervish's duty is to disappear and meanwhile not to quarrel with synchronicities. He doesn't even question how she heard his scat-song.

Guessing who she is, Bo introduces himself as Soren Tired, an insult. Not directed solely at her, because he's done it before, or he wouldn't be carrying Soren's cards. And she, understanding the nature of the insult, introduces herself as Destine Espionné, an East River nymph. Then the two dervishes set out down Spring Street, hustled by a coarse March wind, arm in arm, certain only that the vast veil of illusion has incurred something like retinal pinholes.

22

Eastward in a greasy flat on the northwest corner of 18th Street and First Avenue, near the birthplace of Antonin Dvorak's *New World Symphony*, Klement Gruber, the Bison, sits in a doggy armchair, holding an ice pack to his face and speaking on the phone to Commodus da Cunha, his boss. He dips his stinging bottom lip in Four Roses as he listens: "I am sure, Klement, that you are ashamed to reward my generosity with this disturbing report. I continue to count on your ingenuity. Good night, Klement."

One too many Klements. Herr Gruber knows he better not bungle again.

Khaled ibn al Qwarzimi, Addie's Crane, chain-smoking Helmuts in the Omani consulate, makes a less embarrassing report to his superior. He is, after all, the assistant director of Omani intelligence, and his nominal boss is an idiot. His true boss, Bayazid Qadir ben Saadi, a pan-Arabist Algerian marabout who dreams of restoring the caliphate, will simply intone that doing Allah's work requires patience.

Klement Gruber's ardor for restoring *The Book of Secrets* to its rightful owner, the Omani sultanate, is as nominal as Khaled's. Khaled and the marabout regard the sultanate as corrupt and little different from the Islamists, whom the marabout sees as witless thugs with no understanding of the immense grace of Islam. The book, in their view, belongs to a caliphate interrupted by a hapless Ottoman interregnum. Gruber and his conniving boss will be dealt with in due time. Meanwhile Commodus da Cunha's resourcefulness is useful.

Alchemical contraptions—Moor's heads, aludels, and alembics—hang from fishing lines at varying heights in Bo's loft. Addie thinks of the consecrated sacramental lamps representing the seven churches of Asia Minor in high Anglican churches. She doesn't guess the devices are connected to the attack they just fended off. Bo has dived for alchemical artifacts off the coast of Oman. That's how he met the sultan who years later bequeathed to him *The Book of Secrets*. The artifacts are actually replicas he commissioned from a metalworker who followed his drawings. She stands in front of his freight elevator watching the strange devices turn slowly in the draft from the elevator shaft. His quarters are as arcane as hers. Her heart pounds. She and Bo like pieces of ancient things.

The predictable choreography is for Bo to falsely bustle while Addie decides if she wants to be here. But he isn't like that, nor is she. He stands three yards from her, watching. She believes he could have stood there for hours, enjoying her framed against the cavern that connects him to the world. She has never sensed herself on the threshold of anything until now. She has none of Margaret's concerns about Amir Cavalieri. She has no concerns. Her life falls away behind her. Goodbye, her heart says. She doesn't even wonder where Crane and Bison have gone, but she thinks that the time before they return should be well spent. She looks at Bo and knows the only thing on his mind is that he likes her. She feels like a reckless flower with only one day to bloom.

Addie knows how men are taken by Margaret Wadeleigh. But she knows nothing of the ways the elect are seized by her. Old men and immigrant peddlers want from her what a listless people wanted from Jack Kennedy. Wounded men find her as soothing as plantain. Addie doesn't cost men their dignity—there's no contempt in her. The athletes who've wanted her aerobically might as well have wanted each other. She's never wanted a man, but she's taken on a few. Now, standing in the black light of Bo's gaze, revealing her fluorescences, she thinks, What difference does it make if he's a man? If Margaret calls him Bo, I'll dissent and call him Amir. A man whose stare is so northerly it would make a wolf whine, he frisks her etheric field, that subtle aura that stands out an inch or two from our bodies. He stares clockwise, counterclockwise, stopping, moving on, retracing, seeing what others can't. She feels energy reshape and regroup about her—heat clapping her ears, sparks in the groin, tinkling between her eyes, a pulsing signal from the spleen. He's a draftsman—perhaps he's drawing her. Her reverie lasts a long time, until she sees his gaze roll down her arm and rest on her legs, now slanted on the couch—then she understands and her formidably composed face blossoms with delight—he feels about her the way she feels about instruments, about the inviolability of line and grain. This is not a lewd stare at fine legs, it's a prayer of thanks for such tendons, such chiaroscuro, such subtle articulation. Yes, she knows it well, this limning sense one must have to rescue an instrument from disrepair. And now, thanks to Dacia Wadeleigh's first and only love, she knows the difference between her own sexuality and Margaret's. Margaret inflames desperation to get in the bone, the wood, the steel, the glass, the secret caches of the flesh, but she, Adeline Compton, stirs the (greater?) need to see, to admire, to collaborate in a venture. She—but she can't handle the thought—ennobles.

Sweat beads at her hairline, along the ridge of her calligraphic upper lip, under her blouse. Her eyes yaw and break from her mind's buoy. When Amir looks up into her face he sees Dacia's clowning looniness. Only a cantankerous god would give such an austere face a Mongol bow for an upper lip, a mouth that looks like a raised curtain and invites adventure when all the rest of her says perhaps not. Unlike Margaret she has never hunched her shoulders to drape erect nipples, but now she feels her boyishness become unreliable, rebellious.

He leans forward and kisses her. She thinks of a swallowtail butterfly alighting on a wet leaf. What kind of leaf am I? She doesn't think he will let his tongue ask, ask anything, but she smiles when she realizes it couldn't resist the way her lip tugs at the curtain of her mouth. His tongue in the bow of her lip pushes up at her mind and topples it and she falls over backwards, somersaulting past burning bushes and galaxies. Too late. Everything is too late. She can't see over the Himalayas of her nipples. Are those mine? They've never seemed so arrogant. How have they gone on such a march? She can't lift her head, dangling over the arm of the couch. Why are all the hairs of her body, especially the sticky ones, reporting for census?

Amir has been enjoying the comfort of the eunuch for a long time. He has no stomach for troubling it. It is, like death, underrated. But he has the notion that he might touch Addie without entraining the usual baggage, like fondling a Bernini when the museum guard isn't looking. He thinks she understands, like the Bernini. But now he's about to rearrange her furniture, like the horny grunt he'd once been, poking, prizing, prodding, picking. It happens so fast he can't remember how he's gotten past her panties. She wonders the same thing. His urgency flamencos on the brink of chaos, then plummets into a secret firmament of sizzling stars and choirs of flowers. Over and over he falls. The stars and their navigator lose their moorings. He laughs to die this way. She laughs to find herself a vast sea surrounding a lovely, fragile ship. She feels wet enough to float a fleet. She marvels that neither her organs are grazed nor her nerve ends frayed. No, she's being navigated, her buoys noted and obeyed. She begins to quake, to heave off bridges, break up interchanges, crack cathedrals, shatter glass. Then she faints.

"Hey? C'mon, open your eyes."

She sees long fire opals imbedded in his green irises. She sees her face in his obsidian pupils, her face, not Addie Compton's.

"That's my real face."

He says nothing, not wanting to skew the mirrors she is using. After a while, when she has memorized a face wiser than she has ever been, she studies his, and he begins using his thumbs to knead the gnarls of pressure packed in her brows and cheekbones. He never has to search for them. He finds them unerringly, triggers their charged pain and smoothes it away.

"We're navigators, aren't we? I shoot stars and steer by them. You find how wood wants to work, what it wants to say. You discover how things want to be and then you allow them."

109

"Liberate them?"

"Yes, I like that."

But not as much as she likes his words about being navigators. She hears him speak of the wont of wood and now her lips silently form the phrase. He has found her wont. Where other men might think of a bony fuck, as Peter Harkness is reported to have tattled about her, or an agile lay, Amir Cavalieri has slipped almost unnoticed into a great night sky. They've become undocked, galactic, star beasts cavorting. And yet not really that either.

And you, Amir, did I liberate you? Yes, I did. And look what you've done. I thought I had some appliances to tickle, bump and rub, I thought I was supposed to be grateful for a little internal Rolfing, and you—you did some kind of espionage, you slipped past all my defenses and set charges, like the frogman you are. But even as she indulges her metaphors, plays with them like dolls, she know they aren't about what's happened—no, no, they have made a tumultuous night journey in some sector that had never appeared on the charts. They've fallen through the ice of McKee's Pond, the ice that covers traumas, that freezes over disappointments and denials. She will never skate on McKee's Pond again, not past the encroaching woods or over the entrapped artifacts. No, not when gravity-free space waits with its momentous songs, its blessed disorientations and pitiless grace. And now . . .

"So?"

"How 'bout a cigar?"

They sit crosslegged on the floor puffing contraband green Cohibas.

"I don't smoke."

"Don't tell."

"I won't. I won't tell Addie anything."

They laugh till they choke.

Then Bo grows still and seems to be looking within.

"What are you considering, Amir?"

"There are people whose features reflect a plan, an attitude, and then there are a few people, a very few, whose features lead the way while the soul listens. Do you know what I mean?"

"No."

"I'd like to sketch you. May I?"

"Now?" she asks.

"Always."

"Always now?"

"No, just always."

He wants to sketch her always. If he registers what he's said he doesn't show it. She understands. It isn't a request, it's a declaration. The orchestration of her body, attuned by years of Aikido, has promised a sketch that can be completed with a few clean lines: her body is as functional as rope. Seamen call rope line, which appeals to the artist in Bo. But instead of holding still for the sketch, she crawls towards him, takes the pad out of his hand, touches her brow to his and looks into his eyes. I will treat him fondly, arch my back and give him hard release. But that's before he takes her shoulders and bends her back. She arches her back and bends like a bow about to fire heavenward. The arrow sings before it fires.

Addie studies his face as unselfconsciously as a cat. He touches her bangs, which have grown too long, her eyebrows, her lips, the hair in front of her ears.

"You look, you look, well, amazed. You look amazed, Amir."

"I'm—I don't rise to these occasions."

"Well, you did. Truly, you did. I would know. I'm not sure I like being an occasion."

"I was being circumspect."

"I thought it was lust. It felt like lust."

She pulls his head to her childish bosom. "I think your body likes me, Amir. Does your head?"

He pulls up and stares at her and slowly a tear carries away some of the green of his eye and stumbles down his gaunt cheek.

"I see," she says. "Well, that's settled."

She crawls over to his woolen Navy watch shirt and takes out two more cigars. She lights them both and hands one to Bo. She sits crosslegged facing him, blowing smoke rings. He laughs. She looks down between her legs. "Trust me, Cavalieri, you're the first man I've ever favored with a beaver shot."

Another tear runs down his face. He licks it away as it passes his mouth. She leans over and licks it for good measure and they kiss.

"What's your idea of hell, Amir?"

"A place where your fantasies come true instantly."

Addie sits up on his mattress, which is laid like a bedroll on the floor, her nipples frisking the ceiling. Her eyes engulf him. She already knows that nothing prompts him to speak unless he has something to say. She sits there remembering Dacia's eyes, the light and whim. The green of his eyes is dark and steady. She has despaired of her nipples holding up the ceiling by the time he speaks: "I'm sure our friendship is over if I can't fathom your look," he says.

It doesn't occur to her, as it might to most women, to complain within, if not aloud, that this is no way to treat someone who has just made love to you.

"Yes," she says after a while, "there would be no friendships at all, everything would crumble, it would be a place of impermanence, untrustworthiness, hell. You're a dangerous man, Cavalieri."

"Not as dangerous as you are, not by a long shot. I can kill or walk away, but you erase things."

Her gemmy nipples perk to the very thing she has despaired of in men, emotional commerce. And even more important, he knows something about her not even Doctor Wadeleigh knows. She can erase the perimeters of things with her long green eyes.

She crawls across the mattress and takes his face in both hands. "I don't want to erase you accidentally, Amir. Do I dare ask you what your idea of heaven is?"

He jumps up, walks a few feet, and picks up a box of charcoals on a rolling stand. "Yeah, it's not to be erased by you."

She stands up naked, like a brazen girl flashing her panties at a boy. She squeezes her throat with both hands and smiles. "I never thought . . ."

He puts his forefinger to his lips. "Neither did I."

She props her head on a few pillows, a shirttail rising above a thigh that would have broken the heart of Praxiteles.

Her honeyed cache opens to him as irresistibly as a rose to the sun. Honeysuckle tipsiness comes over her like the shocking arrival of spring. They're people, Adeline and Amir, who have no need whatever to know anybody's mind. They're content to be told, or not. She falls in love with the sugar of this recognition. Amir is a man who can stare at her center without imperiling her, stare at it because it's there.

★

"What're you, some kind of monster?"

She knows he doesn't mean her. She waits.

"That's what my mother used to say to me. I just remembered. I guess I remember because I'm happy and that's when she always shows up in my head. She used to say it as if I smelled bad."

"Obviously she did, Amir. Smell bad."

His gaze whispers thanks in the fine hair of her legs. "I wish it would snow," he says.

24

Margaret leaves Block Beautiful bracing for fresh hell, in this case the five hundred block of Broadway south of Houston Street in an area once called Hell's Hundred Acres because of the sweatshop fire that destroyed it.

She resents the New World for its indifference to her arrival.

She likes the long dogleg walk from Irving Place to Soho. She passes Grace Church at Twelfth and Broadway in the hope of benediction, but the church is too busy trying to survive Manhattan's restless shape-changing. The sun flares on the huge arched windows of Bo's building when she looks up, so she can see nothing inside.

In three days of taking up various stations near his building she hasn't caught him at any of his four east-facing windows. At night a steady light glows from way back in the loft, but there are no moving shadows. On the fourth day, as she sits in the steamy window of Café Aslan—three doors up from the Diderot, Addie's post—Bo, wearing his Navy watch cap, bursts out of his red graffitied steel door. He wears blue cotton sweats splotched with white paint. He looks straight over to Café Aslan, then sprints south about twenty yards and turns west onto Spring Street.

Do I really expect to shadow him in sandals? The sadness of her enterprise falls in on her. She imagines telling him how she proposed to track him in pumps, but she can't imagine him smiling. He might think it tacky to call attention to her legs. His humor is entirely kept for whimsy, she remembers. Every thought of him somehow turns to ash, incinerated by uncertainty. And yet the sight of him elicits in her something like watching one's horse cross the finish line first.

She hurries up to Houston Street and buys herself a pair of Nikes and a new Yankees cap to trap her golden free-fall. She isn't sure that these and her white sweats will help her keep up with Bo. If he's a generation older, he's a generation faster. But, with luck, he'll be distracted by passersby. He seems to enjoy nothing as much as watching others, and she has contracted this contagion too.

★

The next day he bolts onto Broadway and turns north towards Houston, saluting a sinister balloon vendor in top hat who relentlessly chants, *Make the children hap-pee, make the children hap-pee.* She leaves five dollars for luck on the vendor's card table and sets out after Bo, noticing after a few blocks that he seems to be wearing some sort of brace under his waistband. Is he ill? Has he hurt himself? He jogs west on Houston toward the Hudson, the lame March sun behind him. The city reeks of its chief addiction, coffee. He's running at something like a seven-minute mile, much too fast for Margaret. He doesn't run so much as lope, head up, hands loose. Sometimes he spins around and bobbles backwards to reconsider something. Often he glances to the right or left. As she struggles to stay within fifty yards she thinks of him as a wolf. He's a seaman, and if he's certain about anything, it's that she's not her mother's daughter. She's not the very thing she most wanted to be, and now, this moment, tracking Bo Cavalieri, it makes her ineffably sad. Why, she wonders, as the Hudson piers heave into view, does she think him a wolf? Wolf pack? Is he like a U-boat? Yes, he's rigged for silent running and not for doubts. These thoughts too she wants to share with him. If only he'd stop. He's like a U-boat. They don't stop, do they? No, they go on inhabiting our minds because we know the seas we ply are full of them. Sharks, killing machines, are always in motion, but U-boats do stop, and look and listen. And when they're under attack, when they've done their worst and await retribution, they sit still and listen. Like Bo. What is Bo's worst? If she knew that, they could talk again, have commerce. But for all they shared three years ago she knows

115

nothing about him except that he lived his entire life in the breadth of a few years enjoying the sweetness of her mother's breath. That's too much to know of anyone.

The Hudson blinds the city. No boat or ship or ferry can be seen in the flash of its teeth. New Jersey can hardly be imagined. Manhattan need not imagine anything but itself. The rest of the world is an unfounded rumor.

At Ninth Avenue, just north of the Holland Tunnel, Bo eases into a run Margaret likens to a giraffe's. He quickly loses her. And as she leans on a lamppost with one arm she guesses resentfully that Dacia would have overhauled him and glanced back with that daffy grin of hers. Does he think of Dacia when he runs?

Bo's own imagining is that he is both war camel and rider, racing at forty miles an hour, sweeping the air with his curved sword and crying, *Allahu akbar wa Muhammed rasul-Allah.* Not, admittedly, an apt fantasy for an Episcopalian, but such is lifelong in him. He takes communion casually, ignoring God's popsicles, just as he stands at latrines with strangers at sea. In fact the one memory guaranteed to make him laugh is losing his identity for one good crap while he sat over a seawater trough and glanced to the right to see his wallet go to sea. He thinks the incident a perfect metaphor for his life—he hardly gives a crap for his identity.

A man whose senses man all battle stations and never think of an alert as a drill might be expected to detect Wadeleigh's espionage—he does detect surveillance, but not then, and not hers. She walks the world like an elf. Few people ever sense her scrutiny. Her gaze rests on people and their collectibles like dew. She knows this and is grateful. It's not Dacia's legacy, it's Colin's, a gift that made his life an easy if brief passage. It helps her sort her way through the academic hedgerows of fiefdoms and egos.

The sun loses its pallor on saw-toothed Manhattan and bleeds on New Jersey when Margaret finds him by accident. She has stopped for a vomitous red chowder on West Broadway and is walking south. The great liners, those implausible layer cakes, are gone and will not return. Bloody New Jersey can be seen withdrawing through the yawns of the covered piers. He's seated on a bollard, looking towards the Palisades—or so she thinks, but when she begins crossing the cobblestones under the rickety West Side Highway she sees that he's sketching a chestnut vendor who seems to be greasing the wheels of his yellow cart. The man and his cart are both lying on their sides. The man turns to look at Bo and Bo shoots him with his forefinger. They laugh and Bo resumes sketching.

She feels like a child who has discovered little people at tea under a mushroom. She's enthralled and lurks behind a steel pillar. There's no danger of her concentration turning Bo's head. Her existence in the world is not that substantial. And Bo's like a heron, seemingly unaware of any presence until he pounces. Easily as athletic as Addie, he seems to practice a physical economy Margaret ascribes to seamen. And killers. But in fact it's innate; he's merely found professions to camouflage it.

She notices again that his sketch hand—he's left-handed— rarely busies itself shading and smudging and erasing. Instead it forms slow arabesques, not retracing itself. Margaret doesn't know enough about art to know this is a skill for which the great Picasso has been praised too lavishly. It's the mark of a sure draftsman, a kind of Zen. She does notice something different: Bo keeps going to his pocket for another—charcoal, pencil, crayon? She remembers him using only pencil. She doesn't know that with Ulrike Theiss's death color has crept into his drawing. Wan and timid, to be sure, but color nonetheless. This isn't the Amir Cavalieri she ditched, only to deposit a hundred hang-ups in his answering machine. This is an Amir Cavalieri who sits a few yards from where he deep-sixed her hang-ups in their box.

She's struck by how Manhattan gathers him, yet gives him creaturely berth as if he were a wolf, while she's sometimes not even sure her cottage in Lechlade belongs to her or she to it. And yet he's spent so little of his life here. He's wandered around the world seafaring and murdering. Is it because he belongs everywhere and she nowhere? How can this half-caste at odds with his genes belong and not she, who is as much one thing as genealogy can warrant? He's a wog, or half a wog, the other half

117

detestably iron-headed and kraut. She comforts herself with the pure damned perverse racism of her rumination: I am superior, I belong, I am untainted. Only people whose papers are not in order, people who are out of order, need to pass. I have a royal passport. He is a wog. A raghead. His papers are doctored. He may be stopped at a checkpoint. He may be expelled. He should be deported. God knows what diseases he carries. He shouldn't be allowed to crossbreed.

Under the ruined highway she titillates herself with her perversities. Outrages entertain her, like a secret vice. They're like having a beautiful slave. How would I know that, she wonders, and then she remembers that her only sexual fantasy about men, a dogged one, is that in a flat somewhere in Kensington she keeps a man totally for her sexual pleasure and his humiliation. She tries to picture him. Has she ever seen his face? Trucks jolt over her head as she forces her mind up from his torso to his face. But she can't see it. A truck rattles a manhole cover and in that instant she knows her compulsion to hurt Bo is rooted in this fantasy. She draws back into the shadows trying to recapture the urgency of her fantasy, but tears race between her breasts to her navel. A river of tears opens to her pubis. She can't stem it. She begins to hiccup. She's not at all the person she's chosen to be. Under civility and ice lurks this racist, this sadist. She shakes her head violently. No, I am what I seem to be, but I'm also in love. Damn Dacia. Damn me.

★

Margaret. She hears Addie's voice, Addie throwing the lever, shutting down her smoking gears—the Addie of her mind, companionable, yet hieratic. *Margaret, for the love of God, get a grip.* Her flight of superiority, safe superiority, the reassuring snobbery her battered soldiery always rediscovers in England upon returning, cools to a slow march. Yes, she harbors these Nietzschean reveries. Who has watched the human palette of his native land change and not harbored them? She enjoys them as the supercilious General Allenby enjoyed himself when he watched the Bedouin conquerors of Damascus abandon it for

118

the desert and called them magnificent beggars. She enjoys the armor of her prejudices. Why had icy Dacia not indulged them? She too saw the complexion of England change, but she regarded the changes as precious treats—candy from Pakistan, from Trinidad, from Mysore and Hong Kong. What a magical shop England has become. The crumbling of empire amused Dacia. She savored the crumbs. Damned Dacia. Had it never occurred to her that Amir was wholly unacceptable? Perhaps it had, and Dacia found it delicious. She was like that. But, as much as sights delighted, she'd found only one delicacy, and he's sitting on a bollard across the cobblestones from her daughter. There is Dacia's sole delight, her Greensleeves. And her daughter can't hold it straight in her perfectly mathematical mind long enough to say a few words, to start a Platonic dialogue. That was the Greek way, wasn't it? To see what might ensue of dialogue? And she can't do it, for the same reason Dacia didn't have to do it, because thoughts of Amir make her damp and awkward. So much for Platonic dialogue and the Greek way. The Greek way is not what Dacia or her daughter have in mind. But worse than being in this fix is knowledge that she can just stride across the avenue and blurt it all out and he'll say, Hello, Margaret, and listen to her till the cows come home and walk her around Manhattan and make her a fine dinner and bathe in her resplendence as if it were aromatherapy. That's exactly what she can do, and then who will she be? Margaret Wadeleigh, respected mathematician? Margaret Wadeleigh, the damned fool? Margaret Wadeleigh, the miscegenist? Fornicator? Who will she become by simply letting Bo Cavalieri like her? She has no one in her new spy world to ask. Not Addie. But if Addie, what would Addie say? Addie is as haunted by Dacia as she is. Margaret is ambushed by an immense mystery: she has no idea what Addie would say. It frightens her. She always knows what Addie would say. It frightens her even more that Addie might not know what to say. Once after a casual tryst Addie said to Margaret, "I polished his spigot." And when Margaret spluttered with laughter she elaborated, "I let him take a little poke." And when she saw Margaret helpless with laughter she said, "Very little." A freshet of Addie's *bons mots* came to her: "Well, Margaret, the poor man just wants to smell the roses" and "Let him have a good thought for his old age." They'd always talked like this, encountering the odd good man and dealing with him well—as the unneedy gods should. But Amir does not need to be primed or polished or pumped or permitted a sniff. What does he need? The answer is more deafening than West Street. He needs nothing, wants nothing except Dacia. And therein he's a problem, and she doesn't like any of her blackboard problems as much. But none of this, with all its allures and glamours, has brought her here. Something else is at play. Addie and Margaret make their own safety in a palpably unsafe world. No one else has a role, except to amuse or rattle. But from the moment Margaret discovers Bo in Cairnhall he represents safety from all without and all danger within. In his company, or alone with her memory of him, she feels safe.

He sits there on a bollard, drawing a chestnut vendor, sure in his knowledge that she's living her arcane life at a safe distance. She pities him that this is no longer true. She feels like Hermes about to deliver a blow. Poor misbegotten wog, he's being stalked by his colonial orientalist—ooh, she knows that would make him smile, uppity wog that he is. Superior wog. She looks at him as T.E. Lawrence looked at the Arabs, knowing the English had once been the wogs and the Saracens the masters. Amir, Bo . . . her mind again slips its track when he rises—she thinks she hears his knees creaking—tucks his sketch book under his belt and begins his warmups for the run eastward and home.

PART 2

24

The way people confront is their bill of lading. How they express what they've read and seen measures their comity as unfathomable nations.

"Addie," Margaret whispers as Addie turns the key to the entry of Bo's building.

Addie doesn't want to turn to face her, to recompose her face to suit a moment she can't define. She doesn't want to deal with this fellow stalker, to wonder if their love has become erstwhile. Nor does she wish Margaret to go away.

★

There are two kinds of merchant seamen, those who disappear and those who turn up like bad pennies. None of the latter ever shipped with Bo twice. They knew that for them he'd find the dirtiest jobs and the meanest watches. They're not seamen but grifters and he has no use for them.

Addie knows Bo likes inconvenient people—fools and klutzes, gifted kvetches, scalawags, loners as loony as himself— but perhaps she and Margaret are entirely too inconvenient.

Margaret has glimpsed this Bo, the gravitation of improbable people to him—shopgirls leaning towards him as if falling, old men who think they recognize him, waiters who treat him like a nabob. She mentioned this to Hettie Warshaw and Hettie said that the elect recognize each other but dimly as through a veil. She wants this connection to him to be free of Dacia. She wants to open the door and sweep that dread girl out. And then she remembers the absent-minded Reverend Frobisher Card who often started the wrong sermon or lost his way mid-sentence.

Senile since my ordination, God's fool said, and Margaret made a mental note to listen to him carefully. One day, as she loitered in the narthex listening to him instruct Sunday school children, Frobisher Card told a listless little fellow, "Angels are not at all what you think, my boy, no indeed, they're dangerous and always disguised. Forget about the lutes and the harps, you never recognize them, no, never, I assure you." And then, mumbling and shuffling papers, he vanished into the sacristy and the misery of his name.

She indulges a manic vision of herself dragging Bo by his ear to the professionally distracted Reverend Frobisher Card and saying, Is this your bloody angel then? For she had, upon leaving Bo, an eerie sense of having entertained something alien unawares. Can one love something alien as Magdalene had? If anyone can, a mathematician can.

★

With her unturned key in the lock, Addie says, "If he doesn't know what eleven-year-old Dacia would do, he doesn't know what to do himself."

"He told me once he never knows what to do in emotionally complex moments unless he's seen it in a British movie."

"What was so wrong, so difficult being Dacia's surrogate? You should have been. If he'd asked, you would have, but you thought it was Dacia asking," Addie said.

"Whooo! I've seen formulae and equations that have daunted me, but yours—should have been Dacia's surrogate, you say? Should have been? It's just what I bloody well refuse to be. You think it's written I have to requite them? I don't think he gives a damn."

"He does and you do, and I don't want to hear any lucubrations from one who spends her life cutting to the chase. Wasn't it you who complained that Einstein spent too much of his *élan vitale* bullshitting?"

"Lucubrations?" Margaret puts her hand on Addie's chest and they collapse in each other's arms laughing.

"Well, we're agreed then, are we, that something's wrong? He wouldn't have just shoved off," Margaret says.

"Especially as he's retired. I may have had a bad-breath morning, but . . ."

"But how could he forgo those legs?"

At such times Addie wishes she had the kind of lips that would purse, like Margaret's, but hers are unsubtle, made to express startledness. Margaret knows exactly what Addie is thinking and traces Addie's upper lip with her forefinger. "We'll just have to find him, won't we?"

It doesn't fret the two young women that their quest for a middle-aged wanderer might finick the order of things. They see it not as an interruption of their lives but as the one thing their natures call on them to do.

Suddenly Addie feels immense compassion for Margaret. She has Mutawakkil ibn al-Qureishi to protect her from Dacia's caprices. Margaret has no one but Addie.

Margaret sets her left hand lightly on Addie's shoulder and Addie lays her own hand over it. Then Margaret does exactly what her friend had wished. Addie feels the heat lightning of Margaret's pelvic girdle surging down between her legs and rising in front to her navel. She turns the key and pushes.

"I think he's gone missing," she says. "I'd call the police, except I'm sure they'd go off in the wrong direction."

Recognizing finally that Margaret won't speak again until Addie tells her more, she turns and says, "I think it's about a book. We could bivouac here and try to sort it out."

She tries to fathom Margaret's state of mind. I know that Margaret never imagined I would be the one who would bring her here. No, this isn't how she imagined getting here. I must find a way to withdraw, to turn over Bo's world to her for a while, to behave as we've always tried to behave, like Arthur's knights. Addie draws back into the shadows of an unlit foyer hung with photographs of a shockingly blonde young woman and a solemn, curly-haired boy. Staring at Ute-Britt Broghammer and her nine-year-old son Tariq, she thinks, I'll find him, Ute-Britt, and I'll keep him for you.

She watches Margaret touch the contraptions festooning the loft. Margaret touches a hundred things—a watch cap, a sketchbook, a coffee mug, socks, a cigar box, a pair of boxer shorts left on his bed, a pair of panties... Addie waits for her to say something, but she keeps moving as in a pavane, and when she comes back to the foyer she says, "Who are these people?"

"Ute-Britt was a barmaid in Hamburg when Amir met her. She was in love with a Moroccan guest boy named Lakhdar Ali Wahab. Amir liked to sit in a dark corner and sketch her and Lakhdar as they worked. He tried to catch the glances they exchanged. One night his friend and shipmate offered Ute-Britt two hundred American dollars to sleep with him. She accepted to buy her lover a falafel cart. When Lakhdar found out he hung himself in his garret. Amir was broken-hearted and so was Ute-Britt. They kept watch together one night in Lakhdar's garret, just holding each other, not making love. Then Amir quit his ship and took the boy's body back to his small home village in Morocco and buried him. He didn't want a fellow Saracen to be buried among strangers who despised him, you see. It's only recently he's been able to resume his friendship with his old shipmate. For a long time he wanted to kill him. He started sending money to Ute-Britt. She sends him photographs of her son, Lakhdar's son."

"God in heaven, I don't know what to make of the man."

"What's there to make, Margaret? How many men would do such a thing? It's the way he's made. Ute-Britt Broghammer and Tariq are his family."

A silver thread of pain runs from the foyer back to Amir's bed as Margaret sees that her lover and Dacia's only love have been in each other's arms there. They're drawn to the bed, to the requited and unrequited. But the dark foyer holds them, Margaret, Addie and Ute-Britt, and Margaret is swamped in the fellowship of the German girl.

Did he enjoy the comfort of the eunuch, as he ruefully put it, or did he rise to the occasion in Addie's arms? Here's where Addie purloined—only the antique word will do—my lover, swooped down like an eagle and snatched him in front of the fox. But that isn't the way it happened, is it? It can't have happened like that. No, this is celebratory, not predatory. They celebrated me in that military bed. Me and Dacia. And if Addie met any eunuch she'd have put him to use. And if she met someone, something else . . .

Margaret weeps and hides it from Addie as long as she can. Celebrated me, how do I feel about that? Left out, for starters. Yes, I should tell Addie that. She'd laugh. But I should tell her nothing till I know how I feel, how I really feel. And I suppose that means I need to know how she feels, how she felt when she intruded. Isn't that what she did? Intrude? But how angry can I be when I've depended so much on her directitude? Well, anger's not about rights, is it? And where the hell was Dacia? If I had been in that bed, under those bizarre pots, she'd have been there pouring ice water on my muffin—that's a lie—she'd have been there buttering my muffin. How can Addie have let me see her underthings in that bed? It's cruel. I'd never do that. But those underthings there, smirched and taunting, don't hurt or anger me. They should. I wish they did. But what they really do, what Addie meant them to, is excite me. What can men ever be to us but excursions.

The crisis passes. Margaret understands that Addie has carried out a mission like an excellent subaltern. She understands the consequences are not here but with Bo, because Addie can never be mined for anything so personal. Addie is safer than a Swiss bank account. She doesn't sell or trade other people's moments.

Swift Addie, like Diana, has finally consummated their long agony. She laughs aloud. Oh for crying out loud, Addie probably said, and went and did it. She launches a dangling alembic with her finger and laughs again and turns to face Addie.

"It is funny," Addie says. "I wonder what Dacia will do."

"Well, I thought she might give it a rest if I did it. But come to think of it, maybe she'll punish us both. Maybe she really wants him"—should she mention the comfort of the eunuch?—"to go without."

"Go without what?"

"Us."

"I see," says Addie. "Perhaps that's why he's gone missing then, d'you think? Dacia has taken him."

"Oh, I don't think so, Adeline. She isn't as smart as we are, but she's stronger. One thing she knows: she owns Amir Cavalieri forever."

"Ooooph . . ." Addie shudders and hugs herself. "It's that wet wind blowing in from East Anglia."

Margaret smiles and embraces Diana, protectress of women, for the first time in a long time. "It will be hard enough to warm our own bones tonight without worrying about hers."

★

Because first light rapes the loft, Bo installed white canvas sails to hoist up to cover the huge windows. This softened light finds the women in their habitual embrace, thighs locked, their breath lifting each other's eyelids. Margaret blows Addie's hair from her eyes. "He doesn't resent the game, you know."

"What game?"

"People trying to be popular, participants. He's not rancid deep down where it's dark. There's something wrong with him, Addie. Did you discover it? He emits light, but it's such a full spectrum you mistake it for daylight or somebody else's. Does that make sense?"

"No. But I understand. He leaves everything as he finds it. Once he's seen it, that's it, that's his reward. He doesn't have to have it. That's why we like him."

"But you went ahead and gave him a reward anyway, didn't you?"

"No. I took what I wanted. Actually, Margaret, I took what you wanted."

25

The angel of crisis is more unwelcome than the angel of death. This is the torturer angel. Deferential, comforting, so all the more frightening. Do you wish this and do you wish that? And are you aware of the consequences of this and that? Does this feel good? That hurt? What kind of hurt? Would you rather I do that?

They don't sleep.

They sip the soured Marsala that Bo kept too long for cooking.

The angel waits on them hand and foot, setting out its instruments, following the protocols of an operating theater: scalpel for separating, calipers for pulling, gauze for sopping, hose for sucking, screens for monitoring, electrodes for alarming.

By noon, sore in love again, aching to preserve their childhood bond, troubled by each other's scent, they stare into each other's eyes and know their torturer's name: he's masked in his disappearance, but his manners give him away. Let us pretend we don't know who he is and depart. They smile in the wickedness of their conspiracy. Margaret speaks first, sitting crosslegged and naked: "Lord, lettest now thy servant depart in peace, for mine eyes have seen thy salvation. Salvation is going while the going's good, *n'est-ce pas?*"

"But we swore we should never be wicked, and you've already been wicked, Margaret, and this would be two strikes against you. I don't want to keep you company in purgatory."

"Darling, kindness is not the Stockholm Syndrome. Whatever a tormentor's intent, it still is torment. We're not wicked, love, we're smart."

"That's what brings you here, your smarts?"

"No more than yours brought you to this bed, but we must recover our senses. It's no sin to lose them, but it's a sin not to look for them. Don't be truculent, Addie, this isn't for us. It's hackneyed. We're originals. And we're young. Sometimes our twats trick our brains."

"Oh for the love of Christ, Margaret, be yourself. We can't pretend it all hasn't happened. We can't dismiss it. Gems are always rough where they're found."

"What do you like about him?" She instantly regrets asking—what, after all, does she like about Bo?—because she catches Addie at one of those rare moments when synapses fire impossibly well.

"He's completely devoid of a handler's jocularity, you know, the kind that masks a certain deafness."

"Addie! Were you lying in wait for that one forlorn question?"

"Yes, of course. For a long time. I reformulate it every time a man even looks as if he may keep me at bay. That's what they do, you know."

"And Bo doesn't? And we don't?"

"I don't need to tell you, Margaret, he's scary, but he has no defenses. Either he doesn't need them or he's made some kind of decision to be there."

"It's the latter, Addie. I remember his phrase—inhabit the moment. That what he does. That's why he's dangerous. You're off somewhere calculating the odds, remembering something, and he's right there with no dust in his head. I don't think you can post a sentry he can't slip by, because he doesn't care."

"Mmm."

"Meaning that now you know him better than I do?"

Addie looks surprised. "No, Margaret, that can never be, simply because you are Dacia's daughter and you are the reason we're here. We never know a person better than someone else. That's a presumption. We each apprehend something, that's all. The rest is nonsense. We're quite conceited."

"You and I?"

"All of us. On the one hand we know much more than we admit, for safety's sake, but on the other hand we claim to know much more than we do know, especially about those nearest if not dearest."

Margaret looks at Addie as if she's discovered a Cézanne in a dump. This is not the Adeline Compton she has loved so long. Their relationship now stands where adult children stand with their parents. Renegotiate or let it wither.

Margaret puckers her lips, rises and walks to the bathroom, leaving Addie to consider the grace in her departure and the grander beauty of the departure for which she'd argued. Yes, it would be so elegant to leave, to renegotiate the distance and the difference between Chelsea and Lechlade, to arrive at a place exorcised of this unbelonging sailor. That's his fate, to unbelong, isn't it? But Margaret at her toilet, finding philters belonging to Addie, and Addie, distracting herself, each consider the life the sailor has made for himself here, the places he visits, and they're overcome in their separate places by the poignancy of his struggle to make himself a home.

When Margaret emerges from a shower that sounds like a furious neighbor banging the wall, Addie says, "I have to go home and pluck a few chords, Margaret. I don't hear the pitch of it. You know what I mean? If I don't hear the pitch I can't deal with it. You figure things out, I hear them out. Why don't we meet back here this evening, say seven? Maybe by then we'll know what to do. Maybe by then Amir will reappear."

"You call him Amir?"

"You can rummage any part of my body, Margaret, but not my head. *Wine Eintritt verboten, verstehe?*"

With this reminder of the taiga sprung between them, Margaret dresses and leaves silently. Addie considers the field after the engagement. Then she begins opening and shutting drawers, rifling the huge walk-in closet Amir built, even checking the oven and kitchen cabinets. She pulls books out from shelves to see if The Book is behind them. No, it must be at the Irving Trust or the Morgan Library. She cuts the lights and leaves.

131

26

It's her habit not to sleep in the same spot too long. She likes to be near things she's restoring, various parts, an open book, a small sculpture. She doesn't like to boss them around—they resent it—so she camps in a bedroll beside them. She lets moonlight and lamplight and ambient sound find her. For this reason she always cleans her own spaces, to spare her communicants the dictatorial ways of others. In the rude light of morning between the windows of the upstairs back wall she parks herself under a blanket at the foot of a statuette of Osiris, king of the dead, and sleeps.

By four she's dressed and ready to jog down Ninth Avenue to Amir's loft. She doesn't call Margaret. Margaret will either be there or not.

★

"Adeline, you barmy Brit!" Joe says, holding his broom at port. "Jaysus!" he says under his breath. He's wanted, always wanted to call Addie beautiful, because, Irish palaverer that he is, he can't think of the right words. The only words he can ever think of are "bright" and "clean," and they won't do, so he calls her barmy while the right word—heroic—hides behind his tongue. He knows not every man thinks Adeline Compton beautiful, certainly not pretty, and this gives him the proprietary sense of a conquistador. She's like some glory stumbled upon by Ponce de Leon. She shoots rays of light in all the dark places of Joe's soul. His days are noted by her passages. And now she passes slow-footed and falling in upon herself. "Adeline, you barmy Brit!" he says again, his Limerick accent salted by Noo

Yawk's Yiddish humors. She stops dutifully, and he gives her his characteristic drunken Cockney sailor salute. She tries to smile, to return his salute as usual, but her hand droops at her shoulder and falls.

"Adeline, gal, come in and talk to Doctor Minihan."

She shakes her head.

"Amazin' it is how resourceful I am, gal, didja forget it? C'mon now, follow Joseph."

Joe Minihan looks like the Aztec sun. So radiant is his red hair that Adeline resents his ears for interrupting its circuit. But his eyes are too quick to support his avuncular persona. Joe is not what he seems to be, and Addie knows it. He tends bar like a man on a lark. One night late last November Addie's throat got scratchy while she was threading through the diesel fumes and she slipped into Parnell's Hat for a glass of mineral water. The bar was crowded and rowdy. Joe spotted her looking for an opening. "Shove off, ya great sloth of a man," he said to one of the roisterers, "make room for my gal here."

"Ya got a gal friend then, Joseph?"

"I'm not talkin to ya, ya daft sot," Joe said, winking at Addie and sopping the mahogany in front of her. This was not quite the Joe Minihan she knew, but it was more like the one she suspected. She drank slowly, ears turning like a rabbit's.

"Joseph," said a newcomer perfunctorily, "I'll be passin' the hat for the lads."

"Ye'll not be passin' the hat for the bloody IRA or the constabulary or the B-Specials or the fuckin' queen, ya sack of shit. These are the United States, and they'll be stayin' that way, and a Protestant's as welcome in this establishment as any damn Catholic if he minds his manners. And that goes for the Jews and all the other blighted sots o'the world."

Addie pulled at her chin and gave Joe a mock-querulous look. But he stared back blind.

She liked to hear the firemen and the cops, the orderlies up from Saint Vincent's, the rescue crews, the quick fiftyish women embittered by their bosses' three-martini abuses. She lingered safe from importuning under Joseph's aegis, and she lingered still when from the bowels of the mirrored gloaming she heard the baneful strain ". . . 'n Ireland'll still be Ireland when England's buggin' up."

"Last call, last call, drink up, g'wan home and beat up th'ole lady, ya lard-ass heroes," Joe said. They didn't take him seriously. His habitual genial demeanor lulled them. "Give us a cold one, Joseph," they called, or, "Joseph, pour yerself a smile, lad." They saw the same hard-bitten cynic she saw, but alcohol and denial go down well together.

He ducked and came up with a baseball bat. Then he reached in back of a row of Three Feathers and flicked the main breaker with his right hand while rapping the bar with his bat. "Goo nite, ladies, goo nite, gents," down the bar he went. "Goo night, Patrick, goo nite, Alice. Take a cab now, James. Sleep on the sofa, Harry." He emptied the place, deft as a drill sergeant.

"You're not who you seem to be, Joseph Minihan," she said.

"And who the hell is, Adeline?"

"I am, Joseph. I am what I seem to be."

"Ay, so y'are, gal, I'm sure. It's like winnin' the lottery, a rare thing."

"I believe you are a silent man, Joseph. The blarney is your cover story."

He leaned over the bar into her face. "I am a Republican assassin, Adeline, a bloody-handed Limerick slum boy, and I get sick of saloon soldiers of every stripe, for they would fight to the last drop of a slum boy's blood, Tommy and Paddy, it matters not. I've heard the yellow-livered lot of 'em, I 'av. The Tommies who jailed and tortured me, they were no worse than the fascist IRA gunmen and the lying Sinn Fein. Ay, all of 'em cowards and haters, Catholics and Protestants alike, not good enough to shit on, not a one."

She listened enthralled, listened to bent Ireland speak, and she had hoped it would go on, but he stopped. "Drink slow, Adeline, keep the bloody Irishman company as he cleans up Parnell's mess."

★

She remembers that November night now as Joe coaxes her in. Following him into the rubbed and scoured gloom, Addie remembers she's following an assassin, a man who thinks his torturers no worse than his confederates. She watches his shoulder blades swim under his striped sailor shirt. Years of confinement, working with weights, doing push-ups in cells, inform this catamount's gait.

"So what's yer story, luv?"

She gives him one of those sea-washed looks. He gives her a mug of coffee, pats her hand and begins washing glasses, a mindless task he prefers to bartending. "The three-legged species has three sorts, luv: men blessed enough to want ya for a sister, men who wish ya could be a little twisty, and ya know the other."

"Twisty?" Joe Minihan makes her smile.

"Ay, some flaw that lifts the third leg, luv."

"I think it's pheromones, Joseph. It's all in the nose."

"Ah, so that's it then. This beak's been broken so often it's confused. But, ya see, if I thought ya was a bit twisty, Adeline, ya couldn't tell me anythin' now, could ya, 'cause ya'd be steppin' around this third leg."

"This inconvenient third leg, yes, I understand. So you're a blessed man with some regrets, Joe?"

"It's sort of like that, Adeline, like yer a queen. Nah, queens're bloody troublemakers, I should know. But it's more like yer a"— he swings away so she won't see him blush—"a goddess, I'd say."

"Joseph, if a goddess confides in a mortal it's usually fatal."

"What could a mere goddess, even a Brit, do that the SAS hasn't already done, luv? Can ya tell me that?"

"I met a man . . . "

"Bloor!"

"A dangerous man, like you, Joe. You could say I stole him from my best friend."

"Interrogators say you could say, but I don't say, Addie. Damned fools think there's words for everything. There's not a dime's worth of difference between the bass-mouthed Sinn Fein and the Home Office, except Brits lie better. Really, they do lie better."

"Yes, we sound so authoritative, it must be true if it's in a British accent." Addie warms to the subject, as one with perfect pitch does, in spite of her despair. "My friend, Bo Cavalieri, has gone missing."

"Yer sure he's not been stolen back?"

"I deserved that."

"No, ya did not. It's just I hate to see a goddess messed over. Even a British goddess."

Addie weeps as she always does when she weeps, looking straight ahead, silent. This is how goddesses weep, he thinks, like statues. He wishes he hadn't invited her in to hear she'd met a man. But he's foolishly grateful for her company. And so he wipes everything he can lay hands on, like a tugboat oiler, as if nothing will work if he doesn't. A clock he's never heard before crazies the air with its ticking. "Well," he bucks himself up, "let's find the lucky son-of-a-bitch and bang some sense into his head."

She pinches her nose and stares at him. "Lucky?"

"Well, if you care about him, Adeline, I'd damn well say so. I'd not be gettin' myself lost if it was me." He can't believe what he's said. He shuffles towards her and whispers, "I did say what I think I said, did I not?"

Addie holds his face in her hands. "Dear Joe." But she can't find words. He watches tears trudge down under her jaw and reappear along the long cords of her throat, and he knows they're as much for him as for her missing man.

"Ah, Adeline, my cougar, I'll help ya find this awful man, I will. So what's his story then?"

"In New York what's your story means what're you up to. This man has never been up to a damned thing in his whole life. He just gets by. He was a, how do you call them, a frogman, then a merchant seaman. He's an artist, he draws, but he doesn't paint. He has this priceless manuscript an old sultan gave him. I think someone wants it and may have taken him to get it. But I'm sure it's still here, maybe in the Irving Trust or the Morgan Library."

Joe reaches under the bar and pins a black and white Yankees button on Addie's sweatshirt. "Lemme give ya a medal, Addie, for the goddamnedest mouthful I ever heard, and I've heard the biggest blowhards in the world. Never been up to a damned thing, you say? What is it then ya think frogmen do, Adeline? They're up to no good night and day, that's a fact. They slit gizzards and cut throats. This guy's too much by definition— dump 'im and give yerself a break. It gives me a headache hearin' about 'im."

"Then I'll not bother you further, Joseph."

"Ye'd not be botherin' me further, Addie, if ya came in here to kill me, and that's the truth. So get off yer high horse, for I said I'd help ya."

"It's your high horse I'm worried about. I don't trust people who claim things are too complicated for them to deal with. No, I don't, Joseph, so put that in your pipe and smoke it, you professional Mick. And by the way, if I can do the Yanks the honor of speaking the way they do, so can you, you damned phony, but you'd rather wear the green and hornswoggle the masses with your bum-fuck Irishness, so no thanks and to hell with you."

Snot, tears and remorse blow up on his face. He groans within himself. She's nailed him dead to rights. Yes, he wears his Irishness, and yes he's pissed all over her love for this lucky sailor, and no she's not a girl to take it, not at all. She's Britannia, trident in hand, and the Brits are a bad people to mess with, as any Irishman knows.

"Adeline, I can help you find this man if you can find it in yerself to forgive me."

"Well, can you find it in yourself to be something more than a caricature of yourself, Joseph?"

"Ay."

27

"He lives in Soho. I helped him fight off two blokes the other night. Foreigners. Well, more foreign than the rest of us, that is. They jumped him at Spring and Broadway. Right out in the open. I think they were planning to chloroform him and pack him into a car. They were after a manuscript an old Arab sultan died and left him. But I rushed in to help. Turns out he's pretty good at Tae Kwon Do and I do Aikido."

"You were going to meet him or something?"

"It's a long story. I was stalking him. I didn't know him. But my friend Margaret Wadeleigh did. She dumped him and it pissed me off. I'll explain later. I was curious about him. When I jumped in and we fought off these guys we got . . . we got friendly."

"Friendly."

"We became lovers."

"This is one lucky assassin."

"Assassin?"

"Yeah, Addie, that's what frogmen do, ye know. Nowadays they call them Seals, so I reckon this bloke's old enough to be yer father."

"Sure you didn't work for Dublin intelligence?"

"And what intelligence would that be? He could be dead, yer friend."

"No, I don't think so. The manuscript is hidden, and that's what they want, I think. But I have to help him soon or they may kill him, because he's not the sort of person who's likely to give them what they want. I'm afraid he may have an inflated opinion of death, in any case."

"Ha, well, a man after me own heart, after all. Maybe it wasn't the sultan's to be so generous with, didja think of that?"

"Yes, there's good reason to think so. If my friend thought so, he would give it back, but there's some queer bond between him and the old sultan. I'm sure he doesn't want the old man's will thwarted. He never had a father, so maybe that's it, I don't know. I think it was something deeper. Maybe the old sultan saw something in him he himself couldn't see. He's been studying the manuscript, trying to understand why it was given to him."

"Well, it's an odd thing we're talkin' Arabs, Adeline. Old Joseph knows a few of them. Villains, like me. The IRA and the PLO are cut of the same cloth. They like to kill more than what they're killin' for, and nobody knows it better'n me. Rage is more addictive than heroin. They're not about a country, they're about killin' and bein' killed. Any country that comes from them will have to kill 'em, that's for sure."

"My friend says the same thing. His hands are not clean either."

"Here's the good part, Adeline, a soul that's damned is easiest to rescue—the upright are so full of shit you can't get near them. It's a fact. Ireland's tragedy is not the booze, it's the bullshit. Assassins are not like barkeeps and bus drivers, they have a lot of time to think. I have this pal, Si Larbi ben Hamrouche. Al Fatah kisses his ass. They think he's a mujahad, they call it, a warrior for the faith. They're full of it, he's a mechanic like me. He's Algerian. They're like the Limeys, they have a long history of being mercenaries. One day we're crawling under razor wire—it's beautiful stuff, ya know—and this Spetznaz instructor is giving us haircuts with his machine gun, and Larbi says to me, 'Yusuf, I don't like to kill Jews. No Jews, no civilization. That's their job, civilization. I want to kill Arafat. He's too ugly. If he looked like Omar Sharif the shit-eating Palestinians would have a country by now. Iranians are good to kill too, but not with your hands, they're too oily.'

"I ask him, 'Ever kill an Irishman or a Brit?'

"He says, 'No, Yusuf, I will never kill an Irish, because I like you.'

139

"That was a relief because the bastard is almost seven feet tall, and I noticed he didn't promise not to kill any Brits. Then he says, 'But I would like to kill an Ivan. I think maybe this machine gunner. He looks hostile and stupid. We don't need so many of them, what do you think, Yusuf?'"

"He said all this under fire?"

"Yeah, it was the only time he got chatty. Now he's an Al Fatah hockey puck. I know goddam well they think Mossad has killed somebody Larbi has killed—that would be his idea of a joke. His other idea of a joke is to kill everybody but the Jews. He's the best friend they have, but of course he's on their hit list because he looks the part. He's Hollywood's idea of a bad Arab. Well, there are no good Arabs as far as Hollywood goes. When they want to cast a murdering IRA man they find some handsome Anglo-Irishman. It's his big chance. But a murdering Arab has to look ugly enough to stop a mortar. We need Larbi, Addie. Especially as there seems to be some kind of Arab connection here."

"Joe, we may be getting into much deeper waters than you think."

"They're the only kind, Adeline. Ask the sharks. This dago boyo of yours is getting the best."

"He's not a dago, anymore than you're a boyo. He's a Yank of German and Arab extraction. Have you got all this straight, Joseph?"

"You're hard on a man, Adeline."

"I'm hard on the blarney, and I thought you were too, or do you like being a Hollywood Irishman?"

"Ya get used to disguises. Yer right, yer right, Adeline, let's dispense with the blarney then and get down to it."

"This Si Larbi ben Hamrouche, it's not a small thing you'd be asking him to do, Joseph."

"I hope not. He blew up a lot of froggies when he was a mere lad, and years later the Sûreté grabbed him in Rome. They held him in Marseilles and grilled him and God knows what else. His pals got word out and I got him out."

"Just like that, you got him out."

"I back-channelled a message to the Sûreté saying that General Jacques Massu wanted to look the famous bomber Larbi in the eye. Massu was the paratroop commander in Algiers during the generals' revolt. He took part in a coup because Paris got antsy about torturing the dirty Arabs. The Sûreté naturally understood that Monsieur le Tortionnaire would like to get a look at Larbi. Three of them were driving him from Lyons to a house in Argenteuil. I set up a rendezvous on a country road, found a guy who looked like Massu and sat him in the back seat. When the Sûreté pulled up, two of them got out. They saluted Massu. The dummy and I saluted them like old veterans. Then I walked over to the car where Larbi sat. They had him shackled in the back seat. One of the frogs sat behind the wheel. I cut his throat before he could figure out what was going on, pulled a semi-automatic from under my coat, spun around and shot the other two. Poor bastards. I had Irish papers for Larbi and that's that, so he owes me one, ya see."

She presses her cool left hand to his face and they brave each other across the Irish Sea until the raillery covering his disappointment in her liaison with Amir subsides and their fondness for each other regains its footing.

"I'll be off to meet my friend Margaret at his loft, Joe," she says in French.

"She's still yer friend?"

"We're lovers."

He opens the hot water tap, grateful for its commotion. "I'll see about Larbi." He loses his face in steam. "I may have to promise him some Ivans to kill. I toldja, didn't I, he likes to kill the wrong people? Like Wrong Way Corrigan, ever hear of him?"

She soothes him with her eyes: shush, Joe, it's not every man I trust with such knowledge. Be your usual deadly self now. Find us this Larbi and the four of us will go find Amir Cavalieri. You wouldn't try to sort the consequences of the battle of the Boyne before you decided what to do next, now would you? And Tommy wouldn't give you time, would he?

"Larbi may like yer friend, ya know. Their people seem to breed assassins."

"Yes, so unlike Ireland or England."

"Ha, ya got me there, Addie. I see this is goin' to be quite a trip, wherever we're goin'."

She scribbles Amir's address and phone number on the back of a bank deposit slip and hands it to him. "This is where to go when you close up."

"In the wee hours?"

"Unless you have something more interesting to do."

28

She'd ransacked Amir's drawers, files, cabinets, closets, suitcases and sea bag the night before. Everything of interest met the eye: drawings, books, alchemical gewgaws, admiralty charts of Manhattan and Omani waters, star charts, pencils, charcoals, crayons, a tray of unopened paint tubes, palette knives, easels, an apron hung on an easel, a rag hung on each easel, evidence of an orderly man.

The wide-planked floors are sanded, bleached, polished and bare except for three Kermanshah carpets. They're handsome but out of place. She tugs one of them with her foot. It won't budge. She takes a palette knife off a porcelain paint tray and loosens a corner of the carpet. Amir has glued it down. She grabs both ends and rips it up. Dead center is a brass pull-ring recessed into a two-foot plank. She lifts the ring and jerks up the plank, revealing a black metal compartment filled with letters, postcards, snapshots and sheaves of lined paper with a child's scrawl in German. Why conceal letters from Ute-Britt and Tariq?

By the time she takes the freight elevator down to let Margaret in she has gotten into similar compartments under the other two carpets. Margaret arrives in time to help sort the contents of all three. Even Ute-Britt might offer a clue to Amir's whereabouts.

"I don't know if he packed, I don't think so. The bathroom looks as if he's still here. His empty sea bag's still here. There's no wallet or keys, but there wouldn't be if he was out walking."

"He wouldn't leave without telling you, Addie. He's not like me."

"Well, he's good at leaving. It's his profession. But, yes, I think he would have told me."

"Yes," Margaret says ruefully.

"We have to go through everything in these boxes, Margaret. I think at this point you still know more about him than I do—you had more time to talk to him—so you might be able to cull something from Ute-Britt's box. There's always a chance there's some other stuff in there."

Margaret nods. It's not a task to her liking: she envies Ute-Britt and fears Bo belongs with her. She plops down on the floor disconsolately and dumps the contents of the box between her legs.

The next box holds Bo's seafaring papers: Z card from the Coast Guard, officer's licenses, expired passports, commendations from the Navy and shipping companies, some kind of military medal—a silver star on a ribbon, two rows of campaign ribbons, some with stars on them, photographs of ships and sailors, an unloaded Browning 45mm handgun, a folding knife with a marlin spike, foreign coins and paper money, a French birth certificate.

"His passport, Margaret! It's current. If he's left the country, it's under duress."

The third box is filled with letterhead correspondence: the Omani embassy in London, Tomlinson Distilleries, Ltd., The Morgan Library, The University of Exeter Centre for Arab Gulf Studies, Oriental and India Office Collections of The British Library, the manuscripts division of Princeton University, the collection of Arabic manuscripts in the National Library of the Czech Republic, the Near Eastern Collection at Yale University, the Islamic Studies Library at McGill University, the John Rylands University Library of Arabic manuscripts. The correspondence is voluminous. To each letterhead is stapled Bo's own inquiries. His respondents reveal a barely concealed enthusiasm; they're wild to see *Al Kitab as Sirr, The Book of Secrets*.

The phone jangles. Bo's outgoing message comes on: "Cavalieri. Leave a message after the beep." Then: "Hey, I found her. Swann 45 with a Rhodes diesel. She's got enough sail to keep us out of trouble. A one-seventy jenny, can ya stand it? Needs work." The caller laughed. "She's over at City Island. Gimme a call."

"Weybrandt Gundersen, his closest friend. Lives in Weehawken," Margaret says. "They've sailed together for a long time. I guess they're planning to buy a boat. A Swann is a British boat. Maybe we should call him."

"No," Addie says. "He's not what we need. He's a seaman. We need an operative."

"You mean someone from MI-6, that sort of thing?"

"The IRA actually. And Al Fatah."

"Compton, what've you gotten us into?"

"His name is Joseph Minihan. He's a former IRA assassin. He's recruiting Si Larbi ben Hamrouche, an Al Fatah bigwig of Algerian origin."

Margaret flops backwards on the floor in mock collapse. Addie gets up and stands over her. They look at each other poker-faced for a while and start laughing. "It will be all right, Margaret. He's a rare soul. I'm quite fond of him."

"It's your fondnesses I worry about, Addie. And what's with these collectible Algerians? First Si Sliman, then Cavalieri, and now this Al Fatah ghoulie?"

"I don't know, Margaret. I'm puzzled about that myself. Like our motherland, I seem to collect Arabs. You don't know the half of it. Someday I'll introduce you to Mutawakkil ibn al-Quereishi. Then you can introduce him to Al Razi and Averroes."

"In for a penny, in a for pound."

"He can take care of himself," Addie says.

"Yes, that's why he needed you to rescue him feet first, I suppose. One says people can take care of themselves when one's done something doubtful to them, dumping them perhaps."

Nothing is ever dead-filed in Margaret's mind, Addie thinks. She will never declare herself grown up, so no one will ever be comfortable with her. Except me. "I meant only that he's more capable than most of handling trouble."

"He has fits of unworthiness, of unbelonging, Addie, and at such moments he's helpless."

Why, if you cared to go so close to the man's soul, Addie wonders, am I his lover? But immediately the answer visits her: Margaret, her friend, her lover, has suffered a third-degree burn of the spirit. She has broken her way into a sacred fire left untended by Dacia and Amir and stood for a moment in the middle, bewildered, dismayed. This fire burns in a weatherless world where it can never be put out. Something happened and didn't happen between Dacia and Amir that instills despair in everyone who knows them. Two abandoned children built a kingdom and then exiled everyone. They opened their hearts once, only once, and so it might be better to leave Bo to the uncertainties of his life. He's indifferent to his drama and reliable in a way no safe man ever is.

Margaret has more of his data than Addie, but Addie has been lying on the ineradicable sob in his chest, and she's not sure how much of him she wishes to share with Margaret.

Their heads can be turned only by a man capable of casting a cold eye on Sturm und Drang, a man likely to pass them by unless they catch him by the sleeve. They're nobody's casualties. Margaret quit him, inventing reasons as she ran. Addie caught him by the sleeve. Their own relationship had always been like brushing hair, pungent and above all voluntary. But now they feel like Little Red Riding Hood, clothed in doubtful innocence. They're where they want to be, and a hundred years from saying so. They no longer understand their roles: Addie has seized too much initiative and Margaret for the first time inhabits her own beauty and no longer regards it strangely.

29

It's ten a.m. in Algiers when Joe closes Parnell's Hat. The chauvinists and wannabes think a group of secretive Dubliners own it. Like Si Larbi ben Hamrouche killing the wrong people, it's Joe's little joke. He owns Parnell's Hat and knows his lie gives the place cachet. It isn't just cynicism that binds him and Larbi, it's their perverse humor. He plays Doris Day's *Once I Had a Secret Love* on the juke, not because he had one, but because he hadn't and thinks he was just as well off for it. He hadn't even loved Ireland that much, and he has nothing against Protestants he doesn't have against Catholics. Being a bad ass was fun, and when it wasn't fun any more he became too sad to think of anything better to do than pour drinks for fools not much smarter than himself. It's an evil-priestly thing to do, as he likes to say. He sits now on the end of the bar, chin on his knees, looking out on the street. He's for the most part a teetotaler, having already made enough of a fool of himself. Guess I had a secret love, didn't I, Adeline?

Si Larbi is looking out onto a rainy bay of Algiers when the phone rings. "Yusuf, my old friend, what's the name of the game?"

"Not what, whose, it's whose game, ya murderous villain."

Si Larbi ben Hamrouche listens to Joe's story and then turns around in Al Fatah's Algiers office to stare bleakly at the comic mug of Yasser Arafat pinned to the wall. He hasn't heard from Joe Minihan in a long time. The Irishman wouldn't know him now. "The Irish are a curious people, Yusuf. One minute they're in love with C3, the next it's a book, an Arab book. Yusuf, as I sit here looking at my ugly leader I praise Allah for a good joke."

"Larbi, yer talkin' English like a toff. Ya been hangin' out with the bloody SAS then?"

"It's the ambition of every wog to speak like a toff, and then to kill him, Yusuf."

"So ya can help me, Mister PLO, is it?"

"I'd like to strangle someone soon."

"Anything might come to that, ya know. But I don't think there'll be any Ivans involved, or have ya had yer fill of 'em?"

"I'll see what I can do, Yusuf. I'm coming to New York, you know. Yes, I have diplomatic papers, do you believe it? That's something you murdering bastards in the IRA could never get. I'm part of the PLO delegation. Be there next week, flags flying."

"Most murdering bastards have papers, ya great camel."

"You have to tell me about this book, Yusuf. Is it some kind of fancy Quran? Some of them are worth a fortune."

"I don't think so. I don't know. I should know more this morning."

"A lot more, I hope. And what about this Bo Cavalieri? Not an Arab name, you know."

"Yeah, I know. Long story. I'll call you back soon. I just wanna ask if I can count on you."

"Always, Yusuf. We've done a lot of things together. Besides, I like Irish girls."

"Aw ya big dumb fuck, g'wan with ya, New York is full of the best lookin' women in the world, and ya tellin' me about Irish girls. And all that stuff we done together, Larbi, well, ya better hope yer Allah has a good sense of humor, my boy. As for me, I'm not convinced. I'm not convinced of anything."

"You're convinced, Yusuf, you're a convinced idiot. You're going to help this Limey bird find an Arab with an Italian name, and for what—the love of God?"

"For the love of what is it that ya run around makin' trouble for the world? It ain't the PLO, I'm damn sure. And it was not the IRA for me. Near as I can tell it's for the love of trouble. So what're ya goin' do, lecture me about Limey birds and missin' Arabs? If it comes to that, I'd rather blow up a bus full of strutting Orangemen for a crazy girl than for the IRA, Larbi."

"The love of trouble, Yusuf? That could be, yes. But I like to think I'm the only true revolutionary because I kill the people I work for. I haven't got to that little toad Arafat yet, but I'm working on it. Okay, my friend, I'll see you soon. Meantime, information, I need information."

30

They're still sorting papers when the buzzer razzes them. Addie goes down to let Joe in. "Margaret, this is Joseph Minihan. Margaret Wadeleigh, Joseph."

"Pleased to meet ya, Miss Wadeleigh." He pumps Margaret's hand peremptorily. "Addie, I spoke with the dreadful Larbi. I dunno what's come over the man, he sounds like one of yer Oxford dons. He wants information. I told him that's what we're short of. How short are we?"

Addie turns to Margaret. "Si Larbi ben Hamrouche, I told you about him. I think we've found what we're looking for, Joe. At least we can piece it together. It's the book, as I thought. *Kitab as Sirr.* It's an alchemical workbook. Well, I could be wrong about that. It could be a metaphysical work, or both. In any case, it's famous, fabled, like *The Book of Kells*, you might say. It's alleged to contain alchemical secrets, but I think that even in Arabic they need to be deciphered or interpreted. The book is literally priceless. The late sultan of Oman gave it to"—she considers the pronoun to use—"our friend. He doesn't know why, but it touched him deeply, and he won't give up this book, even if it kills him. He's been teaching himself Arabic, trying to read it in the original. What's clear from these letters, Joe, is that Oman wants the book back, as I suspected. They claim it shouldn't have been given to him. A bunch of institutes and the like want to see it—of course, they'd like to have it—and at least one collector wants it, which probably means others do too. I think the book is still here in New York, probably at the Irving Trust or the Morgan Library. But they're not likely to talk to any of us. What I fear is that someone has abducted

150

Amir to wring the book out of him, and then who knows, they'll kill him."

"I think ya can bank on that, Addie," Joe says. "Well, I'd be surprised if Larbi couldn't squeeze something out of the Omanis. But maybe yer friend can't have it both ways, maybe it's him or the book. We'll see. What can I show Larbi?"

The women trade puzzled looks. "Well, I think we have to keep these papers in our possession, Joe, don't you?" says Addie. "But I see no harm in letting him look them over."

"There's always harm where Larbi's concerned, that's the good of 'im. This collector sounds a likely villain, doncha think? And I don't think the Omanis will be sittin' on their hands either. But why would they be in cahoots?"

"There may be a quid pro quo somewhere, Joe. We don't know anything about the collector. He may have Arab connections."

"Let's hope so. That will make Larbi's work easier. Well, what wouldja think of copying this stuff and givin' Larbi the copies?"

Margaret purses her lips and nods. Addie nods too.

"Well, lemme look them over, will ya? All of a sudden Larbi sounds like he's blathering for the BBC, but I dunno if the great camel can read."

31

The great camel looks more like a malevolent djinni. When he barges out of a white stretch limousine on First Avenue and Thirty-Ninth Street Addie wishes she hadn't rubbed his lamp. Up close, her middle finger twitches to trace the parchment scar that runs from the left side of his hairline down to his right jawline. She wants its secrets before she wants to be introduced. Larbi's upside down grin says he understands such compulsions.

When Joe announces, "Adeline Compton, Si Larbi ben Hamrouche," she reaches out her hand, but the giant grabs her wrist and lays her hand against his scar. He laughs. Addie feels an immense bond, as if she's walked through ancient streets with him. He has been blind, like Samson, following her. This life would have been bereft if she hadn't met Si Larbi. Something is going right.

"Mr. Ben Hamrouche killed many Crusaders fighting for the sultan Baybars," she tells Joe.

"Not Saladin?" Joe asks.

"He was a filthy Kurd," Si Larbi interrupts, confirming his recent mastery of English.

"We're all filthy somebodies, ya great camel." The men trade Kung Fu stances and laugh. Then Joe peeks at Addie sheepishly, remembering she knows more about Aikido than they know about Kung Fu.

Addie stands between her assassins, making ready to find a third. She's forgotten Margaret.

"My name is Margaret Wadeleigh, Mr. Ben Hamrouche." She gives him her hand. At the same moment a tremulous aide taps his arm. Si Larbi doesn't turn. He looks at Margaret for a long time before taking her hand. "You're the cause of this trouble," he says, smiling.

"Mr. Minihan said that?" she asks, glancing at Joe.

"No," he grunts, as if that were an absurd idea. "A man in my line of work always knows where the trouble is coming from. I like trouble. Trouble is funny. That's where Yusuf and I are different. He doesn't like trouble. He really doesn't. That's rare. You don't either, I can tell. But you are the cause of this trouble. This makes you unhappy."

"Very."

"Too bad. I like your face. Yes, it is a good face, and you have good friends. Where is my information?"

Addie hands him a padded mailing envelope filled with copies of the letters they sorted in Bo's loft.

Si Larbi whispers some hoarse Arabic to his aide, who gets back in the limo, cowed. "The fool thinks a schedule is important. Schedules get people killed, isn't that right, Yusuf?"

Joe nods. "Let's sit down over some coffee, Larbi, and we'll watch you read this stuff. I told the ladies I wasn't sure you knew how to read."

"I read English better than you read Gaelic, my friend. You have to kill people in English these days. Actually, I like English, it's like Arabic, it's a big vacuum, sucks everything up. That's why French will die—the frogs think it's a fortress. They're a narrow people, the frogs, almost as narrow as the Irish."

Addie and Margaret exchange amused glances. A philosophical assassin is holding forth hard by the United Nations.

"Never mind about the Irish, will ya, ya crock fulla shit," says Joe. "We don't want yer jokes, we want yer help finding this awful sailor, though for the life of me it seems t'me these nice young women would be better off without 'im."

Si Larbi regards the women. He tucks the envelope under his arm, takes Addie's arm, motioning the flunky to stay in the limo, and steers her across the avenue where they enter a small café.

"Miss Wadeleigh," Joe says when he sees they are inside the café, "Miss Compton and Mr. Ben Hamrouche have some catching up to do. Let's you and I have ourselves a little stroll. If we're getting into trouble we ought to know more than each other's names."

Margaret dips her head, turns, walks back out onto the street and waits for Joe. She's not unlike Bo in her dealings. She listens and waits for people to show themselves. Joe Minihan surprises her. He comes out of the café, locks arms with her, and silently propels her uphill on First Avenue. The sun has crossed the avenue and streaks the storefronts on its east side. They walk ten blocks, waiting each other out. Finally she steps ahead of him and cranes her head around to look in his face. He winks and they laugh.

"What is it that you do, Mr. Minihan?"

"Joseph, it's Joseph. Joe's okay. Lemme see, what do I do? I'm an Irishman. Naturally I'm perverse, so I'll tell ya what I don't do, Margaret. I don't do booze and I don't do Irish. Being Irish is an accident; acting Irish is a low profession. It means a man doesn't know who he is, so he borrows a joke. Gimme an Irishman or an Arab or an anything an' I'll give you a two-inch prick and a stupid bastard to boot."

Margaret gulps as if she'd swallowed a bone. "You're a citizen of the world, Joseph?"

"A citizen of the world, what's that but what some political pot of shit said for the medication of the asses? Ya think it's bullets and bombs that're killin' every mother's son in Ireland? God no, it's words. They canna' keep their bloody mouths shut, orange or green. And you Brits are not much better."

What fun, she thinks—the medication of the asses. What a marvelous man. "Why not booze, Joseph?"

"Well, if you would not go away willingly with the constabulary or the SAS or the IRA or the Hezbollah or the Mossad, why in the name of the Christ almighty would you put the cuffs on and throw yerself in prison? Who in the hell wants ya to drink except yer enemies? The drink is nothin' but a deceitful face. I'm not so obliging as to drink, Margaret. I do not intend to make life that easy for the lazy assholes of the world. I'm Joe Minihan, full of difficulty and surprises."

"And here I thought you were the friendly neighborhood bomber."

"You did not, or you wouldn't be here. You and Adeline have keen eyes for doughty men, like yer friend, this Calvary."

Doughty men? She grips his arm tighter and leans on him fondly. "I hope your bad pun on his name proves to be just that."

"We'll see. Don't ever count dangerous men out. The trick is to know how they're dangerous. Not how dangerous, but how they're dangerous."

"How are they dangerous, Joseph? You and Bo Cavalieri?"

"Well, I don't know 'im, do I, Margaret? But I'd say from what Addie tells me we indulge the damn fool notion that we ought to grow up before we die. What face is it can handle that, I ask ya?"

For the first time in her life Margaret thinks she might not have the grit to go on drawing out people like Minihan. His help means his truth, a price higher than any ransom. Like all noble people, he's not for using and discarding, not a means to an end, not unless it becomes his own. Bo's disappearance falls in on her like scaffolding. The cost of rescuing him will be as high as the cost of abandoning him.

32

Addie too is calculating cost as she sits watching Si Larbi leaf through Amir's papers. She imagines winding the oblong petals of his irises like chakras, whorling them into a storm. She knows that she has known this stranger for a thousand years. No barrier of time or race stands in the way of their tried companionability. The adventure upon which she and Margaret embarked at Saint Agnes has turned stranger than the opening of a continent. Time runs backwards and forwards and swirls around them, carrying histories like debris. They're dervishes whirling faster and faster. When they swoon where will they be?

Si Larbi knows the pissed-off of the world; they all pay lip service to the dispossessed Palestinians. The dissident game is as cynical as the establishment game. Most of the Arabs would as soon be rid of the Palestinians as the Jews. If there are Omanis determined to recover the sultan's profligate gift it's not because they give a damn about the book. So the key to finding Bo, he reasons, is finding someone who gives a damn.

"I like the Omanis," he tells Addie as if they'd been chitchatting for a long time, "they're so arrogant. You can pass anything under the nose of an arrogant man; he won't look down."

He feels no duty to linear thinking, to sticking to a subject. His life has been devoted to overthrowing order, to smashing things, so he feels anything that pops into his head is as interesting as what institutions say. He knows that the wiliest tongue is silenced by a single bullet.

He slams both hands down on the heap of correspondence. "This man, Commodus da Cunha, he's an arms dealer. That's not all. He trades in weapons designs. You need enough money to buy Switzerland to do that. And even that's not all. He buys and sells information about defects in weapons. If you want to blow anybody up, you know Commodus da Cunha. The CIA knows him. The KGB knows him. If he didn't exist, they'd invent him. He fills a vacuum. He's the fourth world. And he wants the book. Forget about the Omanis. They need da Cunha more than they need the book."

Addie remembers holding Si Larbi's hand in a narrow street arched by latticed windows. Not in Ali Baba's or Sindbad's world, not fabled and therefore suspect. It has the cinematic feel of memory, the patina and melancholy of a ruined garden. Si Larbi ben Hamrouche is not his true and eternal name. She feels that name flitting around her, just out of reach. Joe Minihan said his own name itched like an Aran sweater and he'd be grateful for another, and Addie thought, Stick with me, and I'll fetch it for you. And now she thinks the same thing about Si Larbi ben Hamrouche. But who am I to fetch true names? I am Mutawakkil ibn al-Quereishi's apprentice, and all this, and Amir too, is within my reach. "Okay, Larbi, how do we find the arms dealer?"

"Finding him's no problem. Do you know why Bedouins love falcons? It's because all plans take the low road. But not the falcon. The Bedouin and the falcon share each other's disdain. They love random opportunity. That's why Bedouins think politicians are comedians. The politicians always have a plan to eat your lunch. While they're talking the Bedouins eat theirs. You have to make your plan in the twinkling of an eye. You have to give it up just as fast."

"An assassin's wisdom is frightening, Larbi."

"It would be more frightening, little girl, if he thought he had any. The Bedouins know a few things. Any more would offend Allah. "

"He's easily offended?"

"The God of the Jews is a sorehead. Allah, the one, is the order of things. It takes a lot to offend the order of things. That's why Bedouins follow marabouts, not politicians."

Joe's the falcon, I'm the nomad, she thinks. Together we will find more than Bo. Is this my truth, that I recklessly open doors and don't know how to flinch? Words hide, but her thoughts hit their mark anyway. Is this a good truth? Who can live with it besides me and Alexander the Great? Not Margaret, cloistered in numbers—no, she can't live among the stars, but she steps out to them from Wind Harp and her chalky classrooms. The stars won't get her killed, as they did Giordano Bruno. I could get her killed. Not Amir's getting lost. Lost is where he likes to be. But by going after him I could get her killed, get us all killed. I live my life as her retainer, savoring her spices. But this is my day, my voyage. Joe is signing on because I'm me, and because he's signed on I have this reunion with Si Larbi ben Hamrouche.

She glances across the table at Si Larbi. He's still staring at her, both hands flat on Amir's papers as if holding them down in a gust. She begins rubbing her chest, not realizing her heart is railing at its cage. She squints at Si Larbi as if he were the sun. "Who are you?"

"Shall I show you how to make a bomb, Miss Compton?"

"Shall I show you how to toss a thug, Mr. Ben Hamrouche?"

And it's done, signed, sealed and delivered. She no longer needs Joe to get Si Larbi's help. He no longer needs a reason, because, against odds and explanations, they're happy to see each other again.

33

Bo comes to in a small Bauhaus salon. The walls, obviously
plumbed by Frodo Baggins, are lined with stainless steel and
green glass shelves. The brushed aluminum fiddles, designed to
keep things from sliding off the shelves, invite him to think he's
in a sailboat's salon, but other things are wrong: the rectangular
ports are landlubberly, and the beam of such a long space is too
narrow. He gets up from a white leather couch and staggers
around. His wrists show no evidence of having been tied, taped
or shackled. He's groggy. A white-coated steward enters with
fragrant coffee and a croissant. "What time is it?" Bo asks. The
steward says nothing, flicks a switch under one of the shelves,
and gestures to Bo to be seated.

"Good morning, Mr. Cavalieri," a voice comes from a
speaker. "Allow me to introduce myself. My name is Commodus
da Cunha. I am your host. I regret not being there to greet
you, but I will soon have the pleasure of welcoming you as an
honored guest and fellow bibliophile when you arrive at Fabrica
de Ouro, my estate. Meanwhile, I trust you will be comfortable.
You'll be taking off from a small airfield in New Jersey in a
minute or two. It may interest you to know that you are flying
in *The Balkan Wars,* a Heinkel 111A medium bomber. It went
into production in 1936 as a ten-passenger commercial airliner.
Hitler's Luftwaffe despised it. Too slow. So the Germans sold the
first Heinkels to China to raise much-needed hard currency. It
is a lovely machine, Mr. Cavalieri. Overdesigned and overbuilt
in the German manner. After all these years, it shows no signs
of metal fatigue. This particular airplane, which I bought from
Generalissimo Franco's air force, has been modified for distance.

It may well have been one of the bombers over Guernica. Please let the steward know when you wish to eat. The menu is limited but excellent. I assure you that you are in no danger, Mr. Cavalieri. I am sure that we will conduct our business pleasurably and be on our ways. Please enjoy your journey. Adieu."

Language refined, voice coarse, accent slippery. Because he knows about Tristao da Cunha, the famous Portuguese navigator, Bo knows that Da Cunha is a Portuguese name, but the accent, wherever it comes from, doesn't fit. And Commodus? That's another story. What sort of big shot would fly around in an antique Heinkel? The sort of man who cherishes wooden character boats. An antiquarian, a romantic. He examines the books in the salon. An eclectic lot: G. K. Chesterton's *The Man Who Was Thursday*, Charles M. Doughty's *Travels in Arabia Deserta*, Robertson's Davies's *What's Bred in the Bone,* William Carlos Williams's *In the American Grain,* the Marcus Aurelius *Meditations*—ha, a clue—Commodus was Marcus's son and unworthy successor. But a clue to what? Well, Marcus was a Stoic. Bo likes the *Meditations* himself. And he's read a little Chesterton, but not this. He's read Doughty. And *What's Bred in the Bone*, a book about betrayal and indomitability, drew tears. Williams? Well, there's that poem about so much depending on a little red wheelbarrow, yeah, he remembers Williams's demeanor as a poet: clean, spare, startling. Yes! George Nobbe at Columbia had prodded him to read *In the American Grain*, especially the essay about Aaron Burr, noble and maligned. He was a lightning rod, the professor said, like you, Amir. People took unfathomable likes and dislikes to him. But unlike you, Amir, Burr had filters in his soul. He knew how to file his impressions, how to keep them from swamping him. Washington disliked him instantly, preferring the bootlick Hamilton, and it blighted Burr's career. Has this man, Da Cunha, read that essay? Does it mean something to him? Does he sympathize with the admirable Francis in the Davies book? If so, what might that say about him? These books notwithstanding, the man's an abductor. Bo's fingers remember the paper meadows and ink glades of *Al Kitab as Sirr,* the only thing of value he owns. That's what this is about, the sultan's gift.

He sits by a port window, shuts his eyes, and addresses the old sultan, his benefactor: Well, your majesty, or whatever they called you, this is a fine howdy-do. Got any advice for me? Shall I jump the steward and see if I can commandeer this old war horse? Is this kismet? Nah, that's a Turkish word. The Arabs say nasib, right? So I just ride this old camel to the oasis and see who's hanging out, is that it? Listen, Addie said something about some kind of marabout and alchemy, so d'you think you could tell the marabout in her head that I'm okay? I am okay, aren't I? Oh, I get it, that's not knowable at the present time. Patience and all that happy horseshit. Well, old man, I can't say I was a picture of contentment before you met me, but I sure hope you know what you're doing because I don't want to check out in the manner prescribed by a Commodus da Cunha, I want to check out in the manner prescribed by me. That's not a lot to ask, is it? So what do I think, that you're God? Nah, they say you were a bad guy, but I'm real familiar with 'they say'—hell, Ulrike Theiss, my own mother, said I was a bad guy. They'd have to say you were a bad guy after throwing you out, wouldn't they? The British seemed to think you were okay, but they like bad guys. Come to think of it, so do we. Why in hell did you give me that book? Do you know? Was it just an impulse? It was, wasn't it? You just saw something in my face that reminded you—of what? You as a young man? Somebody you liked? It wasn't that, was it? It was something else. You saw something you were supposed to see, as if you were waiting for me. Like I feel about Addie Compton. She doesn't need men to jerk her around and rearrange her furniture. Hell, I don't know why any woman needs men. And she doesn't need me, she just saw something she wanted to be around for a while, something she felt she ought to have, something that had been waiting. I know that feeling. So you won't tell me why you gave me the book. I'm not sure the book will tell me either. Did you know this Commodus guy? I bet you knew most of the wheeler-dealers. Weren't they all trying to get their hands in your pockets? So why did a guy like you give an American sea bum a priceless chunk of Arab history? Was it a joke? Will I see the humor in it some day? Is

161

there gonna be a some day? I dunno, your majesty, but I have this feeling that you knew right off this would be one helluva trip, and I have a feeling you're smiling somewhere behind your whiskers. But not at my expense. I know you liked me.

He chokes on the last thought, as men without fathers do.

Through a lunch of caviar tea sandwiches, his apostrophes to the late Said bin Taimur continue into the evening. He's dozing when the twin-engined Heinkel banks sharply. He looks down and recognizes the harbor of Lisbon. He has flown into Lisbon to pick up ships and he has picked up pilots in the outer harbor who then steered his ship to an anchorage or to the Alcantara Dock.

On the ground the steward gestures him out onto the runway. He never sees the crew. On the runway the Bison points to a black Bentley and says, "This way, Mr. Cavalieri, please." His right hoof is stuck in his trench coat pocket, so Bo assumes he holds a gun. The Bentley whooshes to a marina where a white three-masted schooner is docked, her twin diesels grumbling in sync. They sound like Mercedes diesels. Bo makes her out to be more than a hundred and twenty feet long. A classic. He wishes Gundy could see her.

"I understand you have sailed this harbor many times, Mr. Cavalieri," the Bison says. "Would you care to steer *Bartolomeo Diaz* upriver, oh about six kilometers? I believe you are familiar with the Rio Tejo."

They climb the gangway. A distinguished-looking captain with the pointed silver beard of an Iberian grandee appears. He bows slightly and shows Bo to the wheelhouse. There he produces the relevant Admiralty chart and gives Bo the wheel. "My crew understands English," he says. But they aren't English. Well, one of them might be, but he might be German or Scandinavian as well. This man seems to be the mate. Bo studies the controls. Then he sits and reads the chart. A steward brings a decanter of something amber, but the Bison waves it off and orders tea "for Mr. Cavalieri." Bo glances at him and grins. The Bison has done his homework. Bo walks the *Diaz* from bow to stern, examining her eight lines. Each line has its own bollard on shore, except Four and Five midship. He motions with his forefinger and thumb for the gangplank to be taken aboard. The *Diaz* is laid up along her port side with a quartering northwest breeze nudging her up the Tagus.

"Cast off number one," Bo says. Then a crewman darts a questioning look. "The bow line," Bo adds helpfully. "Let go the spring lines," he says. "Cast off the stern line." He could have let go the lines all at once, but he thinks the crew will better understand a more methodical approach. The five- or six-knot wind eases the *Diaz* off the dock. The mate relaxes. He can see this captain is a seaman. Bo wonders if this is the last ship he'll ever sail. Is it? he asks the sultan. But the old man has business elsewhere. Bo eases the ship out into the current and brings her around upstream. He smiles at the syrupy growl of the hundred-and-fifty-horsepower engines and turns to the chart. Someone has marked a landing upstream. This scenario has been plotted well. His teacup is refilled. He wishes he could be sailing this elegant vessel with Gundy. And with Addie. From Heinkel to turn-of-the-century schooner, moving back in time, past the Moorish relics along the shores of the Tagus, upland to meet a well-spoken thug. To torture and death? He shrugs. It's been a long run, Scat. Who needs old age? Still, I'd like to go out my own way. Who knows? Maybe this fuck will oblige. Probably not. He's not getting what he wants, that's for sure. That's his problem, isn't it? He wants. What do I want? What did I ever want? Well, not getting raped and damn-near lynched at Cairnhall would've been nice. A little approval from Frau Theiss would've been okay too. And Dacia. Yeah, a lot more time with Dacia. But not enough to go looking for her. Unh, unh, that would've been too scary. Once you get hung and raped you're not hot for surprises, or anything else, and it would've been too big a surprise even if she'd been happy to see me. So I guess I could say I didn't want anything. Well, my next drink, I wanted that. A good cigar. A clean ship. Oh, I forgot—I wanted to kill Gundy. He just had to screw Ute-Britt, didn't he, the greedy cocksucker. But, wouldja believe it, he finally asked me about Lakhdar, what was he like, and so on. Like he cared. That's nice.

Yeah, I do like that—Gundy cared. So I can't say I didn't ask for much. I asked for a lot, come to think of it. And, come to think of it, I got a lot of what I asked for. Altogether, I'd have to say this is as good a time to go as any. I mean, who gets to cross the Styx on a ship called *Bartolomeo Diaz*? Let's hope I do it right. I'm gonna do it right. This Portuguese fuck is not gonna get me to let down the old man. What would you say about this, Marcus? Give him the book? I don't think so. No, you old Stoic. You'd burn your arm off right in front of him, just like that Roman general did in front of the Carthaginians. I'll bet he called them Punies. Scare you maybe, defeat you never. So, Marcus, lend me a little of your Stoicism here, okay? I mean, hell, nobody promised us a ball. I remember what pissed you off about your generals, that they were so worried about the Christians. What kind of Roman generals were they anyway? And what about that Pontius Pilate? They sure didn't send their best out there to Palestine, did they? What kind of Roman procurator, you asked, would let a bunch of feather merchants and sea lawyers talk him into killing a mad carpenter, huh? So much for Roman justice. Of course your canny successor Constantine was kind of glad Pilate was a schmuck, wasn't he? How else to set up the Jews?

The dock comes into view sooner than he would have liked, just as he's enjoying his death song. Now he has to starch his hawk's face and cast a cold eye. And that's a little harder since meeting Addie.

The copper caps of the dock pilings glow like embers in the setting sun. Bo takes account of the falling wind on the starboard quarter of the *Diaz*. It and the current alone will lay her nicely up against Fabrica de Ouro's long dock, requiring little maneuvering. Bo puts the engines into neutral, then backs to slow the *Diaz*. He comes around from the wheel, runs forward and heaves the bow line to a waiting hand.

Commodus da Cunha, descending a pink Carrara marble stairway to the dock, takes pleasure in this seamanship. He's round without being fat, the kind of man hard to imagine without a cigar in his face, and it would have to be in his face because his mouth is disturbingly indistinct, a darkness that serves for a mouth, two straight slabs of flesh without refinement. Under a powder blue burnoose, its hood set back, he wears a Nehru shirt and cotton trousers, both white. His round balding head wears a halo of gray hair. His face seems bleached, accentuating intelligent yellow eyes. A retinue comes up behind him with torches that flirt with the copper crowns of the pilings.

Bo returns to the wheel, snuffs the engines, then inspects the dock lines. He frowns at the lubberly way they're secured to their bollards and cleats and jumps off the *Diaz* to do them right, flemishing the remnant line in neat flat coils on the dock. When he's finished he finds Commodus watching him from about six feet away. Bo guesses he'll say, Welcome to Fabrica de Ouro. Commodus closes the distance between them, takes Bo's hand, which has not been offered, holds it firmly and then grasps his forearm, looking directly into his eyes. He says nothing. Bo is disarmed. The man knows there's nothing he can say that won't be disingenuous and acts accordingly. He guides Bo to the stairs and they ascend silently. Bo has not been allowed to bring anything, so nothing follows them up from the *Diaz*.

34

The Arabe Moderne design of The Gold Factory beguiles the eye in dreams of Granada and conceals such newfangled features as breezy air-and-light tunnels, prismed skylights and round opening ports. It perches on a broad promontory of the Tagus's north shore four miles up from Lisbon. Golden gonfalons stream from domes set in four crenelated towers. In the center of the rectangular complex a patinaed breast-like dome rises to the level of the towers. Where a Muslim would have crowned this with a crescent, Commodus da Cunha salutes Portugal's seafaring feats with an armillary sphere that his servants are at pains to keep polished for the pleasure of the reflected sun and moon. The southern pearl limestone facade of The Gold Factory seems to emit rather than reflect light.

But The Gold Factory's glory is its hydrological genius: it's a neurology of running waters, an ecstasy of ionized air. The complex springs of Portugal's northern mountains have been tapped to channel water through its labyrinthine interior, as if to pan out impurities, leaving gold. The garden, enfolded in four lime-green ceramic walls, is an islet held by a surround of running water. Tiled azure waterways pierce each side of the enclosure to end in oval garden-copses of fountains. Beside each waterway run mosaic walks and over them the second floor of the palace floats on Moorish horseshoe arches.

At night gas torches choreograph a dance of shadows.

Oneness lies at the heart of the Arab garden, reuniting lover and beloved. The aquarist Da Cunha infuses his gardens with the notion of the Sufi master Ibn al-Arabi that we and God are co-creators of an ever-changing universe: at intervals along this encapsulated water system he has positioned stone models of the harbors of Lisbon, Ceuta, Tangier, Algiers, Naples, Barcelona, Alexandria, Palermo, Venice, Genoa, Rio, New York, and many others. They're illuminated from within and without. These exquisite port cities with their boats and ships are the gardens' lamps.

Here too is a marvel, for these waters flow by gravity, hinting at the hermetic engineering of the tilt of the channel bottoms.

The estate rests on the first of two terraces. The upper terrace is more than twice the breadth of the palace itself and hosts a vast crescent-shaped reflecting pool. From the concavity of the pool a veil of water falls down a retaining crescent of black granite about four feet high. White incised calligraphies in Chinese, Arabic, English, Sanskrit, Cyrillic and Hebrew shimmer behind the watery veil. There in the glory of silence are remembered Gautama Buddha, Confucius, Lao-tzu, Pythagoras, Muhammad, Jesus, Isaiah, and others. At each end of the wall white stairsteps wind up to the reflecting pool.

Bo understands immediately that Fabrica de Ouro has been built to keep a secret, but Commodus has no secret worthy of such a keep, and that's why he wants *Al Kitab as Sirr*. Bo is drawn to this elegant ambition but not at the cost of betraying the old sultan, who thought him deserving of treasures, and so he accepts Fabrica de Ouro as the last grandeur he will see. He regrets only disappointing Addie, for he has already provided for Ute-Britt and her son Tariq in his will.

35

Everything is a cooperative venture. But the venture is not as important as the co-operators. Druids and alchemists and Sufis like Ibn al-Arabi know this. But all those who sing the arias of their dogmas—scientists, economists, politicians—glorify the venture, preaching their best-seller lists and top tens like the Gospel—and wasting the time of civilizations. Colleagues and peers and merchant bankers may pass for co-operators, but elves and djinn have less to say and more power.

In this sense Bo Cavalieri is exactly where his cooperation with otherlings has led him.

As Sandro Cavalieri chose the comforts of a cuckold in his old age over the friendship of Bo, his stepson, Bo chooses the reprobate sultan over Sandro. He met the old curmudgeon only twice—once to help Peter Tomlinson obtain consent to dive on coastal wrecks and a little later, when he had deserted Tomlinson, to ask his help in finding work on a trading dhow— but their improbable liking for each other proved indelible and rewrote their lives. Exiled by his reformist son, the old man sat in the Dorchester Hotel in London thinking how to show this taciturn American whom he had called Sindbad that he'd taken his measure and not found him wanting. It was, to Bo at least, a heartbreaking thing for a broken old man to do. It pleased the old man in his twilight to wonder where Bo was and what his circumstances were. Bo can't say the same for Sandro or Ulrike. Given two bare encounters, the old sultan had to imagine what this Sindbad wanted. Sitting in the lobby of the Dorchester he regretted calling him Sindbad, because Sindbad sailed from Basra in search of wealth, and fabulists endowed him with myth. No, the old man decided, Amir Cavalieri sailed for other reasons. He thought merchant seamen were miserably misnamed: they sailed to make their fatted masters rich; they themselves were not merchants. He didn't wish to think of Amir this way. He wished for him a more honorable old age than his own, however hospitable Perfidious Albion was to its captive. He detested the imperialist dogs—the red ones and the red-white-and-blue ones. Sacks of pig shit, he called their embassies. He wished he could speak with Amir, that Barbary corsair born out of his proper time. Yes, that would be a relief from beefeating liars with their purple noses and angelic eyes. He must give Amir something to show he'd seen substance in him—that was the word that triggered the gift, substance.

There were two premier books in his matchless library—the library Lloyds admitted it could hardly insure—one he would describe as the ruby in the sultan's turban and the other the emerald in the sultana's navel. Sindbad fought the roc to lug treasures back to cushy Basra in a ship whose design was worth more than any of his treasures—and the greedy Vasco da Gama couldn't see the worth of that design when it was under his nose. What an irony, the sultan mused when he had little else to do—Amir's rocs and djinn and sirens were more dangerous and cruel, and their designs were charted like the modern seas on his forbidding face. The old man remembered the suffering in that face. And all the fame that Peter Tomlinson bumbled into by discovering the Portuguese caravel wreck, the now celebrated *Sao Tiago*, was owed to the sultan's liking that face, for had Amir not accompanied Tomlinson that day to the sultan's palace the sultan would have remembered the odor of British perfidy and would have forbidden Tomlinson to dive on Omani wrecks. Indeed as he sat in the Dorchester in his final years, entertaining his fetch, he wasn't sure but that he'd twice seen the face of God. He remembered that early in his exile a homeless man had risen out of his cardboard box one wintry morning before the sultan's bodyguards had time to react, looked straight into his eyes and shouted, "You-are-God, don't-deny-it."

169

"I don't deny it, but my son does," he'd said to the laughter of his bodyguards.

Undeterred, the derelict waved his finger back and forth in front of the sultan's face, insisting that the sultan consider his own true nature. Said bin Taimur whispered to a bodyguard, "Give him 200 pounds sterling." The bodyguard turned up his palms to say he didn't have such a sum. "Fetch it while I wait here," the sultan said.

The *Sao Tiago* had electrified the world of marine archaeology. It became a four-eyed industry. Archaeologists and naval architects had been waiting centuries to study a real caravel, for none of the drawings of the *Nina* and *Pinta* and other caravels were detailed. It made Tomlinson and Moira Sayre celebrities. But Bo and his wretched friend Uthman al-Biruni found the wreck. Uthman had been under a death sentence for fighting to install a Marxist regime in feudal Oman and only Bo's intercession stopped his beheading.

Said bin Taimur mused that the modern baghala Bo had sailed and whose slaving captain he killed was the prototype of the *Sao Tiago,* but the murdering Da Gama was too busy looting to notice its qualities. The Portuguese later saw the handling virtues of Arab ships off the Barbary coast, incorporated them in the caravel and set off on the random pillaging they called discovery. This armed merchantman, capable of sailing hard on the wind, is the mother of the global economy. Tomlinson was looking for alchemical artifacts, but Bo made him famous by grasping the importance of Uthman's *Sao Tiago.* The old sultan allowed to himself that he'd misjudged the Englishman, for when Tomlinson wrote his now famous book about the caravel and its revelatory architecture he took pains to credit Bo and Uthman not only with its discovery but with making the case for its significance: "The ghostly epitome of honor," he called Bo. And then, in a remarkable epilogue, he wrote that he regretted his role as a British agent in the palace coup that sent the old man into exile. "A decent oligarch whose like we shall not see again," he wrote of the sultan. A decent oligarch? A sultan, damn it, no more nor less. Let the Greeks and their obsequious heirs have their damned word. I am a sultan and as good as their presidents and kings and oligarchs. Still, I wish I had treated Tomlinson better: the English are terrible friends but wonderful enemies.

36

Commodus da Cunha isn't as pig-eyed as Vasco da Gama: he's beginning to suspect the ship might be more important than its cargo. Not that he thinks of *Al Kitab as Sirr* as the ship. He's smarter than that. He sees that the ship is the dynamic his abduction of Amir has set up, a ship taking everyone involved to richer ports by far than those he has replicated on the shores of the miniature seas of Fabrica de Ouro. Anyone who deals for long with Gulf Arabs begins thinking about Vasco da Gama, who thought that going and getting were paramount. Commodus, who's much richer, has begun to recognize that a man is born with all the wealth he'll ever need, but he must learn to repossess it from his mentors. That's what he thinks to obtain from the book and might instead—or so he now hopes—obtain by extorting it. In comparison, the chicanery involved in arming the jackals and hyenas of the world is child's play. Most men want nothing so much as power. Money and murder traipse after it. The fastest way to get rich is to help con men seize power. If they fail, so what?

Commodus has no chance of getting the book from Amir unless he discovers the man's secrets. Women? Boys? Money? He quickly sees these are crass considerations. Torture? This man will die under torture simply because the worst of it pales in light of what he's already endured. Amir reminds Commodus of a heron, inhabiting the moment, careless of tomorrow, contemptuous of yesterday. Why in God's name did the damned old sultan give such a man these incalculable treasures? He keeps asking himself that question until he becomes aware he knows the answer. It's because Amir Cavalieri intrigued the sultan as much as he does Da Cunha. When this recognition blooms fully in his head he finds himself staring down the central fact of Christianity: Jesus was killed by men he'd driven crazy. Not because they didn't understand but because they did. Not understanding was their cover story, which is why Marcus thought Pilate a blockhead.

Da Cunha understands all this—his recognitions pile onto each other in the wake of Amir's arrival—but he wants the book more than he wants his own soul, and knowing this chagrins him and cheapens his dealings with Amir. He's embarked on a plot, and changing course incurs the risk of sailing straight off the table of the medieval earth. He wants desperately to tell Amir about these feelings, but that would be changing course.

The kidnapped guest—Commodus doesn't know his guest is in fact The Hanged Man—is an archetype, like the vampire. The menacing yet cultured host probes for the guest's vulnerabilities and finds his own. The chemistry of the predicament is dangerous. All possible resolutions are operatic: there, just there, is what Commodus likes about the game—its utter contempt for resolution.

The Omani Crane and Da Cunha's goon, the Bison, have been useless except in managing Amir's extraction from Manhattan. Their lunatic reports on his doings exasperate Commodus. They're like the heaps of trivia we pile on people who scare us. The Omani entertains the ridiculous notion he has the upper hand and is motivated by a higher purpose. There's no point disabusing him. Oman needs Commodus more than it wants the manuscripts. Bison and Crane think they know where the texts are, but they can't steal them. The only solution is to entertain the owner in Portugal, see what he's made of, what he wants—a good idea going nowhere. The man doesn't want anything. He enjoys civilized discourse but not so much that depriving him of it will do any good.

★

"Have you noticed the similarity between the births of Alexander the Great and Jesus Christ?" he asks Amir one evening. They sit on the great south terrace of Fabrica de Ouro overlooking the Tagus. "Mary had Joseph, Olympias had her snake. In either case paternity was in doubt."

"Their only similarity, do you think?" says Bo.

"Neither god suffered fools, but only fools would have thought of killing Alexander."

"You say *but* only fools where you should have said *and* only fools."

Ha, Commodus thinks, I'm getting somewhere. He's not indulging me. This subject engages him. "Marcus never would have crucified the loony carpenter and so we should have had no Christianity."

"Yes, if history is Marxist and Darwinian you'd be right, but the Eastern version is that it all happened as it had to happen."

"And that's why you're here!" Commodus cries.

"To end up on a cross or stretched out devastated by alcohol and syphilis and old wounds? Well, Commodus, that would make you irrelevant and I don't think that's what you want, is it?"

Check. No, checkmate. Commodus relishes this game, but he wants to awe Cavalieri and instead he's finding him a formidable autodidact. If Bo's pedigree is haphazard Commodus da Cunha's is decidedly whimsical. He might as well have been Tristan or Vasco. He's a cobbled man. Born a Muslim Chechen, he bought his identity and treats it like the connoisseur he is. He is, with the Saudi Adnan Kashoggi, a mythical merchant of death. Wherever Kalashnikovs are needed Commodus is on the scene. Katyushka rockets? A squadron of Mirages? Commodus will provide them. No Zurich bank fails to give him obsequious treatment that would make a Prussian butler puke. At least three movies feature mystery men suspiciously like him. He has high hopes for one of these films. He even shuffled money to it, imagining himself played by Roger Moore or Omar Sharif. He was hurt when they cast Bob Hoskins. But Hoskins, he admits, captures his whimsicality.

As he runs his finger around the rim of his brandy glass, circling a secret, he glances up to see Bo considering him. "The British empire was financed by opium, you know that, don't you? Yes. Your two biggest American banks would collapse in a fortnight if they were made to stop laundering drug money. Whole nations, including yours, would implode into poverty without the drug trade. The money spent fighting it is the most expensive charade in history."

He draws back a curtain and drapery, revealing a courtyard. "Look at that Nazi bug out there. It never uses gasoline. It runs on a concoction of hydrogen and chlorine, distilled water and oxygen activated by ultraviolet. And the patent isn't worth the paper it's written on because the world is run on oil and drugs. That's the way it's arranged. It's not the poverty that stinks so badly in Mexico City, it's the hypocrisy. An English banker once told me that if the Cold War were to end I'd be out of business. Can you imagine anyone making a moron like that the president of a bank? If the Cold War were to end tomorrow I'd become richer than I am now. And do you know who would replace Ivan on your enemies list? Abdul, be sure of it. It has been difficult to demonize Ivan, but the West shall have no difficulty whatsoever demonizing Abdul. He's the dark other. What fun the West will have! A hundred Peter-the-Hermits in tuxes will preach new crusades. And Ivan will join them, oh yes, because the Saracen and the Turk are his old enemies. You'll see. And I'll be there selling arms to the Afghans, the Chechens, the Angolans, the Mexican Indians, the Kosovars, the Islamists, the drug lords, the corrupt little armies fighting them, oppressors and stinkpots everywhere. That's how wrong that idiot banker is. He probably looked like a banker, so they made him one, like your General Bumfuck in Vietnam. That's how the world works, you know. That's how we end up with stupid, stupider and stupidest at the top. But let me tell you something, my little secret, Amir, and then ask yourself this: If this man shares his deepest secret with me and threatens to make me rich, why should I withhold his heart's desire from him?"

Commodus poises like a surgeon with a scalpel.

Bo looks down at the floor, trying to drop his smile, but finally he looks into Commodus's face and grins.

Emboldened, Commodus says, "You have a term—I heard it once from a mercenary in Angola—chump change, that's it. Well, what I make dealing arms is chump change. Really, Amir. It's also a disguise. I hide in plain sight. That's where you must always hide, isn't it? The source of my wealth, what I lay up in those Swiss larders, is an index, a little index that makes the Vatican's look like a bureaucrat's to-do list. And you know what I index? Account numbers, codes, drops, serials, the names of agents? No, nothing like that at all. I index what the world's most important people want even when they don't know they want it. Twelve-year-olds? Famous actresses or rock stars or athletes? Pain? Revenge? That's what power is, Amir, knowing what people want. I don't even have to provide what they want. Sometimes I do, most often not. But knowing is what is precious. Can you imagine the hard work finding out? The time, the money, the skills? And do you know what? Few people put money at the top of their list. They say they do, but that's their cover. No, they want friends' daughters, nieces, nuns, schoolboys, the publication of their wretched scribblings, the love of unworthy people, and death, don't forget death. That's your special problem, Amir, death. To have the power of the Golden Horde is nothing—you have to know how to market it. Sometimes I sell this information to people who don't know they want it. Can you imagine my little index as a book? It would be on the best-seller list long after we're dead. Now, listen Amir, think of the research that goes into such an index. When you discover what people really want you also run across their indiscretions, their scandals. I know what people the princes and princesses and presidents and generals and mullahs are screwing, in addition to the masses of course. I am the lexicographer of their hypocrisies. And think about this, Amir—because you must remember that I am always trying to charm the wretched book from you—I am spending all this time with you because they are boring and you are not. You have no idea how boring they are. They think that what they want, whom they want, is the medicine for their sicknesses, but their wanting is their sickness. Now, ask yourself, is not the man who is capable of understanding this worthy of having your book? I will share its contents. We'll explore it together, if you like."

"I don't think Marcus would have liked you any more than he liked Pilate, Commodus. You're not satisfied with knowledge, you want the book because it's a priceless object and the rest of what you say is bullshit." To Bo's surprise, Commodus's face shows not so much a man caught out as a man considering. For once Commodus feels what he's wanted to feel all his life, himself aligned with his destiny.

37

Commodus provides Bo with a sketchpad and pencils as their conversations continue.

"What do you see to draw?"

"I wonder if I can arrest the expression of a man who feels honor-bound to consider something he hates."

"I'll sit for you awhile in the hope you can. But it will be as difficult as painting a lovely girl who blushes not in embarrassment but in pique because her *modus vivendi* calls to her lesser men and women than her beauty deserves. She can't live up to her looks. She knows that when she does it will be too late and she'll have slept with oafs. Is anything sadder?"

Commodus sounds like a cello and the memory of his words, so many of them, settles on his library like dust. Bo likes listening to him. Commodus builds his speech as if he can't decide on his materials: English for precision, American TV accents for punch, foreign excess, brick on stone, lumber and steel: emerging from his head case it sounds like concerti. How, from such a formless yap, can melodies flow?

Bo is stumped. None of his other subjects kidnapped him, but he doesn't think that's why he can't draw Commodus. You could say a sketch is a search, a painting a generous act. Drawing a sketch, you look for the quintessential in the fleeting. But painting . . . yes, here it is, Commodus wants Bo to draw him with something he lacks. He wants Bo to give him something more important than the book. The book's a pretext. Commodus knows all about pretexts. He deals with people all the time who don't know what they want until he tells them. He wants something much harder to give him than the book. How shall I use this power? Bo wonders. This man is incomplete. He thinks something in the way I acquired *Al Kitab as Sirr* will complete him. It's an impossible task. Doesn't he know that? I'm not God. I don't have what he wants, no one does. And even if I did, I have no right to decide if he deserves it. Your majesty, what have you gotten me into?

Commodus isn't a man to avoid others' eyes. What interests Bo most is that Commodus lingers in the eyes of his underlings, a trait Bo can't remember in any other poohbah, not even the gracious Peter Tomlinson. Commodus cares what servants think. But when he looks into Bo's eyes his own roll up as in samadhi and then he searches Bo's forehead. Bo has seen men, rarely women, scan the walls when talking to him, but he's never seen this elevation of the gaze. It reminds him of a celebrant at Mass commanding the communicants to lift up their hearts.

Tomlinson, the writer for whom Bo captained the *Morgaine*, looked for obvious things, the common coin of commercial books, whereas Commodus da Cunha, the bogus Portuguese, looks for much more than silk and pearl routes and sunken treasures, and is astute enough to know it will be hidden in plain sight, immune to greed.

Bo's sketchpads teem, so he thinks it fair turnabout to be studied, even by an amateur phrenologist. He entertains the notion that Commodus glimpses his third eye, a privilege that has eluded Bo. But what disquiets him is Commodus reading his forehead as if it were a wide screen. More disquieting is the ring of sweat jeweling his friar's halo. A tic in the inner corner of his left eye crazes down to the corner of his anonymous mouth, rendering the composition of his face unreliable. Bo wonders what Goya would do. He thinks of chalk, charcoal and pencil and feels his skills curdle because he can't even settle on a proper medium.

★

Bo falls asleep in his chair, his pad in his lap. Commodus fetches a tapestry of Roualt cartoons, covers him, dims the lights and leaves.

At breakfast the next day they munch on their impasse.

"It's lucky for you profligate Americans that most of the world uses its hands and a spot of water or a few leaves to wipe its ass, otherwise Weyerhauser and Boise Cascade would have perfected more sophisticated kinds of rape long ago and your beautiful country would be a quilt of anthills just as it's now becoming a checkerboard of crates."

"Yeah, well, what about you Chechens, have you stopped beating your wives?"

"No peoples have stopped beating their wives, Amir. But please forgive my vulgarity. Ass-wipes are not a fitting table subject, of course. What about books? Have you considered that in the not too distant future they'll twinkle on and off on little tablets that fit in your pocket, not only because paper costs too much but because books are about to sing, change shape and color, transport readers to libraries and archives, jump back and forth between one another and shape-change at will? And this is because the book has become a cheap semblance of its medieval intent. I see a new iconography of the book, each book an exquisite work of art, a celebration of the original manuscript working out its destiny in the air. Just as there is the painting and the lithograph, there will be the book and its electric tribe wandering the airwaves, making camps, conducting raids, celebrating marriages, burying its dead. The book will fly."

Commodus's words have no tooth. They pelt his brain. No books? Books written on air? What the hell's he talking about? Is it a kind of torture? He fell asleep trying to draw Da Cunha. No aspect of a person bothers Bo more than undrawability. It's worse than noticing that someone has no reflection in a mirror.

Commodus looks at him as if he knows just what he's thinking. "It is not your problem that you cannot seat me in your mind. It is mine, don't you think?"

Bo at this moment is on the pale of human engagement, the point at which we might leapfrog a century or two on our lollygagging way to become something like an angel. Not being able to draw someone is worse than knowing nothing you can ever say to someone will make a difference. Bo owes his survival to learning early that words are lefthanded.

"We wake up stinking of stuff to do, our bluff against truly waking up, against the intuitions we bring here. They're like wolves, these intuitions—they frighten us. We hunt them down when we can muster enough courage to enter their woods. That's our fall, and our fig leaf, fear of our own knowledge. Not the silly apple in the Garden of Eden. I am interested in the operations of the mind, Amir, not the pathology but the glory. If we did not shade the glory, would there be pathology? That is why I deserve your book. I would follow every stroke. I would know the mind and the glory of the maker. Never mind whether it is written in Kufic or bound in leather or illuminated in gold leaf—that's Aristotelian balderdash. We've had two thousand years of logic and deduction. Now it's time to grow up. I would follow the stream from God to the calligrapher's hand. I would appreciate his every caesura and certainty. I would be his celebrant. Can you say that, Amir?"

"I can say you've gone to criminal lengths to talk so fancy."

Bo has never seen a wolfish look on a round face. Can he draw it? There it is, alert to every quickening, yellow-eyed, unpredictable beyond compare. "I understand you quite well," Bo hears himself say. "I understand who you are, but all you know about me is that I understand, and that's not enough for you to get what you want. If there are magic words, you haven't said them."

"But I've come close."

★

Bo tries to recall the old sultan who'd studied him like a man who'd threaded his way through a thronged bazaar to suddenly come face to face with the be-all and end-all. This is what Commodus doesn't get—and can't unless Bo in the left-handedness of words hands it to him. As he looks at Commodus's blanched face it comes to him that he's never had much trouble with pricks—they're just so many telegraph poles buzzing by—and now the people who intrigue him might even be his captors. And what's unusual about that? Glamours and allures are always captors. Part of him wishes to give Commodus what he wants. The other part would rather go to hell.

You can hardly get by as a Chechen posing as a Portuguese esplendorado without making your own justice in this world. That old Omani plutocrat had handed a vulgar sailor an ancient work of incomparable refinement. In the white waters of their dark brown inks one could read the sensibility of the Islamic civilization that made the Renaissance imaginable. And Commodus lusts to sail that ink, to lose himself in the courses and rushes of a lost world. He longs to review the Kufic warriors marching stoically eastward, their red and green and blue and yellow vowel sounds fluttering like standards over their heads. By what stretch of justice should a brute assassin be given this sacred responsibility?

"How do you find your way out of your mind, Commodus?" Bo breaks the silence. Commodus looks up for a smile but finds only a Bedouin's far-flung face.

"It's an arduous journey, which explains why I'm old beyond my years. We're both voyagers, Bo."

"Well, I imagine you walking with a stick, hitting dogs, mopping your face, slapping gnats."

Not the vulgarian I hoped for, Bo thought.

"Mafiosi and gurus, presidents and captains of industry, movie makers and media moguls, venture capitalists and masters of espionage—corruptors all, my little geese laying their golden eggs—I go to feed one of them. I shall be back soon, less than a week. I would offer you *Bartolomeo Diaz*, but I am mindful of your talent for piracy. My library and gardens are at your disposal. Mr. Kovtorashvili is at your beck and call." Aslanbek Kovtorashvili, a fellow Chechen, seems to be the aide de camp to Commodus and the superior of the Bison, whose name still eludes Bo.

38

The message taped to the bathroom mirror at Conaboy Ayton's townhouse is English script rendered in the Kufic style, remarkable handiwork:

Dear Doctor Wadeleigh,

Your presence is urgently and respectfully required in the matter of Senhor Amir Cavalieri. When you have read this message my colleague will instruct you further.

There is no need for alarm. I will introduce myself presently and make known how you may assist me.

She no sooner reads these words than a muftied satyr appears behind her. She stares at his image in the mirror, not turning. He makes the heart-to-mouth-to-mind Muslim peace with the side of a Ruger handgun.

"How many slaves has your master?" she asks.

"As many as there are fools in the world," the satyr says.

"May I pack?"

"For clement weather, yes. Not more than two weeks."

★

She'd gone back to Irving Place to collect a few things and rejoin Addie, Joe and Si Larbi. Twelve hours later Addie and Joe sit side by side in Parnell's Hat glancing at each other in the mirror, afraid to say the obvious.

"I like what I don't understand." Their eyes follow the sound to Si Larbi, who fills the doorway, staring the habitués down. Then he walks down the bar to where they sit. "It deserves more respect than what I do understand. Scotch, please."

"Arabs don't drink, and if they did we wouldn't be servin' 'em here."

"When there's no camel piss or Irish blood, I drink Scotch."

The professional Irishmen hunch over their dank tables along the wall behind them looking half pissed, half cowed. Joe enjoys Si Larbi too much to reassure the drunks.

"He writes to your friend about the book. Why does he do this?" Si Larbi asks. "Why not an intermediary? Now we know who he is. He's a suspect. Then he takes Doctor Wadeleigh—yes, yes, that must be assumed—but the question is what does he want?"

"The fuckin' book, Si Larbi, didja not take in what I said?"

Addie covers Joe's mouth. "Listen, Joseph, to what Si Larbi is saying. This is not the best way to get the book. An intermediary could have learned Amir's mind and reported it to his employer. That would have left his employer free to act in anonymity. This is a game, Joseph. You of all people should understand that. Do you think the fulminators who dispatch children and dunces to blow people up want what they say they want, or do they want to play the game?"

"Ah, he's a slaver then? He wants them because she's a looker and yer man's a cutthroat?"

Si Larbi has played this game with Joe many times. It always amuses him.

"Are you doing your share to prove the British have a place in Ireland, Yusuf? The man wants what's in their heads. You agree, Miss Adeline?"

"I don't know what Margaret has been up to. She's often sought out by people trying to work out advanced technologies. She could be in great danger. It's possible it's not even related to this Da Cunha."

"We're not MI fuckin' 6. If she's got some secret weapon in her crock, let them worry about it. We know about Da Cunha and he's likely got yer beau."

"You are right, Yusuf. Da Cunha is our best bet, but it is too much of a coincidence to ignore Doctor Wadeleigh's disappearance. Our job is to keep this clean."

"Yeah, clean, like a surgical strike in a war, ya mean?" He knows, if Si Larbi forgets, that people get killed when big shots think. He believes the salvation of his soul, if he has one, rests on getting Bo out, both because and in spite of the fact that Bo is Addie's lover. It's a matter of honor. And he's pretty sure it means killing somebody. Si Larbi is entertaining too many thoughts. He's gone soft and will get himself killed. In his usual fashion Joe says so: "I don't want to save yer Arab ass twice, Si Larbi. It's bad luck. Yer noodlin' yerself into yer grave."

Looking straight ahead, wet-eyed, Addie says, "You're as full of it as Sinn Fein, Joseph. I love the sound of you talking, but not when you yourself love it so much."

Si Larbi grins like an uncorked djinni. "By all means, Miss Adeline. It is so boring killing for ugly little pricks. You shall be our leader. We will go and settle an old Arab score with the Portuguese. This man will not kill Doctor Wadeleigh."

"An' yer sure of it, are ya?"

"Shut the fuck up," Addie says.

"Positive," says Si Larbi. "She is one of those people the world would be lonely without, and I think this Portugee has found that out. He is no charismatic half-wit, he is a man who uses charismatic half-wits."

"Si Larbi, you dear man, you've been doing your homework," Addie says.

Si Larbi cautions with an ashen finger. "He is dangerous, make no mistake. He won't invite us. We are no use to him, but he knows about us, he certainly knows about you, Miss Adeline. We must leave this hot target area immediately. We are in his crosshairs. I hope your politics will allow you to depart under PLO cover."

"My politics is me," Joe says. "Si Larbi shits everybody by killing without respect to race or creed. The bloody bastard likes Shin Bet as much as he likes Hamas."

"You're my politics," Addie says, putting her arms around Joe's shoulder and Si Larbi's waist.

They take a cab to Bo's loft.

185

39

Manhattan's wet asphalt reminds Addie that the only way to understanding is hard as anthracite. The way their kamikaze taxi driver negotiates this black terrain reorganizes her innards and heaves up the nasty thought that she's gotten Margaret killed. How might that be so? she asks herself as they lurch over a bump. It is so, the city answers as they land. Never mind, wheeze the springs of their cab.

"What is the address on Houston, mon?" their Rastafarian tormentor says.

"Houston? Did I say Houston? Whatcha been smokin', mon? Broadway, I said Broadway and Spring."

Addie grabs Joe's hand and squeezes. Si Larbi grins.

By the time they reach Bo's loft the rain has stopped, but they're drenched in the knowledge that Margaret too is gone.

Joe takes up a perch on Bo's high rolling worktable. He watches Addie, whose head swarms with unstrung words. She touches things to cajole their messages. She keeps glancing at the windows as if the sentences she wants to speak flew out them. When she looks at him in frustration he raises the palms of his hands towards the ceiling as if bearing a tray, signalling her to speak up, get it out.

Si Larbi settles like an Easter Island monolith on one of Bo's Kermanshahs, his oaken hands clamped on his knees. He watches the moon whiten the windows. "When you want to find someone to kill him, it's easy," he says to the windows. "But when you want to find him to love him, that's different. Where is he hiding? In yourself, probably. Your friend, Doctor Wadeleigh, has been given a gift, Addie. Yes, things have been taken out of her hands. We, we have to make the decisions. We could just leave your friends to their fate. Have you thought of that?"

The inconvenience of getting to know this new Si Larbi, this murdering guru, irks Joe. "Listen to 'im, will ya? Do ya know what yer sayin', y'ignorant wog? You were probably a fat corrupt pasha in another life, werncha?"

Si Larbi shows a silver eyetooth to Addie; they know better than Joe who he was.

"He doesn't take orders from anybody," Joe tells Addie. "They only think he does. It's better to be his enemy than give him a bum set of orders."

The giant turns to Addie as if it is his duty to edify her. "Yusuf doesn't know why we are friends. He hasn't given himself the freedom to think about it. We're friends because he is a dervish and I would like to be a dervish. The purpose of a dervish is to vanish. Yusuf came by this knowledge under torture, betrayed by one of his own. I merely listen to my master. My master knows I'm a dunce. At any moment he may stop instructing me, and then I'll be the person it pleases Joe for me to be."

"Is your master hidden?"

"He appeared on this plane three hundred and thirty years after the prophet left. He wrote nothing because he feared the exegesis of knaves and his own vanity. His name is Mutawakkil ibn al Quereishi. I doubt you have ever heard of him. Other masters, like Ibn Arabi and Rumi, are more famous."

Addie's breath lifts her bangs. Yes, I know Mooty-Whacky quite well. I myself call him shyster. She doesn't dare say that. Nor perhaps would Si Larbi wish to hear it. She screws up her face and battens down her eyes. When she opens them Si Larbi is smiling into them.

"Who's in charge here then, Larbi?" says Joe. "Watch 'im," he tells Addie, "the bloody man will say, 'He who is always in charge,' arncha, boyo?"

"Dervishes fool around," Si Larbi tells the walls.

"Now there are only three of us, we could have ourselves a tidy little democracy then," Joe says.

187

"Yusuf can destroy an army barracks or a truck convoy all by himself," Si Larbi says, "and I have reasons not to cross swords with Da Cunha."

He watches disappointment darken Addie's face. "But I think we are trying to figure something out, and Doctor Wadeleigh and the sailor are our hosts, not Senhor Da Cunha."

Joe Minihan should marvel at the transformation of this giant he's portrayed as a thug, but Addie sees no sign of it. It's as if Joe has always thought there'd be another Si Larbi some day and is merely put off by his appearance now.

"I'd better be the boss," Joe says.

"I'd rather have Miss Compton," Si Larbi says.

"I second the motion," Addie says.

"His or mine?"

"You're a bossy guy, Yusuf," Addie says.

"Well, it's settled then, all in favor grab yer passports," says Joe.

But nobody jumps. Joe remains seated on the worktable. Addie stands in a dark corner fondling an aludel on a fishing line. Si Larbi is crosslegged on the Kermanshah. Addie has an impulse to open one of the big factory windows in case he might wish to fly away on his carpet.

"He has estates in Turkey, Portugal, Morocco and England," Si Larbi tells the windows. "His library is outside Lisbon. I think that's where he would take Mr. Amir. It's called Fabrica de Ouro, The Gold Factory. He wouldn't take Doctor Wadeleigh to England. I don't think he would take her to Turkey. You have to behave in Turkey. That leaves O Zonzeira in Morocco. That's his villa near Tangier. It means The Dizziness. That's where Doctor Wadeleigh would be."

"And you know all this shit because?" Joe says.

"I know who feeds the jackals, Yusuf."

40

The Devil's Prick, the locals call it: a hundred-and-twenty-foot exclamation from the fussed-over remains of a Moorish fort. O Zonzeira, The Dizziness, Commodus da Cunha calls it, a black marble obelisk presiding over the tryst of the Atlantic and Mediterranean at Cape Spartel, ten miles northwest of Tangier. It tapers up to the socket of a huge cat's eye staring straight at the heavens. It's this eye, ablaze in the sun, Margaret sees as *Balkan Wars* banks for its descent. The tower's two-story black glass windows are almost indistinguishable from its facade except that they bear the last embers of the sun. By moonlight The Devil's Prick looks like a stay in the march of things, the shadow of a narrow door ajar. By day, early and late, its shadow parts the ground. A circuit of water forty feet wide girds the tower. A twenty-four-foot-high disk of white limestone radiates from the tower more than a hundred yards. Each eighth of the disk hosts an immense angled skylight. All the Palladian windows of the disk face the watery circle.

The pilot of *Balkan Wars* escorts Margaret to a yellow horse-drawn surrey. He's one of those burnished Germans whose faultless cordiality scares the hell out of you. He gets into the carriage with her, and the driver, a dour Berber wearing a fez and full-sleeved blouse, drives sedately to O Zonzeira. She's taken immediately to the summit of the tower where half the cat's eye she saw from the air rotates under the other half to accommodate a huge Rube Goldberg telescope. It sleepwalks on casters over a white marble turntable. A chambered nautilus of black marble sits in the center of this motorized wheel. Large brass urns hold dwarf acacia, eucalyptus and Marmora wild pear trees. Horned larks, chatty red-billed choughs, two acrobatic booted eagles and other birds occupy three towering aviaries.

Commodus stands behind the telescope, twiddling dials. The pilot confides a few words to him. He pats the pilot's arm and turns to Margaret. "Doctor Wadeleigh, my name is Commodus da Cunha. I am enjoying the company of your acquaintance, Amir Cavalieri. You are here in the expectation that your presence will imbue him with the view that *Al Kitab as Sirr* belongs in my library. In return for it I intend to make him a rich man. It's a simple proposition, but his vision is obscured by some sense of loyalty to an old man he encountered only twice. I apologize for making you a pawn. You deserve to be entertained in your own right, and, pawn or no pawn, you are an honored guest."

"As it turns out, Senhor Da Cunha, it would seem you've taken the wrong hostage," Margaret says.

"Folly does not become you, Doctor Wadeleigh. You are speaking out of chagrin. Miss Compton is not Amir Cavalieri's flash point—you are. You will make your accommodations. I will have my manuscript and its secrets. Far from being a fly in your ointment"—Margaret cringes—"Miss Compton may prove to be simply stirring the pot, preventing its ingredients from sticking to the bottom, as it were."

"What makes you think I am so dear to Mr. Cavalieri that he will give up the book?"

"My dear lady, he would give up the book to protect a bum. You merely dramatize his predicament. Fraulein Broghammer or Miss Compton would have done nicely. But I happened to take an interest in you. It is not every young woman of your education and station who takes a semi-literate Alexandrian cabdriver under her wing and makes him her protégé. I am charmed by this extraordinary act. The obsessive mess in which you and Senhor Cavalieri are entangled interests me much less. You are not real people to each other. You are merely the effluent of your fixations. I would suggest to you that it does not befit your dignity, Doctor Wadeleigh."

With that, emitting a buzz of irritation, he shuts obsidian

sliding doors behind him with a thud and leaves her alone on the head of The Devil's Prick. She shakes with frustration. To be scolded like a wrongheaded child by her abductor is too much. Not real to each other, she and Bo? Damn this son of a bitch. Will Addie always be the only real person in her life? It comes to her with fearful certainty that she has imposed on her relationship with Bo a mindless scenario that doesn't befit her dignity, and she's ashamed. She wonders if like her, Bo is taking this madman's craftings seriously. Of course he is, he takes everyone seriously. Fondness for Bo, more trustworthy than love, thrums in her blood. Then another irrelevant thought piles on: if Bo is here in this place only Addie would sense it. What use is this crank thought? Or for that matter all your unmathematical thoughts? says her second self. And perhaps Commodus overhears it, because now his head appears between the doors saying, "I have an elegant little library here of the Andalusian and Sicilian mathematicians. Where possible I have obtained translations. Wouldn't you like to examine it while we wait for Amir to make the best of things?"

41

Two important meetings languish on Commodus's calendar. Sendero Luminosa, Peru's Shining Path Maoists, wait for him in Tripoli. They need ground-to-air missiles urgently and are shopping for a sea of small arms. Mexico's Zapatistas want weapons too, but, more important, they want his advice about which ones suit them. Can't they get some Spetznaz help? He likes the Zapatistas but thinks the Maoists thugs. The Zaps will wait patiently in Prague, listening to the clocks. He'll give them a break. They're fighting one of the filthiest regimes in the world, right up there with Washington, Beijing, Baghdad and Moscow. Corrupt peoples fruit their wines with hypocrisy.

If he were editing an index of Commodus da Cunha's secret desires he would no longer be able to say that *Al Kitab as Sirr* is any more important than Russian ballerinas. For all his careful research, he's bungled this intrigue. Its outcome depends not on stratagem but on what he does now while the Shining Path and the Zaps and the Belmokhtar and the Cabinda and the Shanti Bahini and everyone whose currency is human disgrace wait for him in grand hotels and palaces. Nor are these insurgencies the worst of them, no, not by a long shot, because they're underfunded. Mossad and the KGB and the CIA and MI-6, the authorized murderers, the ones allowed to fly their rags at the United Nations, are as bad if not worse. And they need him as the church needs the Jews, to project their sanctity over against his villainy.

Shuttling between Fabrica de Ouro and O Zonzeira, Commodus wonders what Margaret Wadeleigh and Amir Cavalieri want. He kidnapped Bo for the book. Then, since Bo so little values his own life, he kidnapped Margaret. Now there are alluring complications. Bo is the sort of fool who might not make any distinction between Doctor Wadeleigh and some bum, and there's a good chance he now cares more for her lover, Adeline Compton, than he does for Margaret. Even Alexander the Great would find this knot too artful to spoil. Commodus has wrecked national economies by speculating in currencies. He understands grand scale. He appreciates that the British called their greed the Great Game because it spared them the details of human suffering. Commodus is a dealer in secrets, always the way to a man's cojones. For now at least he doesn't have to worry about a woman's nether parts. When it comes to women he knows little and lacks the special heartlessness to con them. That is why Margaret Wadeleigh is turning out to be a poor hostage and a wondrous one at the same time. Her gateway is not her twat, however much Commodus imagines its elven wonders, and if her gateway is her mind, her eyes are like wreckers' lanterns leading his inquiries onto shoals. She has that sidelong look by which he imagines Elizabeth I froze the bones of papal nuncios and plotting courtiers, and the only interest she has shown him was when he revealed to her a room covered ceiling to floor and across the ceiling with Giordano Bruno's star beasts painted by the crazy Algerian Si Lamdjed el Ayadi. Lamdjed's paints are as gummy as Van Gogh's, his colors as gemmy as Delacroix's. Commodus sees right away that the little finger of her right hand twitches to touch those sworls of paint, and he invites her to do so. He thinks for a moment she might sleep with him if only it could be in this room, and the current of this notion, feathering his brain, is more wonderful to him than stealing the bust of Queen Nefertiti from the Berlin Museum, his most erotic fantasy. Once he allows Margaret to touch the crimson penis of a gryphon he knows he must share his most erotic fantasy with her.

She purses her lips when he tells her and says, "Yes, I understand. I would give five years of my life to sleep with Nefertiti, to taste that unfathomable dignity."

"Five, not ten?"

"Five," she says.

Commodus loves this exactitude. "And for what man would you steal to sleep with Michelangelo's David perhaps?"

"No man, as you correctly presume. And did you say steal? I am not a thief."

No, but you love one, he wants to say. He's never enjoyed a conversation as much, not even with his other hostage, who is dour where she is trenchant. "Not yet, but it remains to be seen if you will steal your mother's lover, locked away as he is in the high-security vault of his memories."

In that instant he sees Medusa considering a strike. "I regret offending you, Doctor Wadeleigh, but it is germane to our purpose here, is it not?"

"Your purpose, Senhor Da Cunha."

"Yes, of course, yours being simply to survive."

"I shall decide mine."

"I have brought nations to their knees before lunch. I have sent despots and their asslicks into exile, but I have never been more honored or entertained by a guest, professor. I have researched assiduously and I do not think your closest friends appreciate you."

"Pity then your invitation was so rude," Margaret says, her smile glimmering.

"My company is not sought after except by scum in pursuit of bogus ideals." He watches her stroke the side of her right hand with her left, a way to concentrate. Commodus's comment touches her. "There are many kinds of beauty, Doctor Wadeleigh," he ventures, "Not many of them are kind."

She considers his flattery as if it were a Gainesborough. "I would like to sleep with Bruno's beasts. May I?" A test. She'll see if he's worthy of serious commerce. She uses a suggestive euphemism, sleep, to measure his refinement. Both of them think of the gryphon's penis—can Commodus's mind range in a lovelier field? She waits.

"If you can call down their powers, as Bruno instructed, perhaps you and I and Amir Cavalieri may all prosper by my obscene lust for his manuscript. I shall have a bed brought to the beasts' room."

"Shall I take it from your answer that you have not succeeded in calling down their powers?"

"I am not worthy."

"That is the key then, worthiness? Should I not fail if I am guilty of the theft you ascribe to me?"

"It depends on the purpose of your theft. The star beasts never blink and won't respond if your intent is malign. Your mother, on the other hand, is another matter. You know about the curse of Tutankhamun's tomb, of course?"

"So I have nothing to lose by sleeping in their room, since the beasts are not vengeful?"

"They are unconcerned with justice. Men praise justice because they're unjust. In the world Bruno envisioned, justice would be an artifact, like the Ten Commandments or Hammurabi's code, no longer necessary. Obviously the church didn't see a place for itself in this scheme, so it burned him. The church must have injustice. It's a primitive institution. But Bruno's room has other dangers."

"Life is more dangerous than most of us dare to admit. What we do admit is the measure of our trustworthiness."

"Now that is a truly dark view, madam. And the English, with their admit-nothing *sangfroid,* fall far short of that mark."

She smiles again. "I wish I knew as much about Chechens, senhor."

"I will say this, professor, I do not think a night with Si Lamdjed's bestiary will unhinge your mind, because I do not think your mind is as mathematical as it is, shall we say, fey. This is something I sense. I have no evidence."

"Well, that's a blessing. The Greeks, especially Aristotle, were certain of too much. Mathematics has reached the end of its Western branch line, senhor. Analysis can't go the distance. We must look elsewhere, eastward, starward and inward, and that is what you mean, I assume, when you use the word fey."

"Yes, yes, but where is that elsewhere you mention?" In his excitement he draws too close for an Englishwoman's comfort and he backs off apologetically.

"Well, perhaps I'll have some sort of answer in the morning."

"You wouldn't dare speak like this to colleagues, would you? I mean, you would be seen as a quack, yes?"

"Yes. You may take it as a compliment. There are few absolute mathematicians for this very reason. Most mathematical minds are tethered to circumstance. They are not so much pedestrian as timid."

"Is that not true of every pursuit?" he interrupts.

"I wouldn't know. In mathematics it's fatal. We are fond, for example, of saying the Arab mathematicians were hindered by their religious beliefs. That's the riff of Western historians of mathematics. But it's a gross canard, because Islam is far more receptive to the idea of vastness and infinity than Christendom. Islam is profoundly iconoclastic, exactly where great mathematics arises."

"May the star beasts respond to your purity, then, mademoiselle."

Margaret Wadeleigh flinches and stares sightless into his eyes. Who has ever called her pure? "I think you have got my number and therefore I shall have nothing to report in the morning."

"And if you had something to report, would you?"

"Not until I'd worked it out, no."

He begins polishing dials with his handkerchief, readjusting the angle of the telescope, clucking at the birds. Suddenly he wheels around to her in a salmon-sweat of embarrassment and says, "You *are* pure. The beasts will speak to you. They must."

Margaret approaches him like a statue on a dolly. Slowly she runs her fingers through his sparse hair. "Perhaps you should kill me in the morning, Senhor Da Cunha, because I know who you are."

"Otherlings always know, mademoiselle, but they don't care."

"That's so," she says.

He rings for his bald serving man, the one he calls Vasco but whose real name is Cheko Vasconcello, and orders a bed and armoire to be set up in Bruno Giordano's room. "None of my servants will guard you as closely as your own inquisitiveness, mademoiselle," he says. "If I am not here in the morning, I shall have gone to entertain your friend. Remember the Andalusian mathematicians, and when you have had enough of them, come here and listen to the sighs of the stars."

42

Muammar Qaddafi fetes them royally in huge black tents out on the Libyan desert. We are fighting the same fight, he tells the Tupac Amaru. Commodus, nodding assent, wonders sleepily what damned fight the colonel means. Is there anything on which Fat Mao and Allah might agree? In any case, he thinks, I am the only man in the tent who knows it doesn't matter because the Tupac Amaru are returning to Peru with the most gravely defective weapons I've been able to find. He sits there thinking about Giordano Bruno and Margaret Wadeleigh and Amir Cavalieri and Si Lamdjed el Ayadi, waiting for the handsome Libyan gasbag to shut up. His profit from this despicable deal will be enormous. He will blame the weapons' performance on a poor Rumanian work ethic. Seated five or six dignitaries down from the colonel, he's able to return the great leader's smile because he's at that moment fondling the thought that he's sold the Zapatistas enough fine weapons to give the Mexican generals nightmares.

On the flight from Tripoli to Cape Spartel he looks down and imagines the Arab armies, drunk on the Prophet's words, pouring across the African continent toward Spain. The weapons I sell are so primitive compared to words, he thinks. That's why he likes Bo. By listening so well he makes you think about what you are saying.

What can he say to Margaret Wadeleigh that will make a difference? She distrusts words. She trusts numbers.

"I can make you a great mathematician, not just a memorable one," he tells her when he returns to O Zonzeira. "Do you believe that, Doctor Wadeleigh?"

"No more than you do," she says.

"Ah, you see, you have just exhibited your fatal flaw. You cannot look a thing in the eye. You believe a glance catches more. Oh, I know you have that level gaze, but that's a put-on."

She chews her lower lip. Yes, it is a put-on. Bravado. Not like Dacia's straight-on look. Dacia wanted to see. But her daughter doesn't want others to see. "And just how does one look a thing in the eye?"

"Well, first of all, by seizing the spirit of my words, not the letter. If you were trying to speak a difficult thought in my native language I could catch you up, too, but it would be cheap, wouldn't it?"

"I apologize."

"Accepted. But to answer your question, you simply never run away. In fact, you go where you fear to go. Always. The weather vane always points to the storm. So, you see, you did an unmathematical thing when you met Mr. Cavalieri."

"I should have flown into that storm."

He smiles. He's presented a pretty predicament. She can keep up this thrust and parry or she can admit to herself that he's probably examined her life better than she has. She raises the ante: "I don't believe you want Amir Cavalieri's book, I believe you want us, Amir and me."

Her upper lip fights off a smile. Commodus mops his brow.

"Yes, and the pantherish Miss Compton and the savage Minihan."

Has he taken Addie and Joe?

★

There are two ways to approach mathematics or life: go right to what you suspect, like a Zen archer, or dawdle along the way, smelling the flowers, observing the wildlife, tracking, if you will. Margaret enjoys a happy ambivalence in this matter, and Commodus's description of her lover as pantherish invites her down the dawdling path. Nothing excited Margaret more than seeing Addie play basketball like a harried panther, looking for her opening. Dacia and Addie were both superb athletes, but there their similarity ended. Dacia had been the better athlete, being ruthless. Why had Bo loved her so much? Had she not yet become ruthless? What had he seen that she never showed her daughter or Colin, Margaret's father? If Bo can tell her this she will love him forever. Perhaps she will anyway. And then, unbidden and like the benediction of a madman, it comes to her: innocence, they'd tasted each other's innocence, that treasure that is purely evil to steal.

Commodus leans on the brass rail ringing O Zonzeira's heavenly probe. In its white suit his body's patience intrigues her. He's providing the hospitality her question needs. What evil was done to Dacia?

Her grandparents had the money to send her to America to escape the Luftwaffe's bombing of East Anglia. When the war was over they dawdled for a year and then plucked her like a dandelion. Later when she wished to master French they sent her to the Sorbonne. Where was the evil in such protectiveness and indulgence? Margaret sent out to the constellations of puzzlement and brought back a single word: disrespect. They didn't respect the liaisons Dacia made, her right to the friendships she made, her baptism in the dawning Americanism of things, something as simple as her passion for baseball, her love for Amir the half-breed wog. In their tribalism they could not conceive of exotics having a place in the life of their chattel. No good to say they shared this in common with most parents. It didn't make it right. They'd killed the child right then and there in a fit of righteousness in West Islip, New York, in June of 1946. They got away with murder and called their victim difficult and then clucked in self-righteousness all the way to their graves.

She sighs so hard she slumps. She had to be kidnapped to fathom this. She feels tears roll south to the tropic where she struggles and trysts with her mother's lover. Her lips form the words silently, My mother's lover. She glances at Commodus. Not many men are generous enough to hold still for someone's recollection. Yes, Dacia, I will do this for you. I will take him for you. She weeps. Now she understands. All those unindicted murderers patting themselves on the back for all they've done for their children.

43

Samothrace Crucible, a three-hundred-twenty-foot shit-pot Liberian freighter, rides at anchor in a clammy Lisbon harbor. She nowadays carries more trouble than cargo. The Policia Judiciaria wink at her because they don't want any more of it. Addie, Joe and Si Larbi sit on her poop deck watching the city's lights wink. For three days they've cased Fabrica de Ouro, returning in the evening to make sketches. The crew members slink about looking as if they were recruited in San Quentin, but near Si Larbi they skulk.

"We could parachute in at night," Addie says. "Or what about firing grapnels over the walls, I read that somewhere. Or we could sap the walls, you know, blow little holes in them, what about that?"

"Ya missed yer calling, Compton," says Joe, "the SAS would've loved ya." He humors her romantic notions of breaching The Gold Factory for the pleasure of watching her. He dandles each idea attentively. And when she has emptied her mind she looks him over and says, "Why do I have the feeling I haven't impressed the old bomber?"

"Bomber is it? What gave ya such a notion, Compton? Don't I look like yer average full-of-it barkeep?"

"You look like the second most dangerous man I've ever met."

"Well, I can't wait to meet the first, girl. Speaking of which, commandos tend to have these big budgets so the pols can dine out on their pricey incompetence, ya see. Myself, I like the simple ideas. This grandee we're dealing with, he eats by the truckload, didja notice? The kitchen traffic's a regular convoy. We need to hijack a bloody food truck. Yer legs can stop a truck,

Addie. It happens all the time on Ninth Avenue. Yer an awful menace. You stop the truck and then we'll pile on like a bunch of terrorists—we can wear ski masks or keffiyehs or Mickey Mouse masks, take yer pick—we'll strip the kitchen help and set out like a butler, housekeeper and gardener to find the fat fuck and twist his cojones till he coughs up the most dangerous man of yer acquaintance. Then we'll walk him and his guest back to the truck and figure out later where to deposit him."

"Stupid enough to work," says Si Larbi. "But we will not have time to deposit him anywhere. He is the sort of man whose death nobody wants to investigate. We may as well do the honors."

"Were you a successful terrorist, Joe?" Addie asks.

"A successful coward is what I am, which is why I'm here to tell ya, Compton. The only successful terrorists I ever knew are dead, and we're better off for it. There are the sanctioned bastards and the excommunicants, and I'm damned if I know which is better off dead."

When these squalls of remorse darken his eyes Addie wonders if she might honorably love two men. At least with Joe she's not stealing him from a friend. Rescuing him from a friend? And then loving necessarily means owning—for those of us cancered in the bone by a troubled parent. Addie is not such a one, but Margaret is.

Adeline Compton, conservator of instruments, and Joseph Minihan, retired terrorist, have much in common—but only by way of the people who threw them together. Their felicity entertains them. Part of them would like to undertake this venture without Bo Cavalieri and Margaret Wadeleigh and their relationship that's too much like hybridizing roses. A man who outlives SAS torture distrusts the big picture. The worst horrors are committed in the name of the big picture. Decency is the next best excuse.

That's why he appreciates each moment with Addie and most of them without her. Addie too has no use for the big picture. Why would she, who savors a grain of wood or the particularity of catgut?

Joe Minihan's thin lips turn down at the corners, not a good omen for torturers. His blue eyes dizzy like broken glass. His eyebrows crackle like autumn fire on a high ridge. His face is a permanent rebuke to his mock-Irish jocularity, and Addie has to beat past his banter to remember who he is, a man who has delivered suffering and has suffered horribly, a brute with a monk's heart. No one can put Joe Minihan together again. Addie longs to see a picture of him at eight or nine years, but he'd be wary if she asked. He's not one to tinker with or reassemble. Like Bo and Si Larbi, he lives now because yesterday is spoiled.

And Si Larbi, why does he bother to speak well and learn much? What does he believe? He believes in friendship, for sure. Not by any stretch could she have foreseen meeting and liking Si Larbi ben Hamrouche. There he sits moon-shot by the garbage chute of the *Crucible*, whetting a Gurkha kukri, sipping the moment. He doesn't need a future. He's as ready to die as to laugh, like Delacroix's Arabs skirmishing in the mountains. I'm happy, she thinks. How can I be happy? We could all die dumb as drunks punching taxis. Yes, we could, and I am happy.

As Si Larbi slices the air with his kukri Addie folds down to the deck cross-legged and shuts her eyes. Joe and Si Larbi draw back against the stern rail. Her breathing slows and deepens. She exhales up against her palate, loud and hollow. Her mind sails like a fragrance up the Tagus, over the southwest dome of Fabrica de Ouro, and down into its watery garden. Its exquisite sensibility arrests her. She fights to breathe and in that instant hears the place wail and sigh, feels it wince, flinch and hurt. Its emptiness moans in the heart of order and high estate. She enters by the garden's south portal, floating low over the cities of Lilliput that seem to hover like spacecraft. Statues, books, kraters, tapestries, etchings, drawings, paintings ache for touch, yet hurt with fear of it, jumpy like people who were abused. She feels no meanness, no menace, only immense loss. Much has been gathered here to redress profound grief, but it's all fallen victim to grief. This is a woman's place, and yet there are no women, no evidence of them. It's a woman's place because of the palpable fondness with which things are situated. The order of things is intuitive. And always a room or two away she senses not human forms but spiraling nebulae throwing off thoughts and feelings: Bo bemused and wary, and another, desolate and avid. Elsewhere are forms so faint they might be ghosts.

That hurt should dull such opulence confounds her. That human beings should elude—refuse? deny?—their contractual shape intrigues her. She has never encountered it. Why shouldn't they? The Sufi longs to vanish. She herself travels like a wraith. What did Darwin know of this? Tut-tut, this is hocus-pocus, Adeline. Naysayers, have a ball. Tomorrow or the next day or next week I'll come back here toting my body and choking on déja vu.

Until now she's never sensed the danger of her astral self being captured, imprisoned in the place where it has been spying. Somewhere inside the forlorn glory of Fabrica de Ouro a magnet draws her. She resists for a second and then gives in to the pull. It leads to an immense glass vault. Down from its apex hangs an emerald-studded armillary sphere made of brass, stainless steel and aluminum. At its center is the S-shaped Milky Way, Earth's neighborhood in the cosmos. Try as she might she can't find Earth in the vast throw of diamonds caught in a black plasmic cloud. The artistry of the installation stuns her. Her intrusion is a sin.

At first, because she approached the vault as a descending angel might, she doesn't notice the obsidian band turning clockwise around its parameters. The skylines of famous cities appear in their dawns and dusks, brightening, winking, and vanishing like chimera. She spots Istanbul's Santa Sophia. Then she feels a chill like a shove behind her and she looks down. Into the white marble floor of the vault two mosaic global maps have been set: the Mercator and the Peters projections. This is a visual joke. Mercator, the most widely used projection, magnifies European civilization, making Greenland, for example, larger than Africa. Peters tries to rectify this Eurocentrism. The master of this presumptuous pile in a fit of whimsy has turned the Peters projection upside down, as if to ask why not.

She begins to drift away like smoke.

When she opens her eyes Si Larbi and Joe are watching her. She shuts her eyes again to cut her silver tie to Fabrica de Ouro.

Addie seems more than ever beyond Joe, and yet closer. Her preference isn't for men. That distance can't be closed, and yet he likes it. And here's another distance. Something has happened, not just deep thought or fatigue, but Addie's true difference and secret life. A high priestess has performed a sacred ritual as if she doesn't know that oafs are watching her.

Si Larbi is transfigured. Before Islam, women like Zenobia often led the Bedouins, occasionally even after the Hejira. Now he's seen such a woman. Why do men follow buffoons like Habash and Arafat and Sharon and Eden and Eisenhower when the world's true leaders sit on the poops of rotting freighters? He doesn't know what to do, so he hands Addie the kukri. She takes it and holds it blade out between her eyes, a kind of salute. She'll never understand why she did this, but she'll always know it was the perfect thing to do.

44

"Give me a man who sniggers and brays, honks and titters, a man with a hinky laugh, Amir, and I'll give you a man from whom you should walk away backwards. Men like that have withered dicks and thorny tongues."

"I don't laugh," Amir says.

"Of course you don't. For the same reason a child doesn't step on a crack, so as not to break its mother's back."

Amir's grin spreads slowly. He feels as if he himself is Commodus, whose dour half-breed hostage has just turned over the sultan's manuscript to him.

Commodus lets out a drum roll of a laugh.

And yet how can you trust a man who has kidnapped you?

"Has it occurred to you, I wonder, that when people like you and me become what we ought not to have become the cosmos is rattled and won't settle down until we face up to this miscarriage?"

Bo grunts. You expect me to untangle that mess of words? But he understands Commodus and he stares into his face while he decides whether to speak.

"For all I know you're exactly what you ought to have become, and you're certainly what you chose to become."

"And you, Bo Cavalieri?"

"I'm not Sindbad. He had a family."

"Nor are you Odysseus lusting for his laurels and tempting the gods. No, you're a mercenary—you're not an exhibitionist. I appreciate that. Would you care to know how I became an arms dealer?"

Bo nods.

"I was the kind of person who is cut off in mid-sentence. When I opened my mouth people frisked the room for reasons not to hear. Tall people win attention without earning it. Short people have to snare it. People listen to arms dealers. They want what we're selling more than they want girls, drugs or fame. Now I'm the one man even madmen hear. You're tall—you probably never had any trouble being heard. You're severe. You don't look like a Hollywood fathead sucking on a bad idea. That helps."

"Helps what?"

"Helps you get by without having to assert yourself."

Bo remembers the people he's killed.

Commodus says, "People don't interrupt you. You'll give them short shrift and they'll like it. Me, I'll tell them exactly what they worked so hard to avoid hearing, and they know it. Of course they've got you all wrong, because you'll do the same damned thing, and you may draw it for them in case they have trouble hearing."

Bo leans forward. Yes, he knows he draws *memento mori* for people, and they usually pretend not to see what they see. But he holds his peace and waits to hear if Commodus knows it too.

"I wouldn't want you to draw anything for me, Bo. No, it would be too painful. I'll try to terrorize you into yielding lesser secrets in that magnificent book of yours, because the book has the sanction of history. You have no papers except what that Omani autocrat gave you. And that's why you hold on to the book, because it's the only authentication you've ever had. No, you have more to tell me than what's in that book, but I'm not ready to hear it and you're not willing to tell me, *ça va?*"

"If you say so."

"You, Bo, have just said a great deal: you've said you know I'm right."

Bo's surprise and malaise grow.

"Your life is about not belonging. I understand this. I've never belonged, but an arms dealer is almost everybody's new best friend. A Chechen outside of Chechnya doesn't even belong among fellow Muslims, but if he learns how to make the crazies of the world more dangerous he's welcome to pray on anybody's carpet. He can even piss on it. You and I are both auslanders, but the difference is that I have a hot eye and you, Bo, have a cold eye. I know how to make monkeys out of dickheads sitting in their clubs warming their hands at ethnic and religious campfires, strutting on balconies. I enjoy feeding them bananas. But you live in a state of grace and I'd like to know how you found it. You understand that the excluders are riffraff and so you are by nature an aristo. Aristos don't depend on pedigree. They wear their licenses on their faces."

He pours snifters of brandy. "Do you know why I called myself Commodus? He thought he could entertain the Romans out of the notion that their liberties had been taken from them. Sounds familiar, doesn't it? Oh yes, the Nuremberg rallies were much like the gladiatorial extravaganzas Commodus staged. Celebrities are dangerous people, Amir. Whether they're gladiators or airhead film stars or politicians, it doesn't matter. They take your eye off the birdie. And what is the birdie? I think, with my poor and devious brain, that we, not them, are the gods, and whoever doesn't want us to know it is the enemy. I am a puppeteer, like Commodus."

"He was strangled by a wrestler."

And when have I ever sold Kalashnikovs to anybody who knew that? Commodus wonders.

45

It's never mattered to Bo who's right, who's wrong. But he doesn't want his captor to know him better than he knows himself. Worse, he doesn't know how to say so without revealing more. Besides, it doesn't matter. Commodus da Cunha holds all the cards, except that he won't get what he wants. Bo's cold blood courses from childhood wounds. And Commodus's speech feels like rape—he has talked himself into jeopardy. Bo can kill him faster than his dolled-up retainers can get to him. Bo wouldn't leave alive, but neither would Commodus.

He's shown himself a spoilsport mouse to his captor's cat. Commodus seems to feel that if the cat's appetite is so jaded he should be allowed his meal, the better to choke on it. In any case Commodus's interest is turning from the manuscript to its keeper. "I would have wished for more sensitivity to your predicament," he tells Bo, his back turned. Bo isn't a man whose teeth you can hope to see. Neither his mouth nor his disposition are shaped that way, but now grim laughter flashes across his face, baring his teeth. Commodus turns and winces. Bo convulses in silent laughter. "I didn't mean to amuse you," Commodus complains.

"I have an outlaw humor."

"You are an outlaw, you know. Yes, you are wanted in Oman for murder. That was an Omani dhow on which you so recklessly sailed, freeing those wretched Somalis from their hope of three meals a day, enriching the beggar crew and smashing the captain's windpipe. Yes, the Omanis want your head. Well, in a desultory sort of way, I admit, and of course they'd like their manuscript even more. They're arrogant fellows. Their hauteur is rank, unlike the Afghans', which is rather jasmined."

He waits for Bo's reaction to this wordcraft. His words are so freighted Bo hardly knows which delicacy to sniff first. And so, as usual with him, he leaves them alone.

Commodus understands this. He takes great pleasure in entertaining Amir Cavalieri. Only austere audiences are worth playing to. But he doesn't yet grasp that Bo is not an audience but a witness. Bo attracts people who need witnesses. Nor does Commodus understand that he needs a witness far more than he needs Said bin Taimur's manuscript.

A crack of light zigzags across the dark of his machinations. He sees in that instant that the old beleaguered sultan grieved for Bo. He wanted that refined grief. Had the sultan seen in Bo the son he would have liked to have rather than the millennarian who deposed him, or was it something else? Had he perhaps regarded Bo as a falconer his bird? Bo invites people to measure their depths. Most of them, finding themselves wallowing, punish him for it. Bo's presence, Commodus finds, is at once reassuring and menacing, and it's up to Commodus to decide which demon to entertain. These are thoughts he wants to share with his captive, but Bo is unappreciative. Commodus doesn't like feeling like a girl—it's too easy to break whom you would enthrall. You wind up meeting a tart in the mirror.

Bo doesn't know the Chechenness of a Chechen the way he knows the Arabness of a Bedouin or the empty quarter of a sailor. Ethnography interests him the way chisels interest a sculptor. Sailing the North Sea peeled back his mind to the possibility of past lives. Off the Barbary Coast, in the Arabian Gulf—Arab places—he'd been a capable mariner, but in the North Sea he experienced a homecoming. He smelled and felt ice where radar dumbed out. He could have navigated by dead reckoning without charts. His brain filled with old rutters. The redolence of Swan's Road between Sweden and Denmark, of which the *Beowulf* poet sang, swamped him. The North Sea, that Viking lake, was all he'd ever known of joy. So it doesn't surprise him that Commodus da Cunha wears the face not of the son of the great Aurelius but of Caracalla, down to the stray left eye and the demonic cleft sweeping up from its inner corner. He has seen only heads of Caracalla, but they implied a stolid body, where Commodus's is swollen with indulgences. Cracked is the word he'd use to describe Caracalla, not mad like the beautiful Caligula but cracked and aware. What a terrible burden, knowing one's crackedness, like the manic bipolar victim sidelong observing his own antics.

As Bo sketches him Commodus speaks. "You like me, Bo. I am holding you hostage, extorting a fond possession, but you are prey to your funny bone."

How to make Caracalla's obdurate mouth wry? Commodus's words fit him exactly. He likes his hostage more than his scheme. Captor and captive fall victim to their bemusements.

★

Commodus picks up a Roman spoon from a silver tray and gazes into its rock crystal bowl as if it were a miniature mirror. This small First Century A.D. prize is his favorite possession. Its long silver shaft ends in a wicked spearhead and his imagination constellates around the spoon: praetorians, gladiators, senators, proconsuls, generals, courtesans, slaves. "You see this, Bo, it's a cochlear, a kind of spoon. They came in lavish sets. Imagine the fingers that must have held this gem, the mouths into which this almost perfect crystal slid, the lips that closed upon it. Imagine! I am a man who appreciates such things."

"Where did you steal it?"

"A museum actually. It was never reported. They always worry about their insurance. They don't like to admit they're bureaucratic oafs."

★

How to make Caracalla's resolute mouth wry?

Bo paces the outskirts of Commodus's immense study, oiling a black statuette of Anubis with his fingers, stopping before an Haute Provence tapestry depicting the apocryphal encounter of Richard Lionheart and Saladin. For once Commodus keeps his peace, seeing that the tapestry shows the split in Bo's persona, knights of impossibly different realms, each other's admirer and mortal enemy. Bo for his part is trying to decide whether to dredge from his hermit soul the will and the breath to say something Commodus might just have ears to hear. He turns and faces his captor ceremoniously, both of them unsure anything will escape Bo's lips.

"I hear that writers edit when they fear to write," he begins slowly. "Artists draw, poets teach, politicians lie, you collect what people make. You should collect people. I'm a start. You don't want the manuscript, you want the person a sultan thought worthy of it. You want the impulse, Commodus." As he speaks Bo remembers that long ago he'd told a girl something similarly forlorn: You have a grand compulsion to be offended by me.

When Bo begins to speak Commodus is beheading a cigar with a pocket guillotine. Now he chucks the project into a wastebasket. When Bo began to speak Commodus's face was an imperium. Now little by little it's sacked by vandal words. Trying to clear his throat, he pours some more Metaxa and offers it to Bo. When Bo waves it off Commodus gulps it down. Perhaps a homily will ward off the chaos of what Bo said.

Unconvinced, Commodus says, "The trouble with capitalism is that it reduces everything to a horse race. It insists on winners and losers. What does the bestseller list have to do with book reviews or merit? It belongs on the business pages of newspapers, does it not? It's a marketing report. Why should books be regarded as race horses? It's an abdication of the very task of reviewing, isn't it? Given this stupidity of charts and lists and top tens, everyone is disheartened. Why write if you can't win, sell big, be someone? Why paint or sing or dance? Of course the answer is that the top ten of anything is usually crap, but that's cold comfort to the artist, isn't it? Your view is a bit too hard on the individual, Bo. What we hail as egalitarian is really degenerate."

Bo turns his back on Commodus and looks out on the Tagus blushing in the sun.

"Yes, Bo, I am bullshitting, as you say, in order to distract myself from the pain of what you say. Yes, I am interested primarily, solely I should say, in the rare light that arcs between people and makes them so much more than they seem to be. And how does one collect that? What lepidopterist can pin that down and preserve it? That is what that apocryphal tapestry is about, is it not? You are right, but so what, since what you suggest is impossible?"

"I think you don't know yet if it's impossible, Commodus, and that's why you haven't coerced me, because if you did, that arc wouldn't fly, would it?"

Bo remembers the *Meditations* by Marcus Aurelius aboard the Heinkel. "I see that you are teaching yourself to collect the arc."

"Do you remember your Roman history?"

"Some," Bo says.

"Commodus was an unworthy successor. He shamed his father's name. I had a perfectly good Chechen name. Ruslan Udaev. I could have given myself a wonderful name. But I thought that this name would chasten me. I have been like Commodus, entertaining the mob with violence. And the surname, Da Cunha, would . . . well, it would fit in here and remind me that one cannot round the horn without minding the shoals."

"Why didn't you call yourself Caligula, that would've chastened you. Still, I have to admit Commodus is a good name for an arms dealer."

"I took this name only recently. Murderers don't care what you call yourself. They call themselves any damned thing that comes into their heads—patriot, holy warrior, liberator, freedom fighter, prophet, visionary, crusader—and the press dutifully plays along because it recognizes fellow hypocrites. I became Commodus when I realized that I was an angry, ignorant orphan masquerading as a grownup."

46

Selling Kalashnikovs and Katyushas in a nattery jungle, an exhausted Eritrean plain or the Cecil Hotel in Alexandria is a simple affair: Endless supply from the world's biggest liars, endless demand from the world's biggest phonies. *Balkan Wars* never departs such company bereft. Such monsters never elicit nostalgia. But as *Balkan Wars* lifts off the Moroccan headlands and Commodus considers how to tell Bo that he's taken Margaret hostage, he is ravished by the nostalgia for them he knows he'll feel when they're gone, when he'll sit fondling *Al Kitab as Sirr* alone, when that arc of which he'd spoken will have eluded him forever. They want nothing from him and yet give him the rich hours of an Eleanor of Aquitaine, a Haroun al-Rashid.

This deal has a defect he can't cure because no one wants what it can produce. You do hear that, Ruslan, he tells himself over the harmonics of the plane's engines: you do hear that no one, especially you, wants what this deal can produce?

What I want, he tells frightened little Ruslan, what I want— he sees Ruslan shiver in the dark corner of a Chechen hovel— what I want is a bit of cognac.

He sits like a punctured balloon, gazing down dejectedly at the up-rush of the Iberian peninsula.

Hrumph, hrumph, hrumph, *Balkan Wars* says as she grumps down to her landing. Hrumph yourself, you old battle-ax. It's not your damned deal going sour. All you ever had to do was shit on frozen Ivans. You don't even have to put up with flak any more. What do you have to put up with, Commodus? Well, for one thing, never getting over your misfortunes. Why have you arranged for me to have no friends? Ruslan asks. Friends are for fools, you little innocent.

"Friends are for fools," he tells Cheko Vasconcello when the servant opens the door of his Bentley. "You don't agree, Cheko?"

"I'm sorry there was turbulence," his servant says.

"Yes, of course, Hercules was poking at his pillars, Cheko, that's why I'm in such a bad mood."

★

Chess pieces are hidden in plain sight. O Zonzeira and its pawn are off the board. To prompt Bo to make his mortal move Margaret must be brought to Fabrica de Ouro. This is chess. "Stop, Cheko—stop."

The Bentley is poised to drive off into space. To keep its footing it will have to turn left, towards Fabrica de Ouro. Commodus gets out. He knows this is one of those interstices of time. The trick is to sense the interstice, to dress yourself in it for a moment. Bringing Margaret to Fabrica de Ouro will . . . Let me see, the man could kill me in a flash, but the worst thing is that I would fall out of grace with them, with myself. Am I in their good graces?

Cheko sits behind him on a rock, like a toad. The answer arrives on the wind, not to his question, but to his dilemma. What is the first rule in arms dealing? Is there a first rule? Of course not. If there were, deals would never be made. Each situation is as mad as its participants. You can't execute a game plan because the thousand exigencies inherent in every deal won't fit the plan. You can't stick to a plan. You have to wait for inspiration, which usually means apprehending the other person's madness. Never mind what the person wants. That's obvious. It's his sickness you have to apprehend. Then you know how to make the deal. Put Margaret in peril, or even show Amir Cavalieri that you have put her in peril, and you lose this game, Commodus. What you want is what arcs between you and Amir, you and Margaret, what can arc between you, what arced between Sultan Said bin Taimur and a sea bum. He listens to the wind for more. Let the game play out. I am not a player. I am playing the players. Do

I understand this? Is it a trick of mind, something that sounds more intelligent than it is? I don't know.

"Cheko, when you drop me off, go back to the airstrip. Take *Balkan Wars* back to O Zonzeira. Fetch the English lady. If she is not ready to come—I invited her to examine certain things there—come at her pleasure. Treat her with the utmost graciousness, Cheko. Understand?"

47

"You have had contact with great wealth before, Amir," he says at dinner. "Peter Tomlinson, then the sultan, and now me. I almost get the sense that you like to watch others enjoying it, if you like them, because instinctively you know that it's more dangerous than an enemy with his face painted black."

"I know money's not benign."

"I should say not. Coin of a phony realm. I laugh when reporters speak of the money trail as if their publishers had the stomach to really follow it."

He planned uplifting conversation, but it turns jaded, and he falls into remorseful silence.

"I've learned something about you while you were gone, Commodus. Your desires are chaste. They don't run to nymphets or the ill fortune of enemies but to a Redon vase of flowers, a deluxe *Le Bateau Ivre,* illuminated Celtic and Arabic manuscripts, Kyoto and Toledo steel, the reports of a caliph's emissary to the Vikings of the Danube, an obscure Arab's report on the Viking fiasco at Seville, Chinese and Korean moveable type, and God knows what you haven't let me see."

"God may well know what," Commodus replies, "but we have an arms-length relationship. You must have learned classical Arabic to know what happened to the Vikings at Seville."

No sooner he says it than his queerest notion rises to the top of his steamy brain: He collects these ancient marvels for a select group of disguised aliens, for their delectation, to entertain them while they wait impatiently for the dawning of a super race with whom they might have something in common. It's a modest job, a niche in the sacred scheme, but the aliens appreciate it.

Until now this was his queerest notion, but now another toots jauntily down a trough of his Alpine brain. Suppose Amir Cavalieri has come in the best disguise yet? Nothing in the Bible exceeds the idea that we traffic with angels unaware. Angels and aliens, is there a difference? So what if this profane sailor is loitering in the predawn of a better race? What if Said bin Taimur identified him? What if the secrets are not in the book but in the events the book inspires? What if the book down through the centuries has been doing just that? Well, that would be it, wouldn't it? The thing I want. The thing I've now been told to want.

Bo watches the shadows of an F.W. Murnau film cross the face of his host. Perhaps Commodus has to be drawn in the Cubist style that reminds us that a world without shadows would be nothing but an operating room.

"Has it ever struck you, Amir, that you look rather like a Lehmbruck?"

"Not as psychotic as a Giacometti, you mean? On second thought, neither. Etruscan, I'd say."

An autodidact for the sake of conversation might say Giacometti, but an alien would say Etruscan because Etruscans haunt a great civilization, Rome, and aliens would prefer such a long view. Yes, I've smoked him out. He's an autodidact, nothing more. Still, an alien would say my desires are chaste. An alien might appreciate the little Redon, the story of Vikings lynched outside the walls of Arab Seville.

"Calvados? You like Calvados and Cohibas, Amir?"

"I told you I don't drink any more. But I'll take a Cohiba, and if not that, a White Owl."

"A white owl?"

"You're spoiled, Commodus. A White Owl is a cheap smoke when you're damn near broke."

"But you're not damn near broke, Amir. You're rich. Not as rich as me, but quite comfortable—if you sell your book. Are we haggling? Have I simply not yet named your price?"

Commodus, he tells himself, if Amir is an alien he must be allowed to see everything. The aliens have no hierarchy.

They are what they become at will. I should take him to O Zonzeira to see the manuscripts, the great telescope. He should see the armillary vault, the projections. No, not the vault. I must have something to withhold, something I don't wantonly throw down at his feet like a bookish boy trying to appease a bully. The vault is the one thing he would wish to see. He's a navigator, and he may be one even among the aliens. But there are other things to show him.

"I want to show you treasures you can never see elsewhere, Amir. I want to show you, not damned curators with their idiotic zeal for fossilizing things."

They trail blue smoke as they drift from room to room, listening to the murmur of the waterways, their cities and fountains, looking at paintings.

"This, this is . . . "

"Bosch, yes," Commodus says. "It disappeared during the war. I'm sure it was soiled by Reichsmarschall Goering's hooves. He would have been drawn to the women's bellies."

"And this, this isn't the Metropolitan's *Toledo.*"

"They would challenge its authenticity because it has been in a private collection for centuries. It's priceless. I think it's better than the one in the Metropolitan, don't you? It's not as cerebral."

Bo can't define Commodus's curatorial strategy. "You've put each of these works . . . "

"Where it belongs! It will tell you if you listen. Curators don't listen. They impose. They're dolts. They follow a dogmatic plan."

Seeing Bo is rapt, he elaborates. "The world would be so much more exciting if they put each work according to its wont. It would be a more dangerous world. Did you know that the wont of a work of art changes over time? Oh yes, the artist has gone on—the work doesn't have to listen to him anymore. You have no idea how unhealthy it has been for us to arrange everything according to Aristotle's boxy mind. It means everything is in the wrong place, imprisoned, angry, bitter. The world has been poisoned by curatorial misconduct. That includes the media,

Amir. These nitwits are telling us that what is best is what sells. They are telling us they have the courage to bring us the truth when they are bringing us curated lies."

"You're preaching to the choir, Commodus. It's your curatorial misconduct that keeps me here. I'm imprisoned, not according to my wont, as you put it."

Their parrying stumbles on buried ordnance. Caught in a dicey piece of hypocrisy, Commodus wings it: "Could we not consider my indefensible behavior an invitation to collaborate?"

★

Seeding the world with explosives, Commodus has learned a great deal about human nature. He's learned, for example, that people who can't wait for you to finish speaking have an incurable illness. He's learned that people who don't feel they owe you an answer are more reliable than those who do. He's learned that the less said about anything the better. He's learned the world is not a void one needs to fill. So he watches Bo going about his usual business of saying nothing, and he turns over in his mind what to do next.

I have become aware, he might say, by virtue of enjoying your company, that no persuasion, however cogent, will induce you to send for the book, even though I am prepared to turn it into untaxable wealth for you. So I have taken something of greater value from you. You cannot live, Amir, with what I have done unless you give me the book. And even under these circumstances, in which you have no choice, I will make you rich.

That's what he might say. He might tell Bo he has taken Margaret Wadeleigh. But Bo, who didn't think twice about killing a slaver and redistributing his booty, would say to himself, This guy has got to kill us. He's gone too far, he's got to kill us. Unless I kill him. That's what Bo would think. And then this exquisite operation would become a charnel.

48

Joe Minihan thinks of women's looks as dandelions, glories on the manicures of life, accidental and celebratory. Of men's good looks he's a bit chary. Bo Cavalieri thinks women creatures of another realm, more dangerous than men. By the time his trials enable him to look on them with dispassion he no longer cares—they might as well be crown vetch by the road. Where were they when he was raped, hung, shot at by strangers, savaged by drink? They didn't even blink. He isn't women's business.

Addie thinks it grace that men like Joe and Bo still think about women at all. She's pleased to talk about her legs, as if they're tools in a bag of tricks. She never has any doubt as to whose they are. When she purses her lips to signal Joe she's willing to flash them to stop a truck she wants time not to consider the plan but to enjoy the difference between Joe's paean and Bo's touch. Or is it the similarity? Bo said nothing of her looks and yet she knows they please his pores like incense. What a pity that she can't make a single lover of Joe and Bo and Margaret. Surely there's a world in which she might.

"Well, Adeline, what is it then? Are we gonna clean this fat fuck's clock and rescue the most dangerous man or what?"

For a moment Addie likes the thought of her triune lover more than the thought of rescuing a third of the whole. "Yes, let's get one of them," she says.

"One is all I was thinkin' of, girl. To tell the truth, I have no use for either one, but since you do we'll get this cavalier guy, okay?"

"You're the cavalier, Joseph."

"What is he then, since I'm riskin' my neck for him?"

"The grim reaper, I think."

"Well, that's two of us. It's strange taste ya have in men, Compton. Bad guys, I'd say. Yer sure yer not a little bit Irish? Because bad taste in men is an Irish preserve, ya know."

"It's entirely English to prefer one's men bloody, Joseph."

"Adeline, ya may be more dangerous than yer pleasant Limey looks suggest, which for sure is an English trait."

Addie studies him with a detachment that invokes a thousand years of Anglo-Irish troubles.

She'd like to continue this banter, but she's fallen down into some cold pit of soul where she's never been and there she contemplates her life. She passes from fixer to maker, maker of what? The answer will occur to her as certain fixes to instruments do. She thinks of the poet Yeats singing,

Cast a cold eye,
On life, on death,
Horseman, pass by.

Merlin had a special place, his crystal cave, and this is hers. Yes, Mutawakkil whispers, you are more dangerous than your looks suggest, and your special place is not in your taste for people but in your contemplation of those you have chosen and those who have chosen you.

And then, standing hidden among trees in view of The Gold Factory, she hears a sing-song exultation that feels like death: there is no God but God, the battle cry of the Saracen horde, lances lowering, curved swords flashing in the sun, falling on Europe like the firmament. Suddenly she understands the seemingly nonsensical cry, No God but God. It means, doesn't it, that she needs no one, nothing but God? And whoever or whatever doesn't matter, as all will be revealed as surely as wood reveals its will, an instrument its true sound, the one it had before the world's bafflements undid it. Nor does it matter why an Arabic truth comes to a Midlands girl, or why an Arab interlocutor and not, say, Merlin, instructs her. She stands next to Joe Minihan feeling the ecstasy of Bernini's Saint Teresa. How has the inner meaning of Islam—surrender—fallen into her hands? She has walked right on past its famous iconoclasm

221

to embrace its truth: we have come to worshiping each other in our tragic emptiness, stupefied by celebrity.

"I can't hear a damned thing with you prattling on," she blurts at Joe.

They stare at each other in shock. Then the preposterousness of her words tickles him and they burst out laughing.

"Can ya hear a damned thing now?"

She shoves his shoulder playfully and they step back deeper among the trees, contemplating The Gold Factory and their next move.

★

Does the luthier hear the sound before he makes the lute? She's spent much of her life wondering what he heard. Imagination calls a thing into existence. She knew that long before she read Ibn al-Arabi. But can a God lonely without us be God? What does The Gold Factory with its jittery pennants want? You are the pot and I'll stir you, she tells Commodus's conceit. Tell me what you want, but who's to say it will be good? Is the alchemist to stand over the pot and ask it what it wants? What a crock! How did it come by its ingredients? She holds out her hands, fingers flirting with fingers, and can't tell their etheric field from the dusk. She turns them up and then—whose hands are more searching than a conservator's?—she feels the prima materia of the situation falling like mist through them, raining on The Gold Factory, on what will come. She shudders with the strangeness of the moment when Joe, staring at her hands, whispers, "I don't know if I could love you if you let me."

Any other woman would answer him according to her nature, but Addie's nature is not her own. She's a changeling, and changelings don't respond to us. She answers strange calls and this cavalier of hers must be of her ilk if he's slept with her. Yes, she won't raise just any man's blood no matter how lovely he thinks she is. Joe's amazed he's not seen this before. Whatever Addie sees with that long, untroubled look, it's not any man Joe Minihan knows, nor does he want to know him. Changelings are not for nothing. An Irishman knows.

If I would let him love me? Would I? Where is the man to fill my head with himself and drive off my preoccupations? Not Bo. I slept with him the way Alexander cut the Gordian knot. It's what occurred to me. Do I love him? What has that to do with anything? We're for each other. Our bodies work in each other's hands, our minds sing to each other. I prefer a woman, but I chose him. He rises to no woman, but he rises to me, and I know as sure as my hands know wood he will again. That's what I know of love. And yet Joe Minihan has plucked a chord I never heard before, a terrorist's chord. Can these men decompose, return to atoms and pour out through my hands outstretched, untouched by my imagination? Is this an alchemist's task? And is this what Joe has just now seen that chills his own cold blood? He's a man of cool appraisals and he'd be dead if he'd been wrong too often.

"They tell me being Irish is like belonging to a club with secret rules, like the Masons," he says with a wink. "Being Italian or Russian or Spanish, that's an accident. But being Irish is like striking the perfect chord on a harp, that's what I hear from the dingbats at the bar. It's the curse of the damned fool Irish that they believe such swill."

"It's the curse of any people to believe they're special, Joe."

He likes wiping glasses. It's the best thing about bartending, the wiping and mopping up and polishing. It gives him time to meditate.

Addie sees that he's dredging and she waits.

"I know when someone is important to me because I dream about such people," he says at last.

"But our dreams are like Japanese sand painting—we're trying to order our minds."

"When you deal with the Brits, Addie, if you'll excuse me, you learn to pay no mind to what people say. One night I dreamed I was standing beside a lorry talking to this guy. I looked up to the top of a mountain and I saw a woman riding a bike along the crest of it, right to left. I knew who she was, I did. Fancy that, I sez to myself in my dream. Being it's my dream, I could say anything, right? Well, I think about it now like this:

you couldn't see anybody at that distance, and even if you could, you damn sure wouldn't recognize them. But I did, and I've been looking for that woman ever since, and I'll recognize her when I see her."

"And if by then you're married and have kids, you'll just say to your wife, Oh there's the woman on the bike, see you later."

"She's the only woman I'm ever gonna marry, the one on the bike."

"But you wouldn't tell her you'd seen her before, would you, Joe? And so she might slip away in the wink of an eye."

"How'd you know that then, Compton?"

Joseph Minihan stares at Adeline Compton as if he's never seen her before. He hasn't. She's amazed the words have tumbled off her tongue. He smooths her right eyebrow with his forefinger, like a parent sending a girl off to school. His touch slows her heart and her translucent eyelids fall over her startled eyes.

"Shush," he says.

"We should carry out your plan," she says at last. "I'll find a short, tight skirt and some spiky heels. What do I do with my hands?"

"Ya wave both of them like a helpless ditz and then ya point to yer car with its bonnet up. I'll see it makes a little steam."

49

The locals think the name Commodus gave his palazzo the offal of a rich man's wit. They couldn't have known the name refers to his larger ambition because at first he didn't know it. He couldn't have known he would be the second rich man in Bo's life to work blindly under the spell of an alchemical dream. He couldn't know that alchemy's catalyst is flesh and bone. Peter Tomlinson, unlike Commodus, recognized that human chemistry is the catalyst that turns dross into gold: finding a trace of glory in an unlikely man and using it to transform him. What Tomlinson didn't know is that he wasn't in charge. Once the old sultan saw Bo's true nature, a path opened straight to The Gold Factory and Commodus da Cunha. Alchemy is to give up the illusion of control, to see that control is against one's nature, a defense against what wants to come.

Tomlinson was born to wealth and station, Commodus to Cossack rapists and Chechen misery. Tomlinson was born in charge; Commodus knows that power is in giving others the illusion of it. But now his dupes dishearten him. To allow them to go on ruling the world is despicable. His own success is in picking his dupes. He chooses not the greedy shits picking the pockets of small investors, not the jerks who pay ten dollars for a Rolex on Times Square, but dictators, generalissimos, presidents-for-life, smarmy Swiss bankers, bloody-handed ideologues, and God-blathering dimwits. Commodus's mother used an AK-47 on her three Red Army rapists when they'd drunk enough to think they'd tamed a Chechen leopard. Then she fled with Commodus to Turkey. Peter Tomlinson's mother assuaged her emptiness ahorse and left Peter to nannies and the perversions of the British public school so that he could entrust his sexual self only to his sister Moira, while Moira could toy with the likes of Bo Cavalieri safe in the nest of brotherly love. It had been the exquisiteness of their relationship that moved Bo to leave. He revered ingenious arrangements, but he wasn't like Picasso—he couldn't despoil what he'd drawn. Peter and Moira invited him into their charmed circle, a solution as good if not better than lesbian love, and it overawed him. He regarded Peter and Moira as magical creatures. He'd been prepared to love them, but his coarseness intruded. For them Bo would have been their charm against a world that had already harmed them.

He was as a captive in Commodus da Cunha's hands deeply indebted to Moira Sayre and Peter Tomlinson. They'd approved him unconditionally and shown him that the path imagined can be followed. He knew that Peter lived indebted to him for finding the *Sao Tiago*, the first intact caravel wreck. He read as much in *The New York Times,* the famous writer-explorer crediting a vagrant seaman with this important find.

Now he entertains the notion that if he could introduce Commodus to Moira and Peter he might give them all the slip while they delighted in his gift. Yes, that would be like the Bo Cavalieri I know, but is it the man I'd like to be? I attract Malay cooks, Omani divers, sultans, dilettantes, balloon men and chestnut vendors for a reason. But if there's no reason, isn't it up to me to make one? And doesn't that means staying put, my anathema? Margaret always stayed except when she ran into me. Then she did what I do and ran. So I must be what I run from? He chuckles. Commodus studies him. "I'm laughing because I can't leave and it's what I do best."

"Yes, yes, I understand that perfectly, Amir. I do. But you may leave at any time. Just allow me to make you rich first."

★

Now Commodus has an inspiration. "You know, I became an arms dealer because people interrupted me in mid-sentence."

"It would have been easier to say less."

Commodus enjoys this economy of words. He's met

it among Kirghiz and Bedouins, but unhappily it excites his garrulity. "Yes, yes, of course, but when I say interrupt I mean they look away, they glance at their watches, they spot someone they know across the room."

Bo empathizes with this forlorn report. He knows there's more than the long and the short of it. Commodus longs for the gravitas that comes naturally to some men and women. He's imprisoned Bo for it. "Being tall is probably better than being short, Commodus, but I doubt his officers or enemies found it much help in dealing with Alexander."

"This wisdom, Amir, where did you get it? You've read the book, after all, haven't you?"

He looks at his captor so bleakly that Commodus wonders if the falcon has survived its captivity. This man has been ready to die all his life and is simply looking for the right moment. On the other hand, he'll give the book up for a busboy or a prostitute. He's researched his captive well. The man supports a poor German barmaid and her son because he liked her lover. This man will not give me his book.

Commodus thinks of Dostoevsky's Prince Myshkin. A citric pleasure fills his nostrils: the story of Bo's sentimentality about Lakhdar the Moroccan guest boy and Ute-Britt Broghammer the barmaid, is better than anything *Al Kitab as Sirr* might offer. What secret could taste better than this little madeleine? It makes Dostoevsky's idiot seem pompous. It's exquisite because it's secret. Surely it ought to be celebrated, illumined by a caliph's calligrapher. Said bin Taimur, the irascible sultan, had not known this about Bo. He, Commodus, has troubled to learn it, and without him it would be lost. The future of the race is hidden between its lines.

"One must learn to cherish the sobrieties of age," Commodus said. "For example, I never wondered why old men are called old farts, but one day I realized it was because they do muchly fart. In fact the whole problem of inflating the body with air could be addressed by simply shutting one's mouth. Think of the benefits to the capitals of the world."

"Yes, it's almost as good as practicing what you preach."

"Touché, Amir. Do you think silence might be the primal goo, the great elixir?"

"I haven't read that far."

"How far have you read?"

"I don't think the truth is extortionable. If you want to turn anything from base to precious you have to start with yourself. I got that from Al Razi. You don't need me or the book to tell you that, which tells me you want its market value, nothing else."

Commodus wags his forefinger in front of Bo, shaking his head, but Bo is undeterred.

"I met a man in Alexandria once," Bo says, "who had a fabulous library. Many of his books were first editions. He had an uncut and signed edition of Walt Whitman's *Leaves of Grass*. He had Hart Crane's *The Bridge* with Crane's marginal notes."

He's rehearsed telling Commodus this. It's what he would have told a good man. He tries to finish the story, but his lips stick. The proper moment comes for him to know that almost no one can remember him speaking or the sound of his voice.

The story is what he'd have told a good man and now Commodus tries to deserve it. "You are like a Bedouin traveling the Sahara at night—you can't even remember the sound of your own voice. If I were a beggar or a whore you would share your thoughts with me instead of bandying this way. The old Omani tyrant saw an emir in you."

"And that's what you want, his fancy about a stranger?"

Commodus looks thunderstruck. "Fancy?"

They stare at each other seeing only the tumbling meteor showers of their thoughts flashing. They're no longer certain of their stations: captor, captive, arms merchant, merchant seaman, aliens in all places, both of them the dark other, strivers for footing, fellow fools. Their eyes slide down their guarded fronts and rest on a lectern between them, and they laugh. Peter Tomlinson and Moira Sayre belong. Taimur bin Said belonged. Ute-Britt Broghammer and Adeline Compton and Margaret Wadeleigh belong, but Commodus and Amir do not, and they laugh.

50

"Your thoughts, Amir, are cleaning my paintings, watering my gardens, aerating my water. Every moment each of us has a chance to change the world, but over and again we choose powerlessness while seeking power. What an insane paradox! We are co-operators of the cosmos, preferring to piss on God's leg. Can you imagine his sadness? No wonder the poles are shifting and the polar caps melting."

Commodus sits in a cavern of bookshelves drawing on a hookah on a silver tray. Bo has found him out and it makes his Margaret Wadeleigh trump card useless. He sits watching Bo. Probably Bo has put this much together: Commodus keeps his retainers in other rooms, inviting Bo to kill him. What conclusion is there except that captor cares as little about his life as captive? Under such circumstances, what's the importance of the game? Commodus, in his frustration, has flown Margaret to Fabrica de Ouro. Now she roams the northeast quarters of the villa fondling the mathematical treatises he has commended to her. But what to do? He's chosen to sing to Amir Cavalieri, not songs but ideas with their own tonalities and melodies.

And Cavalieri listens because he recognizes an old dilemma—listening to the truth from the wrong person. Like all victims of ancient abuse, he either over-reacts or under-reacts. He can't hit the mark. Commodus da Cunha has lifted a huge bloc of truth from the cosmic shelf, but he's the wrong person in the wrong circumstance. There are no plummy British movies to consult, so Bo stands by a far window watching Commodus's smoke haunt the books until some handy thought falls into his hands. But all his thoughts hang up.

And Commodus sings another aria. "Hubris, Amir, the great affliction. Only the mad, like your friend the Macedonian, can get away with it. We must step back from this brink, my friend, and see how we may save each other without killing each other. That is the civilized thing to do, don't you agree?"

"I'm not civilized, Commodus. I never had the luxury. Did you?"

"No, Amir. So won't it be a shame if this comes to nought? Neither of us fear death. That's right, isn't it? Haven't we discovered that about each other? But perhaps we have a modest little reason to give each other for living. You say you never had the luxury. Let me hear about this, Amir."

Bo's incredulous stare strides across the room straight into Commodus's face.

"Now, tell me truly, how many bad guys do you know who really want to hear about your childhood? That's part of my charm. I like people's stories and so do you. How many drawings have you made of me and my minions? I'm tempted to let you keep your book in exchange for them. But that would be rude, as it would impose a disordering choice on you. Yes, you need your drawings to cope with your life."

"You can't charm me with your civility, Commodus."

"Then let me charm you with an inestimable gift, a truth you would never otherwise stumble upon. Civilization rests in each person's hands moment to moment."

"Gimme a cigar, Commodus, I wanna celebrate that one. I dunno that I'd say D'Annunzio smells like hyacinths, but he was pretty good grappa when I was a kid." He laughs from his groin up. Commodus joins the laughter and chokes on his hookah. Camaraderie fills the library. "You're a capitalist, Commodus, the worst kind."

"There are no good *ists* of any kind, Amir. They're all stooges. I used to think myself an anarchist. I sell to ideologues and thugs—is there a difference? But ideologues are pointy and bristly, and I'm a nice round zero. Haven't you noticed? I make ends meet, but ideologues are committed to making sure they never meet. Devils and angels are bad, Amir. They have no mercy on us muddlers. Don't you think it's really impossible to sail under your true colors past the age of fifty-one?"

"Yes."

"And then there is you, Amir. How old are you, fifty-two? Still flying your own flag. A marvel. And only I have the connoisseurship to know it. Surely we ought to celebrate this. I am prepared to reward you. Why should you not reward me? Because I'm wily? Rich? Or because I tell you the truth and you have never known from which mouth you are prepared to accept it?"

Bo feels like a ship lit with Saint Elmo's fire. The hairs of his flesh turn to catch the wavelengths of the moment. Bogeys and genuine menaces blip on his screen. His sonar relays the signatures of unrecognizable submerged propellers. On total alert, he senses everything and can identify nothing, a superb ship of the line whose combat intelligence has gone dyslexic. He has all the information and insight he needs to act. He stands like a hawk over the instant between decision and action where men and their plans die—that heat-wavering instant that the young Macedonian Alexander never knew. Commodus watches the hawk stoop. He rejoices to have lived to watch it. He's finally contrived to put his life in danger. God is merciful, God is compassionate, God has granted this nailed-and-glued-together man the privilege of drawing his fate out of his hookah, of handing it to a magus, a captive djinni.

Commodus resumes his song. "Every treasure has a dark side, Amir. Do the Elgin Marbles belong in London? Does Philip the Arab belong in the Metropolitan? Does Nefertiti belong in Berlin? Museums do not exist to share beauty with the masses. They are the outbuildings of avarice. They are the cover stories for pillage. My wealth stems not from Comrade Kalashnikov, who lives modestly in a Leningrad flat, nor from any other genius. No, it owes entirely to the shabby shamus in me ferreting out the sickness in people. Take your sickness, Amir, it is not that you were a drunkard and may be one again, nor that you have been amnesiac. No, your sickness is a dead child—Dacia, who died to you or rather was killed before your eyes when you were both eleven. She is the light without which you stumble in the dark. She is all you know of how a person ought to be. Had she not lived and laughed with you, you would be dead many times over—in Korea, at sea, off the East African coast, in Manhattan gutters, in the black East River. And now I have her doppelganger, her daughter Margaret. Checkmate, my friend."

51

The green of Bo's eyes clenches around his pupils. Commodus watches Bo's fingers assume a tae-kwon-do urgency. The thin lips draw back against the teeth. Commodus is exhilarated and saddened at the same time. He likes the danger but doesn't want to be killed by someone he wishes to befriend. "My operatives vacuumed her into a limousine at two a.m. six nights ago. A morbid fascination with her mother's leavings, perhaps? She's a mathematician of considerable repute. Yes, quite a reputation for such a flowery girl."

His tone is likely to get him killed. He sounds arch when he's nervous.

"You should be flattered to be under surveillance by such a one. And you and I know she isn't the only woman interested in you. There is that athletic squall who tossed my operative about."

Bo smiles in spite of himself. He likes that description of Addie. It might be nice to live long enough to tell her.

Commodus, on his part, given Bo's body stance, thinks it might be nice to live long enough to bring his hostages together.

"Here Bo, have this wonderful Cohiba while I run a little errand."

★

She steps through the doorway the way the Primavera would quit Botticelli's painting. The sight of her gut-punches Bo. All he can think is that he wants to breathe the air around her. And then he feels someone else's eyes, not bearing down on him in obsession but sizing up the situation. He turns towards two swinging doors upholstered in red and sees a shadow passing in the crack between them. He turns back to Margaret. She stands with her arms limp beside her. The elegant turn of her wrists, caught in light from a recessed lamp above, makes him conscious of a sob. To sob and not think of Dacia is a new sensation.

Commodus feels it first. The air quavers, currents stitch the seams of their clothing, wet spring air breaches windows closed to the winter outside, and Commodus senses against all reason the lifting of the siege of contempt his father laid upon him.

The posh doors swing wide and in seconds a Glock 9mm is under his palate. He recognizes the clarity of Amir Cavalieri's vision.

Joe Minihan, decked out as a Zouave, the uniform of Commodus's housemen, chucks Commodus's chin with the Glock, stares at Bo and says, "Yer the most dangerous man in Adeline Compton's life, then?"

The air ionizes, metal-acrid. Everything is new. Commodus feels like dancing. In a smart world we'd dance at our funerals. He'd dance without Joe's pistol freezing him. He looks at Bo and sees consternation. "Well, are you, Bo?" he says. "That is an arc I should like to collect."

His mind, a merry-go-round, has slipped its gears, each thought faster and more gleeful. A rescue is in progress. Will someone get killed after all? Will I? He lecherously pinches the bottom of this thought.

★

"Si Larbi ben Hamrouche! What contemplated atrocity prompts this unexpected honor?" he asks.

"The fathers of hell always ask rhetorical questions," Si Larbi remarks to Joe.

"Mr. Ben Hamrouche," Commodus tells Margaret, "is one of the few giants left from the fatal marriage of angels to human maidens. The rest have long since become evil spirits like myself."

She notices Si Larbi himself seems interested in this aside.

Surely this is better than lecturing dummies, Margaret thinks, even if it gets us killed. All the action heroes in the world from Ulysses to Antar to Beowulf to their Hollywood facsimiles are used-car salesmen compared to these ghouls.

There's Addie, as if she were dribbling a basketball, looking for a hole. There's Joe fondling the Glock, Si Larbi with arms crossed like a fabled djinni, and Bo taking in Addie's presence. Margaret notices that her own effect on Bo is breathtaking, while Addie's effect is fond and calming.

What is this like? Like? Likening is a cheap way of thinking. Not a mathematician's way. But it's seductive, and so the answer comes all the same: it's like the mysterious Eugene Atget's photo friezes of a lost Paris. The viewer stumbles on a hole in time.

Commodus looks at Margaret. She hears a theremin. She looks at Bo to see how he'd capture the scene. He'd do what eluded Atget, he'd reduce it all—Les Halles, Le Trianon, and this masque—to an economy of line. She smiles a goofy Dacia smile at him. But he and Commodus are listening to something: one of Bruno's star beasts. Yes, one of them is in the room. Commodus called Margaret pure because he knew that only a mathematician, only a certain kind of mathematician, understands the word. Margaret studies the frieze: Si Larbi, his long hair braided over one shoulder, removes players from the field, components from the whole. Joseph, looking over Commodus's sweaty head at Bo, theatricalizes death. What does Addie do? She does this. This is Addie's work. Margaret stares at Addie. Addie nods frugally, having work to do.

Margaret examines Commodus's grand library as if only she notices that the electrons and muons have become unstable. The irrational flash points of her body respond to Bo in their now familiar ague. This is the sensation she planned to leave at Kennedy International years ago and then to her dismay missed.

Bo is looking at her as if she were a distant ship following an uncertain course. His face gathers around his eyes. No one else has his attention, not even Addie. His look is neither warm nor cold. If she has to describe it she'll call it ancient. Addie sees it and is not disappointed, although she feels she ought to be. She loves them both. Commodus sees it and wonders if after all he's won the game. But how can that be, given this intrusion of ruffians?

Joe Minihan sees, too. Jaysus, he swears under his breath. Si Larbi is uninterested. He's considering Commodus for his hit list.

Hours pass in seconds.

"*Salaam aleykum,*" says Bo to Si Larbi.

"Later," says Si Larbi in a grave breach of Muslim etiquette.

"How much later?" asks Bo.

The bloody bastard's going to get into it with Si Larbi, Joe thinks.

Si Larbi repositions himself to judge Bo. "I think your people are from a part of my country where they hate everybody. They think all the other Arabic-speakers are keffirs."

"You'd have done better to say *wa aleykum salaam* and save your breath," Bo replies.

"I think I'm going to like you, you maniac," Si Larbi says.

"I won't hold my breath."

Si Larbi offers his huge hand. Bo looks at the hand, then at Si Larbi, and finally takes it.

Margaret looks like Dacia on a lark, thinking, What have I to do better than this?

"Si Larbi's a connoisseur of villains," Addie says.

"No, no, that cannot be, he's preoccupied being one," says Commodus. "Isn't that right, Mr. Ben Hamrouche?"

"You know why big shots get killed," the giant confides to his countryman Bo, "they don't make you laugh."

Bo winks at Commodus. The arms merchant unaccountably feels as if he's made his biggest deal.

"Do any of you daffodils have the faintest notion what the fuck's going on here?" Joe says. "I'd like to bomb the lot of you just to see where the airy-fairy pieces fall."

Addie leans against Joe and touches his face like a blind woman. Margaret leans towards Bo like a heliotrope, hoping he can smell her gladness.

Is this how it plays out, Commodus wonders, is this how the pieces fall? Is this the great secret of *Al Kitab as Sirr,* that I should know these creatures?

52

He, Commodus, collected these people and now he'll glimpse a glory no gatherer of objects ever sees. And he will see it, won't he? Hasn't he seen it in a mosaic frieze of a moon-eyed Alexander hacking his way towards Darius? But what is it? It's the recognition that arcs between certain people, that fills Amir's sketchpads.

With blue steel chilling his windpipe he teeters on the brink of comprehension. Shoot, he thinks, then maybe in a flash I'll understand, and it will make everything worthwhile.

Joseph Minihan and Amir Cavalieri will go on sizing each other up until Joe makes his next move, but the awe engulfing Commodus da Cunha makes them his witnesses. Commodus sees the tapestry that had arrested Bo come to life. Richard and Saladin stand there face to face, the presages of their apocryphal story trumping fact. Then he sees a gray etheric bar emerge from each man's chest and meet in the middle air, locking them to each other for eternity. Shadows pass along it until at once it turns violet and widens. Commodus draws in his breath and smiles over the butt of Joe's pistol. Finally his fabulous wealth has brought him something worth the work to amass it. Then he feels his father's pleasure in the unworthiness of this thought and he flinches. Joe lifts his chin with the pistol.

In their impasse the assassins Minihan and Cavalieri and Ben Hamrouche measure their years. Amir is not this guy Cavalieri, the only man Addie ever loved. Instead he is the man Joe Minihan can't die without meeting. Insane, this thought, but no more so than all the blood let in Ireland.

The way Joe's gray brush cut stoops at his widow's peak moves Bo's left hand to draw. He's sure Joe is as scarred inside and out as he is. The cracked blue eyes could be caught with graphite alone, and he knows just how to make the torn face. But the compulsion to draw gives way to the lust, no, the ability to disappear. Finally he knows what the Sufis mean—the adept's goal is to vanish, to abandon one's investments. All his adult life, since he turned his back on Manhattan, that neon stew and cackling aviary, and went to sea, he has been close to doing it, but it has eluded him. He turns, breaks the violet bar, and walks to the tapestry. Then he picks up Anubis and sets him down, and finally he walks back towards Commodus and Joe. He puts his right hand on Commodus's shoulder and with his left hand waves off the Glock.

Joe hears a loud crack. A man who's heard gunfire of every kind, he's never heard such a sound. He stares into Bo's eyes to see where his eyes will be directed. His gaze slides down to Bo's thin mouth, which looks as if once it had smiled. Here's a man, Joe thinks, who cares not who he is or what he's come for, but Joe's prepared on those grounds to like him.

"And do ya have the faintest notion then what just happened?" he asks Bo.

"Well, if I did, it wouldn't be so interesting."

"And yer not a damned bit curious, man, who the hell I am?"

"You're somebody Addie knows. That's a plus."

Now it's Joe's turn to let seep a smile. This guy, like Si Larbi, is cut of his own cloth, maybe even that's what Addie loves in him.

"If yer too damn sick of everything to fear, yer gonna get killed, ya know."

"Not today," Bo says.

The two of them clasp hands under Commodus's tapestried chin, and when they glance at him the emperor beams.

Bo rests an arm on Commodus's farthest shoulder. "You haven't lost, Commodus. I will share it with you. I've only half read it, but I know we co-operate the things we set in motion. We're God's conspirators. He can't pull it off without us. That's the gold, the conspiracy, and I know you know it. But it's too simple. It vanishes right in front of you. Every day there's all that junk for us to turn into gold, but we insist we don't have the secret formula because we don't want the responsibility. It's like pretending you don't know somebody you know. We're lying like Crusaders saying they're looking for the Holy Grail, or for a piece of wood, when we're looking for loot with blood in our eyes. We don't like the gold being offered us, we prefer the crap, so we go on saying we have to settle for the crap because we don't know how to turn it into gold. What would the Crusaders have done with the grail? Something as greedy as the lot of them, you can bet on it."

Si Larbi grins. Commodus beams, Joe pockets the Glock wistfully, Addie sticks to Joe for shelter from this gale of musings, Margaret looks wide-eyed as if she's caught a slippery equation. Si Larbi grins and clenches Bo's arm and rattles it. Then he picks Addie up and whirls her around.

★

Joe has a hard time remembering why he's come. If it was for Addie, it doesn't look as if she's getting her heart's desire, so it'll have to be for the hell of it, which invites him to feel like an ass, because where's the hell of it? When you do something this crazy somebody is supposed to die. Didja hear it, barkeep? Somebody is supposed to die. And if that's true, why aren't you in Londonderry loading up a car with bombs? Because we all die soon enough, you bloody bastard. I came because I have nothing better to do and I like the girl. I came because I was curious to see somebody she likes so much. I might've known he'd be crazier'n I am.

Si Larbi has no such second thoughts. He came for Joe. He finds no one to dislike and begins wondering what his reward should be. Usually his reward is to kill the best liar he can find. Then people take to the streets to grieve for the liar, or is it for the lies? The damned fool people get what they deserve: Assad, Sharon, Saddam, Arafat, what difference does it make, since the people don't want truth out of any of them? Friendship always ends in death, Si Larbi. But there are a few things I might like to ask this half-breed here. Why, for example, does he guess that I have a sense of humor? I make babies cry, I dry up mother's milk,

I make dogs whine, I give my stupid bosses the shits, so what does he find in me to amuse himself? But I know where I've seen him before. Sitting cross-legged in bell towers in Jerusalem, in blasted windows in Lebanon, slung with bandoliers, waiting to take the shot. He's all I like about the Bedouin race: fuck you, take the shot, that's their creed. I saw them damned near wipe the blabbering PLO out in nineteen-seventy. Bedouins are the only Arabs I like and they don't even care what an Arab is. He's one of them, this American with the Italian name, he's one of them, waiting for the shot.

He punches Bo's arm, like a shadow boxer, and nods towards one of the oval gardens. The others won't protest the giant stealing their prey. They think there's something here to kill. They don't know he's dead. Not even Yusuf. But this American and I see it in each other. Death is easy to see coming: the dead hide well.

The two sons of Ishmael wander off from the group as if the conclave had been only to bring them together. Bo tells Si Larbi of taking the body of the boy Lakhdar home from Hamburg to Oued Zem in Morocco. The giant nods gravely. "Yes, we should not die among cold hearts."

"You believe they're infidels, these cold hearts?"

"Of course not. Who can believe all the slop that falls from the mouths of mullahs and imams, presidents and generals? All that is true is that we are Bedouins, my friend. I should take you home someday. I see that you are lonely."

"*Inshallah.*"

Si Larbi tells him of his childhood in Ain Rich, of his parents Fatima and Sadiq, who died young of tuberculosis. He speaks of the war against the French, the atrocities. "Who was worse? There's a question I'd like the bullshitters to answer. Heh, not even God can answer it."

In the presence of Si Larbi, without guessing Addie's sense that she has known the giant before, Bo wonders . . . "Do assassins have brothers?" he asks Si Larbi. They have been walking along one of Commodus's waterways, passing famous cities as they walk. Si Larbi swings around to face him, the question striking

240

him like a bullet. "No," he says, "but we two are Bedouins, and that is better." Their teeth flash in the shadows as they grin at each other. This, Bo knows, is as much home as he will ever feel.

53

Joe knows he doesn't want to see Addie sprinting down Ninth Avenue, as she might when she returns to Cushman Row to close up shop or to stay. He doesn't want to long to see her or to jauntily salute her to disguise his love. He wants to close the book of Joseph Minihan on her as he's closed it on Ireland and her verdant grudges. He knows in that blind state under torture when death grants you an opening that there are two people in The Gold Factory who don't belong there: he and Dacia. What a pest she must have been, still is. A pisser beyond compare, the perfect mate for Joe Minihan, a terrorist to the quick, and not even Irish. Dacia, ya daft lass, ya don't even know yer dead. Can ya believe this mess? Lissen, two bombers is better than one, ya know. We can make a lot of trouble together and leave these nut cases to the angels.

Dacia reads this right out of his head and loves it. He knows what all barkeeps know, that damsels in distress are exactly where they choose to be and their rescuers are jerks. He's never lingered to assay the havoc of bombs, and he guesses that Dacia likes to traipse in rubble since she's obviously lost between heaven and the featureless gray plain. He's ready to join her there, but it remains to tell Addie.

"I don't have the playbill, my girl. I don't know how you'll work it out," Joe says. "But it's not for me. We're fond, Adeline, but I think we're like brother and sister. We've been fooling around a little, but we're still brother and sister. As for the sailor, well, he's either the luckiest gob in the world or the most unfortunate. Sorta like bein' an Irishman, ya know." And he would have kept on blabbering in his misery.

But Addie hushed his mouth with her hand. "Hush, Joseph, hush. I would love for you to be my brother. But I wasn't fooling around. We don't know where we're going till we see the road ahead, do we? Do you see that, Joseph?"

"Aye, I do. I am yer brother then, Addie, and ya can count on me."

"I do, Joseph, I do."

★

Commodus orders a banquet in the burbling garden. He calls it the Convivencia, after those fruited years in Iberia when Christian, Jew and Muslim lived under a caliph in peace and concert. Foolishly he feels like a man showered with gifts, not the least of which, he knows, is that Si Larbi has decided not to enroll him on his list of things to do. He stands in the midst of the festivity and says, "I would like to propose something."

"Oh, for the love of God, sit down, Commodus, you've proposed too goddamned much already," Bo says. All laugh at this out-of-character blurt, Commodus more complicitly than the others.

"No, really, I must," he persists. "I want you to sail away, wherever you're going, in *Bartolomeo Diaz*. It will be the sign of my trust. You will share *Al Kitab as Sirr* with me. Yes, I know you will. But the question is, Will I understand it? I thought I would. Why else would I go to such trouble? But I see now that that book is not merely ink on paper, just as the *Zohar* of the Qaballah is not. A fool reads it and remains a fool, but some may only touch it and be changed forever. I have not even touched it and I am changed. But I am not such a fool as not to know that without you, all of you, it would have remained nothing to me but an object of desire. Am I not right? Can you tell me?"

Si Larbi stares across the table at Bo. Margaret rises from her place and stands behind Commodus. She kisses the top of his head and gives Bo her mother's jack-o-lantern grin that had cheered his childish heart.

"Here, here," says Joseph, like a backbencher. And then, unaccountably, they all look at Addie, who for no particular reason presides at the end of the table.

"It's about reverence, Commodus. So, yes, I can tell you. If you were a fool, you're not a fool now. Objects of desire always disappoint you. But not the desire. I know this well, because when I restore an instrument I have had the better part of it. The owner really has nothing of it. If I have been truly able to restore it, it has sung to me in a way it will never sing again to anyone. Do you understand, Commodus?"

He struggles to grasp what she says. "No," he says, feeling miserable.

"You're the restorer, Commodus. See?"

He breathes heavily as if he's about to have a stroke and then a gorgeous smile defines his blurry mouth. "Yes!" He shakes his outspread hands violently.

★

Klement Gruber, the Bison, is off fattening Commodus's index, but Khaled ibn al Qwarzimi, the Crane, remains a guest where Commodus can keep an eye on him. The Omanis want many things more than *Al Kitab as Sirr*. The Crane knows Commodus will not let him leave unhappy. All he really wants to know that night is where Si Larbi ben Hamrouche fits in. Nominally they're allies, Al Qwarzimi and Ben Hamrouche—they enjoy the enmity of the Israelis—but all Arabs regard the Algerians as perverse, and little does the Omani agent know how perverse this particular Algerian is. Commodus wonders if he might enroll the Crane on Si Larbi's list. But the notion does not seem to fit the occasion, and he gives over his contemplations to cracked-heart klezmer, sleazy neon jazz, sweaty blues, and finally the rococo riffs of Couperin. And when the clarinetist falls still, the lute-like Maghrebi oud and trancer drums are heard from a dark corner of the grand garden.

The lights of the fabled port cities come on, and models of baghalas and feluccas hung with lanterns and Beneteau sloops and Bertram motor vessels ply the miniature black waters.

Bo, who thinks man's ideas of heaven tedious, thinks this will do.

The food when it comes—they're silly on champagne—strikes Bo as anticlimactic until he looks over two grand tureens of the cabbage, potato and sausage soup called *caldo verde* and sees the emperor looking like a beloved uncle come to dinner. A sob stops his throat. He's my friend, he thinks, not bothering to taste the strangeness of it.

★

"Well, Saint Brendan, I'll leave ya to yer awful fate," Joe says to Bo. "I have a bar to tend, ya know. I don't know why such a face should attract the ladies, but I'll tell ya this, it's the one girl ya don't see ya have to watch out for, and that's a fact."

He grins to see Addie and Margaret staring at him wide-eyed. Nor are they comforted by his next words. "Every man meets a pixie once. Ha, the ones who don't know it are drinking at my bar. The ones who know it, I'm damned if I know a thing about them, but the ladies here do. Yes, they do, God help them, but He won't, He helps the bastards of this world, don't He? Which is why I don't, because I'm not as mean."

Addie chokes up and turns away weeping. Margaret sighs down to her navel, lowers her head and runs her cool hands down from his forehead to his lips.

Bo sits sideways in a mother-of-pearl Savonarola chair as if shot in the shoulder, one leg sprawled out, the other buckled. His mouth opens as if to answer Joe, but nothing comes.

Commodus marvels at how unemployable Joseph Minihan and Si Larbi ben Hamrouche are. Why is it, he wonders, that people do not put their trust in such men? Why do they prefer fools? And if they did trust such men, I'd be selling chestnuts to Ivan, wouldn't I?

54

Bartolomeo Diaz sails three days later. Bo fully intends to make the great arc, sally up the East River under her gala bridges, the bone in *Bartolomeo's* teeth, and put in at City Island, but the rudder favors starboard and, being superstitious in spite of himself, Bo eases her over and works her northwards to Felixstowe.

Two weeks later they pile out of their rented car and huddle before Wind Harp in a light rain. Marie Lambert has tended it well, but even Margaret is no longer sure it can be her home. They're reluctant to unload the car, to enter the cottage. Margaret, standing in the middle, locks her arms in theirs and, leaning forward, she tugs them along, but she finds their thoughts heavy luggage. Addie will return to Cushman Row or not. She will live in the Cotswolds or not. Margaret will teach at Oxford or Cambridge. Or she'll become a high-priced mercenary, like Si Larbi, solving mathematical problems for boardroom freebooters. Bo will go home to his loft, to Gundy and his wife Jolene, or not. Dacia will come and go.

As the first days after their adventure pass with stowing away their possessions, assigning spaces to each other, bringing in supplies, a sedative routine entices them to put off odds and ends, like recovering the book and sharing it with Commodus. Bo calls Commodus every few days and looks after *Bartolomeo Diaz*.

Only Addie fidgets. She can give a good account for everything and everyone except Sheik Mutawakkil ibn al Quereishi. And then one day she looks up from her plantings in the garden and there he is, frowning.

"You have chosen to ply the alchemist's secret, which I chose to impart to you, not to Ibn al Arabi or Moses de Leon or Averroes or Maimonides. Do you speak like this, even in your imagination? Am I not real, then? Foolish girl, to waste my time fussing about whether I exist. And yet I must thank you for reminding me that even a great lord of the universe can be gulled by a pretty girl."

"Oh, Mooty-Whacky, don't go on so full of yourself, please. Of course I remember what you told me." She pulls off her gloves and throws them on the ground in mock annoyance.

Inside the cottage Margaret motions Bo to the kitchen window where they peer out over the sink. "Don't you think she's a bit young to be so dotty? She's talking to herself."

He takes her shoulders and turns her to his face. "She's talking to Sheik Mutawakkil ibn al Quereishi, her benefactor, her rescuer from a death you and I know nothing about."

Connection arrives at the brink of daring. Margaret has been equal to all but one such moment and now she looks into something very like it again, and there's no England to run back to, no Lechlade to hide in. He knows it too. Such moments crackle. They challenge us to give us a dispensation that has served us well. This is the last inquiry he would ever make of Dacia's daughter, and they both know it. A casual remark, an evasion—and everything will change, perhaps not to their liking. Here, and not in Portugal, is the end of comfort. They stare through the window to see Addie stirring a giant invisible ladle with both hands. She's laughing.

"What is his gift?" Margaret asks.

His hands on her shoulders relax. In an instant their lives change. The apertures of their eyes open wide to let each other in. His kiss would be chaste were hers not hungry. Her tongue invites him back to Cairnhall. She feels him lift up to the fragrant churchly quarter of her being. She thrusts and whispers in his ear, "Everything is all right, Bo, everything."

In the garden Addie stirs her pot, and when her lovers are spent, they sip tea at the window and watch their benefactor.

"He has been teaching her to make gold."

"Has she told you the formula?"

"No, I'm sure she can't. But I suspect that to make it you must be it. We ourselves are the elements of the formula. She's standing out there stirring us, Margaret. Addie fixes what's broken. That's why he chose her."

"And Dacia, Bo, where does she fit?"

"Most of us don't want our mothers watching what we do, but you no longer seem to mind, and that's a great tribute to her. Whatever's happened, she hasn't stood in the way of a good thing, has she? Maybe she's the sheik's apprentice."

"When you make love to me, are you making love to her?"

They stand still and shiver. The walls of the kitchen bow out and the weight of the roof presses. She's spoken too soon: everything will not be all right depending on how he answers.

"Sometimes, when I fear I'm failing, when my blood falls, I think of her." He could have offered up an exculpatory caveat such as "usually not." But he knows Margaret better, much better. She studies the working parts of his eyes and then she whispers, "I'll give you both a hand."

His eyes fill with tears. "We consent to this haunting, Margaret?"

"We consent."

He holds her head to his shoulder, two people who dedicate their sobs to unloving mothers.

"I think Dacia was glad you survived her. It gave her something to do. She made amends. My mother resented my surviving her. She didn't like the ordinary course of anything."

★

Addie is now on her knees, her back turned to them, perhaps weeding, perhaps not. They come up behind her, silent awhile, then Margaret says, "Can an alchemist have lovers, do you think?"

Not turning from Addie, he answers unhesitatingly, "The question is, Can lovers have alchemists?"

"Well," she says, "we shall see, shan't we?"

"Well, it may not be up to us."

They kneel at each side of Addie and see that her eyes are watering the pungent thyme.

★

All her life she has mistaken the ease of doing a thing with doing it well. A conservator of instruments knows not to force a thing. But forcing something is different from its being hard to do, and she has never clearly understood this distinction. If she were to serve as God's alchemist then the ease of doing it ought to signify that she's doing it well. But it's hard, hard and uncertain. What she set out to do did come out well.

In the riot of ions she hears the angels draw in their breath. She leaves Margaret and Bo kneeling on the tearful ground and walks to the back of the lot where he's erected a shed. She turns and glances at him, he nods yes, and she goes in. On the rough floor he's stapled a sheet. It's dappled with his trials in color, dozens of jars and tubes gathered at the foot of an easel by his left hand. The easel itself is covered by another dappled sheet. Warm light from a Lucite skylight ignites this orgy of daubs. She draws the sheet, revealing a fifty-by-thirty-five-inch canvas.

Titian would have thought twice. Twilight is no plein-air tryst for any artist. Bo has moved things around, as artists do, but here's Commodus descending red marble stairs to his dock on the Tagus. The artist would have been pacing *Bartolomeo Diaz*, like Bo when he first saw Commodus. Instead of the copper sheaths of pilings longing after a setting sun, the dock is lit by braziers. Commodus wears a blue burnoose, its white silken lining turned back over his shoulders. The port gunwale of the *Diaz* seems to offer the scene. That's what he would have sketched before turning to paint—the position of the stairs and Commodus's place on them, the concavity of the gunwale, the intervals of the braziers—but what convulses Addie, lungs to crotch, are the subtleties. Even when she begins to grasp these she still doesn't see that a young woman wearing a green turban is hidden in plain sight in the lower right corner, her hands resting on her knees. Her hieratic turn of wrist shows Addie she has been studied reverently. But the etheric fingers hold her eye. They're conducting the painting as if it were still being made. This turbaned changeling is watching Commodus's progress down the stairs. Between her and Commodus is a green arc dusted with gold, an arc so delicately painted it seems at first glance nothing but a specter in the braziers' glow. Only on second look does the viewer see that something is passing between the hidden young woman and the lordly descent of the master, and only then might the viewer suspect that the subject of the painting is not Commodus or his secret watcher but the passing of green gold between them. Bo has painted the arc that burns between fated people, that passed between him and Sultan Said bin Taimur, between him and Commodus, and between all who repossess what we so innocently carry into the world. And when she's done marveling at the colors deployed in the service of allegory she notices sitting atop The Gold Factory's southwestern dome a six-winged seraph whose human expression is not unlike the chiseled grief of Bo's face. The seraph is the color of an aspen leaf and his narrow aura is crimson.

She notes carefully the painting's absentees, Margaret and Dacia, and she wonders if it is, more than anything, a solution to the problem never put: how can they live respecting their feelings for each other and what they know?

★

Next morning Addie unscrews the white mailbox from its post and takes it in to her own studio, a stone barn across the lane from Wind Harp. She paints three curved ribbons, blue, gold and green. Two days later, when the ribbons dry, she letters them in black Palatino type. On the blue ribbon she paints Margaret Wadeleigh. On the gold ribbon she paints Amir Cavalieri. And on the green ribbon she paints *Mutawakkil ibn al Quereishi*.

It's Bo who explains the matter to the postmistress, although neither of them remembers how he explained it.

Glossary

Aikido—a Japanese martial art; a form of self-defense using holds, throws, and the opponent's movements to defeat him.

Al Kitab as Sirr—a priceless alchemical manuscript in Arabic from the tenth century AD.

Al Razi—(n.) (854-925 AD) a Persian polymath, physician, alchemist and philosopher; an important figure in the history of medicine.

alembic—an alchemical still; two vessels connected by a tube, used for distlling chemicals.

aludel—(n.) a pear-shaped earthenware or glass subliming pot, open at both ends, used in a diminishing series in alchemy to trap condensation.

aristo—informal term for aristocrat.

autodidact—a self-educated person.

bloviating—(v.) talking at length in an empty way.

Caracalla—tyrannical Roman emperor from AD 198 to 217, a member of the Severan Dynasty, son of Septimius Severus, known for the many massacres he decreed. He was the fifth emperor after Marcus Aurelius, who was known as the last of the Five Good Emperors and was succeeded by his son Commodus, Pertinax, Didius Julianus, Septimius Severus, then Caracalla.

chiaroscuro—(n.) the treatment of light and shade in drawing and painting;

cockatrice—(n.) a mythical beast, essentially a two-legged dragon or serpent-like creature with a rooster's head.

Convivencia—(n., Spanish) literally, "The Coexistence"—in Andalus, the period in Spain's history from the Muslim conquest of Hispania in the early eighth century, until the expulsion of the Jews, Arabs, and Amazigh in 1492, a period when Muslims, Christians and Jews lived in relative peace and prosperity.

cricoid—(n., adj.) the ring-shaped cartilage around the trachea in the laryx which if fractured causes death.

D'Annunzio—(n., Italian) Gabriele D'Annunzio (1863-1938), Prince of Montenevoso, Duke of Gallese, an Italian writer, poet, journalist, and World War I soldier occupying an important place in Italian literature from 1889 to 1919 and in political life from 1914 to 1924.

dishabille, déshabille—(n.) being dressed in a casual or careless or revealing style; usually applied to women.

dojo—(n.) a place where martial arts are practiced.

dulzian—(n.) an old double-reed insrument, an ancestor of the bassoon.

enfleurage—(n.) a process using odorless fats that become solid at room temperature to capture the odor of plant compounds.

esplendorado—(n., Portuguese) a person who lives in splendor.

euphonium—(n.) a large, conical-bore, baritone-voiced brass instrument developed in the nineteenth century,

Featherstonehaugh—(n.) a surname; pronounced "fanshaw."

F.W. Murnau—(n.) German film director (1888-1931) who made *Nosferatu,* an adaptation of Bram Stoker's *Dracula.*

flageolet—(n.) medieval woodwind instrument in the fipple flute family.

Gordian knot—(n.) a difficult or involved problem; a reference to Alexander the Great's cutting of the knot rather than trying to untie it.

Gurkha kukri—(n.) a traditional curved Nepalese knife, 16 to 19 inches, similar to a machete, used as both a utility tool and a weapon by Gurkha regiments.

Habash, George—(1926-2008). a Palestinian Christian politician and leading member of the Palestinian Liberation Organization until he was sidelined by Fatah leader Yasser Arafat in 1967 and in response founded the left-wing secular Popular Front for the Liberation of Palestine.

Haroun al-Rashid—(n.) literally, "Aaron the Just" (March 763 or February 766 – March 809), the fifth Abbasid Caliph.

Hejira—Mohammed's flight from Mecca to Medina in AD 622, the beginning of the Islamic calendar.

hieratic—(adj.) of or concerning priests or other religious leaders.

Ibn al-Arabi—(n., Arabic) A Sunni Arab Islamic scholar (1165-1240) in Arab Spain, a Sufi mystic and saint, a poet and philosopher.

interregnum—(n.) a break in continuity or a gap in government, monarchy, organization or social order.

jongleur—(n.) a traveling performer in medieval France and Norman England who sang, played music, recited, and often juggled and/or did acrobatics.

Katyusha—(adj.) a Russian-made rocket launcher.

keffiyeh—(n., Arabic) a traditional square checkered Middle Eastern headdress, worn by Arabs, some Mizrahi Jews, and nomads, especially Kurds.

kithara or **cithara**—(n.) an ancient Greek musical instrument in the lyre family. In modern Greece the kithara means guitar; a professional version of the two-stringed lyre.

klezmer—(n.) instrumental Jewish folk music from Eastern Europe.

lira da braccio—(Italian) a bowed string instrument of the Italian Renaissance used by poet-musicians in court in the fifteenth and sixteenth centuries to accompany their recitations.

littoral—(n.) a region lying along a shore; (adj.) related to such a region.

lucubration—(n.) pedantic or overelaborate argument.

luthier—(n.) someone who builds or repairs stringed instruments

magus—(n.) a magician; a Zoroastrian priest.

marabout—(n.) a Muslim hermit or religious leader, especially in North Africa.

memento mori—(n., Latin) remembering that everyone must die; thoughts on mortality; a remembrance of a specific person.

modus vivendi—(n., Latin) an agreement allowing conflicting parties to coexist peacefully.

Moor's head—a distillation apparatus used in alchemy.

ophicleide—(n.) an obsolete bass brass instrument with keys, used in bands in the nineteenth century, superseded by the tuba.

perpetua fortuna—(Lat.) perpetual good fortune.

philter—(n.) a love potion; a drink supposed to arouse the drinker to love and desire for a particular person.

Praxiteles—(n.) Greek sculptor; the most renowned of the Attic sculptors of the Fourth Century BC.

roc—(n.) an enormous bird of prey in the mythology of the Middle East.

Rolfing—(n.) deep tissue manipulation to release tension and realign the body; named for Ida Rolf (1876-1979), who pioneered it.

rutter—(n.) a hand-written medieval navigation guide.

sensei—(n.) a martial arts instructor.

shawm—(n.) a double-reed woodwind instrument from the 12ᵗʰ century resembling a recorder; gradually replaced by the oboe family of instruments.

subaltern—(n.) an officer in the British army below the rank of captain; especially a second lieutenant.

taiga—(n.) a boreal forest or snow forest consisting mostly of pines, spruces and larches.

Viking funeral—the body is laid in a small boat with offerings and is put to sea and burned.

zikhr—(n.) a form of devotion, associated chiefly with Sufism, in which the worshiper is absorbed in the rhythmic repetition of the name of God or his attributes.